Maz Evans

BEYOND THE ODYSSEY

WHO LET THE GODS OUT? BOOK 3

Chicken
House

2 Palmer Street, Frome, Somerset BA11 1DS
chickenhousebooks.com

Text © Mary Evans 2018

First published in Great Britain in 2018
Chicken House
2 Palmer Street
Frome, Somerset BA11 1DS
United Kingdom
www.chickenhousebooks.com

Mary Evans has asserted her right under the Copyright, Designs and
Patents Act 1988 to be identified as the author of this work.

Cover and interior design by Helen Crawford-White
Cover and interior illustrations by Aleksei Bitskoff
Typeset by Dorchester Typesetting Group Ltd
Printed and bound in Great Britain by CPI Group (UK) Ltd, Croydon CR0 4YY

The paper used in this Chicken House book is made from wood
grown in sustainable forests.

1 3 5 7 9 10 8 6 4 2

British Library Cataloguing in Publication data available.

PB ISBN 978-1-910655-99-3
eISBN 978-1-911490-17-3

[A] relentlessly witty, fast-paced middle grade adventure . . . This book is a page-turner littered with belly laughs that any adult will zip through.
M. G. LEONARD

*Blistering humour, mortal danger and immortal heart –
epically clever. Loved it.*
KIRAN MILLWOOD HARGRAVE

I'm really excited about this one. It's laugh-out-loud hilarious, it's super smart (mythology geeks will be in Elysium) it's brilliantly written and it's got some fantastic characters. I totally fell in love with Elliot and the gods, and I think you're all going to love them too.
ROBIN STEVENS

. . . epically brilliant and the funniest children's book I've read in ages!
JAMES NICOL

Maz is fast becoming this generation's Douglas Adams with her ability to effortlessly mix deep erudition and knowledge with outrageous, really, classically British humour. A very, very funny and enthralling adventure about the Greek gods, which children adore.
PIERS TORDAY

This book is packed full of classical gods brought bang up to date with wonderfully ironic humour.
THE GUARDIAN

. . . lashings of adventure, the Olympic gods as you've never seen them before and a wonderfully British sense of humour.
THE BOOKSELLER

Funny, witty, inspired and utterly contemporary, this fantasy thriller/adventure is a magical blend of ancient and modern, with brilliant characterization and a truly human story at its heart.
BOOKTRUST

Welcome to the third instalment in this brilliant series of Greek Gods, mythical mayhem and heart-stopping adventure! I'm not going to try and explain the surprising plot, regale you with the funniest scenes, or lend you a box of tissues for the sad bits. I'm just going to leave you in the capable hands of the brilliant Maz Evans as she tells the tale of what happened next to Elliot and his godly pals. Steel yourself, it's shockingly divine . . .

BARRY CUNNINGHAM
Publisher
Chicken House

PS There's a really useful WHAT'S WHAT on page 359!

For my Lili

Who makes every single day a voyage of discovery.

Thank you for a magical journey, baby girl.

Also by Maz Evans

Who Let the Gods Out?
Simply the Quest

1. Fail to Prepare, Prepare to Fail . . .

'. . . and no one is to froth cappuccinos with a thunderbolt, no one is to turn anyone into a warthog and no one is to fart the national anthem. Are we clear?'

Elliot spoke sternly to the array of ancient Greek immortals cleaning his kitchen. For most people, this might be odd. But for Elliot Hooper, this was just another Friday.

'Roger that – receiving loud and clear, old boy,' said Zeus, King of the Gods, scraping the grease off the oven with the tip of a golden thunderbolt. 'Bestest behaviour. You can count on us.'

'Elly, we wouldn't dream of making today any

harder for you,' said Aphrodite, Goddess of Love, spraying her 'Freshly Baked Bread' air freshener around the kitchen. 'We know everything has to go well. We'll be as silent as Athene's fan club.'

'Absolutely,' said the Goddess of Wisdom, shooting her sister a death stare while crocheting a lace tablecloth from leftover spaghetti. 'We won't let you down.'

Elliot smiled gratefully. He'd been dreading this day ever since he received the Latest Really Scary Letter. Actually, he'd been dreading it a lot longer than that.

'So, I have a few notes,' said Virgo, shuffling a deck of index cards. 'Now when you say I'm not to be – and I quote – "an epic butthead", please clarify, am I allowed to share my peerless opinions?'

'No,' said Elliot.

'Lighten the mood with some well-observed humour?'

'Definitely no.'

'Prepare some refreshments?'

'The carpets still haven't recovered from your last catering attempt.'

'My pigs in blankets were highly optimal!' Virgo huffed.

'They were actual pigs!' Elliot cried. 'In real

blankets! And no.'

'Perhaps I should arrange some entertainment? I could sing . . .'

'No. And please, God, no.'

Virgo's brow furrowed.

'I do not understand,' she said. 'It's almost like you don't want me to say or do anything today.'

'Noooo – you've got it all wrong!' cooed Elliot. 'It's *exactly* like I don't want you to say or do anything today. Epic. Butthead. Don't be one.'

'But I . . .'

Zeus's gentle hand on Virgo's shoulder silenced the former Constellation. It always did. Of all the King of the Gods' divine powers, Elliot was particularly grateful for this one.

Elliot closed his eyes and tried not to think of all the ways today could go wrong. It was all going to be fine. Everything was fine. He just had to convince *them* of that. Who was he kidding? He had to convince *himself* of that . . .

Elliot ticked off a couple of items on his list and put the pencil in his pocket, where it immediately fell through the large hole growing inside.

'When will you let me fix those trousers?' sighed Athene, as she had for weeks.

'When I put them in the wash,' answered Elliot, as he had for weeks.

'Morning, son,' yawned a voice from the stairs.

Elliot smiled up at his father. He immediately felt better. In fact, everything had felt better since Dave Hooper had arrived at Home Farm two months ago. He'd told Elliot so many cool stories about being in prison, he'd taught him how to pick locks, all the places you can safely hide sweets you shouldn't have . . . but most of all, he had insisted on looking after Josie at night.

'You don't sleep much in prison. Besides, I'm more of a night owl. You need your beauty sleep. Lots of it,' he'd said with his cheeky wink.

Elliot didn't know how he'd managed before Dave came home. Now he was getting more sleep, everything seemed more manageable. His moods were brighter, he was doing better at school, his mum was . . .

He tried to ignore the fear that prickled in his throat. It was hard to say what Mum was now. She was so far away from herself, he hardly recognized her. Most of the time she simply sat staring into space. She barely spoke any more. She barely did anything any more.

In fact, there was only one thing that seemed to wake Josie from her conscious slumber.

And that was Dave.

Dave's return might have made Elliot feel

happier, but for Josie, he'd had quite the opposite effect. Every time Dave came near her, she'd snarl and shout at him.

'You're not my husband!' she'd screech. 'You're an imposter! Get out of my house!'

It was so sad. But, Elliot reasoned, she wasn't herself. She was so confused now, and it was over ten years since she'd last seen her husband. All the time Dave had been in prison, Josie's mind had been steadily getting worse. She'd remember him eventually and calm down again, he told himself. Of course she would. She had to.

'How's Mum?' he asked hopefully.

'Asleep,' said Dave. 'Best thing. Listen – I'm going to make myself scarce today. Y'know – like we talked about . . .'

Elliot nodded. His dad knew best. Dave had explained that coming out of prison was a big shock and he needed time to adjust. Besides, he wasn't sure how the Little Motbury community was going to respond to a convicted armed robber returning to the village, so he'd suggested they keep his return quiet for now. It made perfect sense. Elliot hadn't told a soul.

'Good luck today, son,' said Dave, putting his hands on Elliot's shoulders. 'You've got this.'

'Thanks.' Elliot grimaced. He was going to

need a lot more than luck. He wished his dad could stay with him – he could do with his support. But today was not the day to tell the world that his ex-offender father was living with him.

Because today was the day that the school welfare team was coming to assess Elliot's home life.

According to their letter, this was an 'informal visit' that was 'nothing to worry about'; it was purely to make sure that Elliot had everything he needed 'to feel happy and safe'. Dave said that if the authorities knew that a recent convict was living at Home Farm, it would make a lot of things very 'formal', give them 'plenty to worry about' and Elliot would not feel 'happy and safe' if he were taken into care. So Dave was going to stay out of sight in the fields beyond the farm.

'Laters, all,' Dave chirped at the Gods, who waved cordially.

Dave had taken the news of his son's new life surprisingly well. Once he'd got his head around the fact that a family of ancient Greek Gods were living in his home, that an evil Death Daemon would rule the Earth unless Elliot beat him to four Chaos Stones capable of controlling the elements, and that the fate of the world rested on his thirteen-year-old son's shoulders, Dave had slotted into life at Home Farm with impressive ease.

Elliot looked at the Gods' frozen smiles as Dave walked outside. He couldn't quite put his finger on it, but if anyone was struggling to adjust to the new arrangement, it was them.

Elliot returned to his checklist.

'Have all the household devices been sorted?'

'Nearly there,' growled two feet sticking out of the downstairs loo. Elliot peered in to see Hephaestus, God of the Forge, adjusting the toilet with a spanner. 'Dishwasher, fridge, cupboard and oven are all deactivated,' he growled. 'Upstairs loo don't play Mozart no more, but this one still belts out a bit of Beethoven if you do a number two. I'll sort it, never you mind.'

'Thanks,' said Elliot. He was relieved that the kitchen wasn't going to spontaneously cook a roast beef dinner and clean it up, but he really didn't want today's visitors to poop to Beethoven either.

'I've transformed everything in the shed to look like it belongs on a farm,' said Athene, 'and Aphrodite has sprayed her Positivity Potion so that the welfare officers see everything in a good light. Fortunately, it won't be required to work on her outfit. No potion in the world could help that.'

Aphrodite pouted. 'I'm going to check on

Hermes,' she said. '*He* always appreciates my unique style.'

'Especially now he's asleep,' muttered Athene, returning to her crocheted spaghetti.

'I'll come with you,' said Elliot. He needed some fresh air.

He followed Aphrodite up to the shed, where the Messenger God was lying unconscious on a sumptuous feather bed.

Elliot tried to swallow down the sadness he felt every time he saw Hermes. Every day he – they all – hoped that the Messenger God would wake up, after Nyx, Goddess of the Night, shot him with a poisoned arrow at Stonehenge. Since that dreadful night, there had been no sign of Nyx, nor of her sons, Thanatos, Daemon of Death, and Hypnos, Daemon of Sleep. But the Messenger God slept soundly on. Would he ever wake up? Elliot missed his 'bruvva from annuva muvva' so much.

'Hi, bruv,' he whispered, giving Hermes an unrequited fist bump. 'Sorry I've not been up today. It's been a bit ...'

E, mate, he knew Hermes would say if he could. *Not being funny or nothing, but today's gonna be like a porcelain piñata. You're, like, totes gonna smash it! BOOOOOOOOOOM!*

But Hermes didn't say anything. Just like he hadn't yesterday. Just like he probably wouldn't tomorrow.

'Sweetie,' Aphrodite whispered to her brother, 'I just need to hide you away for a bit. I'll be right here. Sleep well.'

The Goddess of Love kissed Hermes softly on the cheek, before removing a translucent spray bottle from her pocket. She sprayed it gently around the Messenger God, and as the vaporous mist settled over him, he slowly started to fade from view.

'Invisibility Potion,' Aphrodite winked at Elliot. 'Remind me to brew you up a batch.'

Before Hermes disappeared entirely, Elliot gave him another gentle fist bump and made his way back towards the farmhouse. He shook the sadness out of his head. He had other things to worry about today.

'Virgo, have you evicted the gorgons from the downstairs bathroom?' Elliot said, consulting his clipboard.

'Absolutely,' said Virgo stiffly, grabbing her school bag and walking quickly towards the stairs. 'Now if you'll just excuse me . . .'

'Open the bag,' sighed Elliot.

'No,' said Virgo firmly. 'I have private things in

here. Girl things.'

Normally Elliot would have run a mile. Girl things were . . . gross. But he wasn't falling for it today.

'You're about as private as Wembley Stadium,' he said. 'Open the bag.'

'I will not, I—'

'Virgo,' said Zeus softly, but firmly. 'Do as he asks. Please.'

Virgo stood motionless as she figured out what to do. She reminded Elliot of the computers at school when they froze with the little wheel spinning in the middle of the screen.

Eventually – reluctantly – she handed Elliot the bag.

'Thank you,' said Elliot, pulling back the zip. 'Now what have you—'

'PLLLLLLLLOP!' squealed a thin little voice. What looked like an enormous green bogie leapt from the bag and started bouncing around the kitchen.

'Gorgy!' said Virgo sternly as the bogie jumped across the Gods' heads like stepping stones.

'Gorgy?!' Elliot winced, swatting the bouncing bogie off his head. 'You don't mean you've—'

'GORGY!' Virgo shouted, bringing the bogie to an abrupt halt. 'Come here at once!'

Gorgy sheepishly unfurled and shuffled back towards Virgo. Elliot looked at the curious creature. He was small, no bigger than a football, and almost as round. His green pot belly stuck out over his ragged trousers, while his wild green hair flowed around his little round face and snouty nose.

'Virgo!' chided Athene. 'That's an infant gorgon! They're dangerous! You can't keep one as a pet!'

'He's not a pet,' said Virgo condescendingly. 'Gorgy—'

'Gorgy the gorgon?' scoffed Elliot. 'Original name for a pet ...'

'He is *not* a pet!' Virgo huffed. 'I am merely studying Gor ... this ... creature to further understand Elementals. Our relationship is purely professional, not emotional. Why, I have no more regard for this creature than—'

'Mama!' cried Gorgy, holding his arms out to Virgo.

'A-ah,' stammered Virgo nervously, 'I am teaching Gor ... the creature ... the basics of language.'

She held up a cup.

'Gorgy – what is this?'

'Plop!' squealed Gorgy.

'You see!' Virgo said triumphantly. 'He said "cup"!'

11

'He said "plop",' said Elliot. 'As in, "You are a great big plop."'

'Gorgy,' Virgo continued, raising a plate. 'Tell Mam . . . Tell *Ms* Virgo what we call this.'

'Plop!' Gorgy squealed again.

'Come along, Gorgy, we practised this.' Virgo scowled, holding up a fork. 'What do we call—'

'THIS!' yelled Hephaestus, charging towards the young gorgon with his bronze axe. 'Come 'ere, you little blighter!'

'Gorgy! No!' cried Virgo, standing defensively in front of her pet gorgon.

But Gorgy had other ideas. He instantly rolled back into his bogie-ball and bounded around the kitchen while Hephaestus charged after him, axe aloft. Within seconds, the neat and tidy kitchen was destroyed: food, plates, mops – anything that Gorgy could lay his hands on – were thrown at the immortal blacksmith, who heaved his axe to no avail.

'STOP!' Elliot yelled, just as Gorgy found a safe spot beyond Hephaestus's axe on top of the cupboards.

Hephaestus froze with his axe above his head and looked apologetically at Elliot. Everyone in the kitchen surveyed the carnage.

'Sorry, young'un,' he said. 'I'll tidy it up. Honest.'

'Gorgy!' Virgo cried. 'Gorgy – come to Mama!'

But Gorgy wasn't going anywhere. He screwed his little face up into a ball, which made him look like an angry pea. Strands of green hair started to wave around his face. Elliot noticed that they weren't hair at all – they were little thin snakes. And they were hissing at Hephaestus.

'Bad! Man!' shouted Gorgy, pointing at Hephaestus's axe.

'You see!' beamed Virgo. 'I taught him that!'

'BAD PLOP MAN!' Gorgy shouted. The snakes stood on end and gave a deafening hiss. The sound travelled in a mass of swirling air, encircling Hephaestus's axe in a blizzard of hissing, until the bronze head started to flop, like butter on a barbecue. The stout wooden handle wilted in Hephaestus's hand, rendering his axe as deadly as a wilted daffodil.

'WHAT HAVE YOU DONE?!' he shouted at Gorgy.

'Er, Gorgy – time to go in your cage,' said Virgo, bundling the baby gorgon into her arms and rushing him upstairs.

'You should count yourself lucky,' sighed Athene. 'An adult gorgon can turn anything to stone. A youngster like Gorgy can only muster softer materials.'

13

'He turned a wasp into a lump of chalk yesterday,' yelled Virgo proudly from upstairs.

'You see!' shouted Elliot. 'This is exactly what I'm talking about! This is what cannot happen today! You guys have got to stop . . . being you!'

The Gods looked mortified. The gentle ring of Hermes's iGod pierced the tense silence.

'Er, shall I?' said Athene quietly.

'Why not?' sighed Elliot, surveying the devastation in his kitchen. How was he ever going to persuade the authorities everything was normal? He couldn't remember the last time it had been.

'Hello?' Athene said into the phone. 'She is . . . Yes, of course . . . Yes, I'll inform her immediately.'

Everyone looked quizzically at the Goddess of Wisdom.

'Virgo, that was the Zodiac Council,' she shouted up the stairs. 'They need you up in Elysium, right away.'

'Now?' said Virgo, reappearing in the kitchen. 'But I can't possibly leave Elliot at this critical time. My presence here is vital. He needs me to support him. He needs me to advise him. He needs me to—'

'Go!' said Elliot forcefully, pushing her towards the door.

'Are you sure?' said Virgo. 'I was planning to

serve some fairy cakes. With genuine fairies . . .'

'Take Peg,' said Zeus, opening the door before Elliot pushed Virgo straight through it. 'We'll see you later.'

'Well, if you think you can manage without—'

The slam of the front door confirmed that he could.

'One down,' muttered Elliot under his breath. He sighed and looked around the chaos as the Gods started to clean up after an angry baby gorgon. Today was going to be a very, very long day.

2. Out Laws

'**V**irgo! How wonderful to see you! Come in, child, come in!'

In the paradise that was Elysium, Virgo entered the glass pyramid chamber of the Zodiac Council and scanned the smiling faces of her former colleagues. They seemed exceptionally pleased to see her. This was most irregular.

'Er, hello,' she said cautiously. 'Is everyone optimal?'

'Super-optimal!' roared Taurus the bull, the current president of the Council, coming forward to shake her hand. 'Delighted to see you again! Have a biscuit!'

Every Councillor had their own style of government during their annual month in office. Taurus was renowned for his austere, no-nonsense leadership; he hated frivolity. During a previous term, he had outlawed balloons. Yet he was offering biscuits? Perhaps Virgo was dreaming. She had begun to do this since she was stripped of her kardia and became mortal. She could no longer always be sure if she was awake or dreaming. She made a mental note to look out for giant singing watermelons – they gave the game away every time.

'Um, where do you want me?' said Virgo, looking around for somewhere to sit. Was she on trial again?

'Why here, of course, child!' bleated Aries the golden ram, pulling out Virgo's red sofa from beneath the golden Zodiac table. 'Where you belong.'

Virgo looked stealthily around the chamber. No watermelons.

'You want me to sit ... with you?' she began.

'Yes,' smiled Aries.

'At my seat?'

'Of course,' grinned Cancer the crab.

'At the table?'

'Well, we're not going to put you in the bin!'

17

laughed Pisces the fish. 'Not again . . .'

Aries patted the sofa with a golden hoof. Virgo sat down cautiously as the other Councillors took their places and smiled at her. It was curiously uncomfortable.

'Well, now, isn't this marvellous?' boomed Taurus, running a hoof through his small clump of auburn hair. 'The whole gang back together. It's just not been the same without you, Virgo.'

'Hear, hear,' was the general mutter of agreement around the table. Virgo sneaked a look under the table. No watermelons there either.

'It's . . . uh . . . very optimal to be back,' she said. 'Has someone lost the stationery catalogue again?'

Her colleagues roared with laughter.

'No, you big silly!' said the Gemini twins. 'We just wanted to see you.'

'Why?' asked Virgo suspiciously.

'Why not?' laughed Capricorn the goat.

Virgo paused. Wasn't it obvious?

'Because . . . you never have before,' she said.

A collective gasp went up around the table.

'How can you say that?' whispered Sagittarius the centaur, with a hoof over his heart. 'Don't you remember that time we all went on holiday?'

'Yes,' said Virgo. 'You left me behind to answer the phones.'

'That's why we brought you that straw unicorn!' shouted Leo the lion. 'And what about the big party we threw for your 1,021st birthday? There were jugglers, acrobats, magicians . . .'

'Which I would have enjoyed very much. If I had gone,' said Virgo.

'You were in charge of invitations,' huffed Aquarius, pouring himself a drink from his water jug. 'If you didn't invite yourself, that's hardly our fault . . .'

'The fact is, Virgo – you are a valued member of our team,' Taurus interrupted. 'And that's very important. We are a *team*. There's no "me" in "team".'

'Er – technically there is,' whispered Cancer. 'Otherwise it would be "ta".'

'Shut your claws!' shouted Taurus. 'The point is, Virgo, that you are still part of our ta . . . our *team*, aren't you?'

'Um, I suppose so,' said Virgo. 'If you overlook the fact that you took my kardia, expelled me from Elysium, won't let me come back until I prove myself a hero, and someone keeps writing sub-optimal things about me on Golden Racebook . . .'

'Excellent!' roared Taurus.

Virgo wasn't sure if her perception was

sub-optimal, but it felt as if everyone leant in towards her.

'So, enough dilly-dallying,' said Taurus, pushing the biscuits beyond the reach of Scorpio's scorpion pincers. 'The fact is, this isn't just a social call. We need you on official business.'

Virgo breathed a sigh of relief. They didn't want her company after all. This was most reassuring.

Cancer pulled out one of the many leather-bound volumes that lined the chamber and threw it on to the table.

'We need to make a small change to the Sacred Code,' she said. 'As you are aware, a unanimous Council vote is required to do this. From every-one. Even you.'

'But I'm suspended,' said Virgo. 'You suspended—'

Aries slung a golden woolly leg around Virgo's shoulder. 'Let's forget about the past. Let's look to a brighter future.'

'A *safer* future!' boomed Taurus. 'And who doesn't want that?'

All the heads around the table nodded so hard they reminded Virgo of Elliot after the time he ran into a wall for a bet. She smiled at the memory of his mortal stupidity.

Taurus cleared his throat and snorted out of his

large nostrils.

'It is possible that your claims about the escape of Thanatos, Daemon of Death from beneath Stonehenge, might not have been as . . . sub-optimal as we first thought.'

'I TOLD YOU SO!' shrieked Virgo, leaping off her sofa in triumph. 'I *knew* it, I *knew* it, I *said* that . . .'

She looked around the disapproving Councillors. As Elliot might observe, this was something of an epic fail.

'Not that it matters,' she mumbled, returning to her seat. 'But what changed your mind?'

'Our network of covert operatives has reported several *unconfirmed* sightings of Thanatos, Daemon of Death, and his mother, Nyx, Goddess of the Night, in the Underworld,' Taurus admitted.

'The fairies are posting pictures of him on Flitter under the hashtag #ThanatosIsAlive AndWellAndWeHaveSeenHimLoads,' said the Gemini twins.

'Be quiet!' roared Taurus. 'However, it is impor-tant to stress that at this moment in time—'

'We know nothing about that,' said Capricorn.

Virgo found her tongue lodged curiously between her teeth.

'But, in the light of these *unsubstantiated*

reports, we feel some ... additional security measures would be advisable,' said Taurus. 'We have a watch list of dangerous immortals that we fear might ally with Thanatos in the *incredibly* unlikely event of a conflict. We think it is in the public interest for them – and any other threatening presences on our radar – to be detained in Tartarus.'

'This is very wise,' nodded Virgo. 'We must summon them for questioning and, if your intelligence is correct, arrange their trials immediately.'

Taurus exchanged a nervous look with the rest of the Council. Pisces stood up and waddled around the table to Virgo's sofa.

'You see, child – there's the issue,' he said, sitting so close to Virgo she had to dangle half her backside off the edge of the sofa. 'Questioning ... trials ... lawyers ... All of these things take time and resources that we feel could be better spent. You know how we hate unnecessary procedures.'

'Quite!' roared Leo, to the encouraging murmurs of his colleagues. 'I've done seven residential courses, thirteen corporate awaydays and twenty-six webinars on how to avoid unnecessary procedures. I can show you my mind map if you like.'

'So, what do you suggest?' said Virgo, with a

furrowed brow.

'Delighted you asked!' bellowed Taurus. 'We just want to make a tiny amendment to the Sacred Code. We're calling it "Cole's Law".'

'It's hardly anything . . .' said Cancer.

'They'll barely notice it . . .' said Aries.

'Everyone loves Cole's Law . . .' chimed the Gemini twins.

'All we want to do is give ourselves the power to take known, dangerous immortals and place them out of harm's way,' said Taurus. 'Immediately.'

'I see,' said Virgo. 'What sort of dangerous immortals are we talking about here? Are there more imprisoned Daemons that you are pretending not to know about?'

'Not exactly,' said Sagittarius, switching on the projector and aiming a beam of light at the wall. 'These ones are all around us — hiding in plain sight. We know that werewolves can be very aggressive . . .'

'I've met several ill-mannered vampires,' Aquarius chimed in.

'Those sprites can be vicious on Flitter,' said the Gemini twins.

'A gnome once barged in front of me at the cheese counter,' huffed Capricorn.

'So, you see,' said Sagittarius, 'it's hard to say

exactly where the threat is coming from. But I have conducted extensive research and have concluded that one sector of the immortal community is harbouring all the most dangerous immortals.'

He flicked a switch and an image of a pie chart filled the wall. Across it in red letters was a single word: 'Elementals'.

'I don't understand,' said Virgo, shaking her head. 'Which Elementals? I mean, that category is huge. It describes any immortal that isn't a Constellation, a God, a Hero, a Neutral or a Daemon. Elementals are the most common immortals. And it shows—'

'Precisely,' growled Taurus, looking grimly into her eyes. 'It could be any of them. That's why we're raising the threat level. We don't think this is quite a Code Black situation. But I am declaring a Code Brown . . .'

'Toilets are that way,' sniggered the Gemini twins.

'So . . . you want the power to detain every Elemental, even those who've done nothing wrong?'

'Yet,' added Aries.

'And you want to imprison them without questioning?' said Virgo.

The Councillors nodded.

'Without a trial?'

They nodded again.

'Just . . . stick them in Tartarus, without giving them a chance to defend themselves?' she whispered.

'The Council feels that Cole's Law is necessary,' said Taurus grimly. 'Eliminating the Daemons has kept us all safe for millennia—'

'Not that we know anything about that,' said Pisces.

'And now it's time to deal with this new threat,' said Taurus. 'We very much hope you agree.'

Virgo turned this around in her mind. The right to a trial was a cornerstone of the Sacred Code. She knew it off by heart: *Rule Aiv7socks): All immortals have the right to a fair trial.* It was written between two equally important laws: *C-49tcucumber): Immortals must never leave the tap running while cleaning their teeth* and *F4Bromley★): Immortals may never go back on an agreed swapsie.* It was fair. It was just. It was right.

Even for Elementals.

'Can I ask a question?' she said quietly.

'Of course,' said Taurus.

'Anything you like,' said Pisces.

'Be our guest,' said Scorpio.

Virgo rose slowly from the table. It was now entirely clear what was going on here.

'WHERE ARE THE SINGING WATER-MELONS?' she cried. 'I know you're here somewhere! Show yourselves!'

But there was no reply. Not a single water-melon in sight.

'Have you quite lost your mind?' asked Aries. 'This is a crucial security matter! Not one of your five a day!'

Virgo slowly sat down again. This was not a dream – it was really happening.

'But what if they don't agree?' she asked. 'Surely you can't force them?'

'Of course not,' laughed Taurus, pushing a small golden button in front of him. 'We've already thought of that. We plan to recruit some . . . enforcement officers.'

'Not the Satyr Squad?' sighed Virgo. 'I've tried to tell you, they are not real law enforcement officers, they just dress like that for hen nights . . .'

'Not the Satyrs,' said Aries.

'Who then?' said Virgo.

Taurus looked to his colleagues for support. They nodded at him encouragingly.

'The Titans,' he said firmly.

Virgo put her finger in her ear. Elliot had once

informed her that he'd put a beetle in her ear while she was sleeping and it was slowly eating her brain. Perhaps that was why her hearing was malfunctioning.

'I'm so sorry,' she laughed. 'I thought you said, "The Titans"!'

No one laughed along.

'Y-you can't be serious?' stuttered Virgo. 'The Titans tried to overthrow the Olympians! They have been locked in the deepest pit of Tartarus for millennia! They were considered such a threat to public safety they were imprisoned so far beneath the Earth that it would take an anvil thrown from the top of Mount Olympus nine days to land there. How would you even reach them?'

A small ping sounded behind her.

'We installed a lift,' said Taurus.

Virgo turned around slowly to see a huge pair of golden doors behind her. A cold draught swept across the chamber as the lift came to a halt. A shiver ran through her.

Taurus walked slowly across the chamber to greet his guests. There was utter stillness as the lift doors opened to reveal . . . four enormous ankles. Two of them had huge golden fetters around them. Virgo gulped.

'Gentlemen!' shouted Taurus to the legs.

'Please, do come in.'

The first pair of knees started to bend, revealing a huge pair of legs that led to a massive, muscular torso. A torn black vest rose up to a vast neck, tattooed with an elaborate blood-red pattern. As the enormous head came into view, the tattoos twisted into the shape of ram's horns that curled up and over the big ears, then encircled the huge black eyes in the middle of the colossal bald head.

'Crius!' cried Taurus, who barely came up to the knees of the giant before him. 'Thank you so much for joining us. Please – invite your brother in.'

Crius slowly turned his head from side to side as he surveyed the chamber, casting a huge shadow across the floor. His gaze fell on Virgo, who suddenly became aware she had been staring at his tattoos. The Titan bent down, drawing his enormous head level with hers. Virgo gulped.

'I carved them in blood.' He smiled, revealing his crooked yellow teeth.

'Th-th-that must have hurt,' stammered Virgo.

The Titan closed in until his eye was the same height as her whole body.

'It wasn't my blood,' he whispered.

A small whimper escaped Virgo's body. It wasn't the only thing looking for the nearest exit.

The Titan slowly rose to his vast height.

'Brother!' he called, with a voice deeper than fear. 'Come!'

A colossal foot took one step forward. But this giant didn't duck. A crashing thud rang around the chamber as the second Titan collided with the top of the lift.

'Ow,' came a slow grunt from inside.

'Duck. You div,' growled Crius, rolling his eyes.

The new Titan manoeuvred himself awkwardly out of the lift. His appearance was no less intimidating than his brother's: he had the same massive muscular torso, if not quite his enormous height. He too was covered in tattoos, his bald head emblazoned with a red skull. Together, they were a truly terrifying sight.

'Welcome!' said Taurus nervously. 'Why don't you introduce yourselves for the benefit of the group?'

Crius surveyed the room again.

'All right,' he growled. 'I'm Crius – but they call me "The Ram".'

'And I'm Coeus,' said his brother. 'But they call me . . . they call me . . . they call me . . .'

He stopped and scratched his head.

'What do they call me again?'

'The Brain. You idiot,' said The Ram, giving his

brother an almighty shove.

'I'm Coeus,' the smaller Titan announced again. 'And they call me . . . "The Brain. You Idiot."'

The Ram stared incredulously at his brother before turning his dark gaze back to the Council.

'Why are we here?' he said.

'We are aware that you have served an exceptionally long sentence,' said Aries. 'You have had time to reflect on your crimes and we're sure you're sorry.'

'We are,' said The Brain. 'Sorry we got caught.'

He received another great shove from his brother.

'Remorse . . . excellent,' floundered Cancer. 'We'd like to give you the opportunity to improve your conditions. If you help us, we are prepared to upgrade your maximum security sentence and allow you to roam openly in Tartarus.'

'Great!' shouted The Brain. 'That'll be much easier to escape from!'

He was silenced by a colossal smack around the ear from The Ram.

'What about these?' said The Ram, pointing to the gold fetter around his left ankle.

The Councillors looked nervously at each other.

'They would be removed,' said Leo. 'Subject to your satisfactory service.'

'What are those?' Virgo whispered to Libra.

'Muscle inhibitors,' said Libra, weighing two scones on her scales. 'They limit their strength. Without them, they'd be unstoppable.'

'And we're going . . . to take them off?' said Virgo.

'Only once they've told us we can trust them,' said Libra, tapping her nose. 'Foolproof.'

Virgo found herself wondering if her fellow Councillors actually knew what fools were. She looked back up at The Ram, who was smiling at his brother.

'At your service,' he said.

'Excellent,' said Taurus, with what sounded suspiciously like a sigh of relief. He signalled to Cancer to continue.

'The law is very clear,' said the crab, balancing her glasses on her head. 'We cannot make a change to the Sacred Code without a unanimous vote from all Council members, even suspended ones. This includes you, Virgo. We are all agreed. We just need one more vote.'

'So,' glowered Taurus. 'Are you with us?'

Virgo slumped back on her sofa with a slow breath. This was immense. If she agreed, anyone could be placed in Tartarus without questioning. By the Titans. This wasn't just sub-optimal. It was wrong.

'I'm sorry,' she said quietly. 'I can't.'

Taurus snorted angrily. He nodded to Aries, who placed a small golden box in front of Virgo.

'We feared you might say that,' he said. 'So might I remind you that we still hold this.'

Taurus flipped the lid open. It contained a necklace with a crystal pendant, a heart within a flame. A kardia. *Her* kardia – the source of her immortality. Virgo felt her heart swell with longing. There was nothing she wanted more in all the worlds than to have her kardia back. Not even the overpriced scented pencil cases she'd observed at school and had been curiously desperate to obtain.

It felt like for ever since she had felt it around her neck. And yet here it was, within her grasp. She could just imagine it back where it belonged. She could just imagine herself, back where she belonged.

She raised her fingers to touch her precious kardia . . .

SNAP!

The box slammed shut. She looked up. Taurus

was looming over her, his nostrils flaring like sails on a stormy ship.

'So,' he said. 'Are you part of the team? Or aren't you?'

Virgo cowered in her seat. She'd never noticed how big Taurus was before. Nor that his tuft of hair was actually a really bad wig.

'Y-you said I had be a hero,' she stammered. 'To regain my kardia – you said I had to be a hero.'

'But can't you see, child?' said Aries, sitting on the other side of her sofa. 'There are many ways to be a hero! What we do here is heroic too! Saving the world from dangerous immortals – what could be more heroic than that?'

'Not all heroes have swords,' said Pisces, sitting on the other side of Virgo. 'Some have staplers.'

'If you vote for this resolution and we successfully round up all these dangerous immortals – well, we'd have no choice but to return your kardia,' said Cancer.

Virgo considered her position. Her kardia back! Her immortality returned! Her silver hair restored! Her need to eat broccoli removed!

She tried to swallow. But her mouth was curiously dry.

Taurus returned to his seat at the head of the table.

'And so, let's put it to a vote,' he said grimly. 'All in favour of Cole's Law, raise a hand.'

Virgo watched as twelve hands shot into the air.

And with a heart that felt as if it had met a full-grown gorgon, Virgo's rose slowly to join them.

3. One of Those Days

Elliot watched the hands on the kitchen clock continue their never-ending journey towards 11 a.m. His heart was quivering, the unpleasant taste of fear clogged the back of his throat.

He looked over at Josie, staring into the flames in her favourite armchair by the fire. She did that a lot now. Just . . . stared. Athene and Aphrodite had done their best to help Josie look her best, fixing her hair and make-up and dressing her in her favourite red dress. But the make-up looked wrong – as though someone had coloured in a fading portrait. Elliot remembered Mum dancing in that dress at one of his birthday parties – the skirt had danced on air around her. But the dress wasn't dancing today. It looked very, very tired.

'Everything OK, Mum?' He smiled and took her hand.

Josie raised her head, as if hearing a forgotten song. She turned slightly towards Elliot, but said nothing. She was having a quiet day. Elliot kissed her softly. Quiet was good, he reassured himself. Or at least better than confused, angry or tearful.

The Gods had hidden themselves in the shed with Hermes, and Dad was out in the fields. It was just him and Mum. It felt like a long time since that had been his life.

The knock at the front door reverberated through his body. Hephaestus had disabled the magical fence that protected Home Farm and Elliot had forgotten that his visitors would be able to come right up to the door. He suddenly felt very, very vulnerable. Perhaps sending the Gods away had been a mistake?

There was a second gentle knock. It was too late now.

He took a slow breath, pinned a smile to his lips and opened the front door.

'Hi, Elliot,' Ms Givings, the school welfare officer, said warmly. 'This is my colleague, Mr Trick.'

Elliot recognized the petite, red-haired Ms

Givings from their last meeting at Brysmore. Mr Trick was new – as were his designer jeans, shirt and jacket. Elliot imagined his nan eyeing the visitor up and down. 'Money can't buy taste,' she would have muttered.

'Hey there, Elliot,' said the man, in that strange tone that adults use when they have no idea how to speak to a child. 'Can we come hang for a bit?'

'Sure,' said Elliot, accepting Mr Trick's high-five. 'Er . . . hang all you want.'

He led them through to the front room.

'Hello, Mrs Hooper.' Ms Givings stretched out her hand to shake Josie's. 'Lovely to meet you.'

Elliot held his breath as Josie stared at Ms Givings's hand. She slowly raised hers and held it. Elliot exhaled. Had that taken too long? Had Ms Givings noticed?

'So, Elliot – cool digs you have here,' said Mr Trick, pointing his fingers like a gun. 'Why don't you give me the grand tour?'

'In a minute,' said Elliot, who had no intention of leaving Mum alone with these people for a single second longer than was absolutely necessary. 'I'll just make some tea.'

'Groovy,' sang Mr Trick, putting both thumbs up. 'Milk, no sugar, purlease. I'm sweet enough!'

Elliot tried to laugh. It wasn't easy.

'Your home is lovely, Mrs Hooper,' said Ms Givings, settling herself on the sofa. 'Have you always lived here?'

'Our family has,' Elliot called from the kitchen, urging the kettle to boil so he could get back in the front room. 'Generations of Hoopers have lived here.'

'How wonderful,' said Ms Givings to Josie. 'I bet these walls could tell a few stories.'

Josie smiled, but said nothing.

'So, as our letter explained,' said Ms Givings, pulling out a notebook, 'today is just an informal chat, a chance to get to know you both and make sure you have everything you need. Is that OK?'

Josie simply stared.

'Great,' said Ms Givings.

Elliot raced back into the room. The kettle was taking too long. He tried not to stare at the welfare officer. If she'd noticed anything was wrong, she was doing a good job of hiding it.

'Hey, El – how's about that tour?' said Mr Trick, with a smile that could strain spaghetti. 'Wanna show me around your bachelor pad?'

'I'd love to,' Elliot lied, opening the biscuit tin. 'Would you like a bisc—Argh!'

'Dude!' said Mr Trick, probably for the first time in his life. 'Everything OK?'

Elliot slammed the lid back on the tin.

'Plop!' came a small squeal from inside.

'Sorry, buddy?' said Mr Trick.

'I said "plop" – please excuse my language,' said Elliot quickly, holding the lid firmly over Gorgy. 'These biscuits are stale. I'll just get some more. They're . . . er, in the shed.'

He looked anxiously over at Josie and Ms Givings. He'd only be a second. And he had to get rid of the infant gorgon belching on Bourbons.

'Cool and the gang!' said Mr Trick. 'Say – mind if I use the little boys' room?'

'Sure,' said Elliot. 'First door on the left.'

Elliot opened the front door as calmly as he could and closed it quietly behind him. As soon as he was clear of any windows, he sprinted over to the shed.

'Zeus!' he hissed. 'Athene! Aphrodite! Anyone!'

'Everything OK?' whispered a nearby pitchfork.

'I need you to take this – I need to get back to Mum. Now!' he hissed urgently.

With a pop, the pitchfork turned back into Zeus, who took the tin from Elliot.

'Lovely thought, old chap – but you really didn't need to bring us a snack,' said Zeus, lifting the lid.

'Nooooo!' cried Elliot, a half-second too late.

39

'PLOP!' squealed Gorgy jubilantly, bouncing out of the tin and running across the shed, leaving a trail of crumbs.

'Argh!' cried Elliot. 'I have to go. Catch him – and don't let him anywhere near the house!'

'All over it,' said Hephaestus, transforming from a table with his repaired axe.

Elliot pelted across the paddock, took a second to steady his breath, then let himself calmly into the house. The opening chords of Beethoven's Fifth Symphony rang out through the hallway.

'What was that?' asked Ms Givings kindly.

'Novelty toilet seat,' said Elliot. 'We love a joke, Mum and I. I'm sorry – the biscuits have . . . run out.'

'You're doing me a favour,' laughed Ms Givings. 'I eat far too many. Occupational hazard . . . So, Josie – may I call you Josie?'

Josie twitched at the sound of her name, but said nothing.

'Of course you can,' said Elliot, taking Josie's hand. 'Mum hates standing on ceremony, don't you, Mum?'

'Yes,' laughed Josie suddenly.

Elliot couldn't resist smiling at Ms Givings. See? Perfectly normal.

'Wow – so let's totally check out the rest of the

house!' said Mr Trick, appearing in the front room again. He was such a freak.

'Listen, this is a bit awkward,' Elliot began, 'but Mum doesn't . . . she doesn't like me being alone with strangers. Do you, Mum?'

He released her hand and noticed it was slightly pink. He hadn't realized how hard he'd been squeezing it.

'Whatever you think,' Josie replied. She often said this when she didn't know what to do. Today, Elliot was very grateful.

'And besides,' said Elliot, warming to his theme, 'at school we were told that we shouldn't be alone with an adult we don't know.'

Ha! A watertight excuse.

'I'm glad you were paying attention,' said Ms Givings, shaking her head slightly at Mr Trick. 'You're a very responsible young man. Let's all stay here. The tea will go cold.'

'Right! The tea!' said Elliot, before Mr Trick could attempt another high-five. He ran into the kitchen, quickly poured the boiled water into the teapot and threw some mugs on a tray.

'Spoons,' he said under his breath.

Immediately, the cutlery drawer shot open and out flew four teaspoons.

Elliot jumped. The Gods were supposed to

have switched all the magic off. Couldn't they do anything right? He froze – no one seemed to have noticed. Lucky escape.

He took the tray through to the front room and laid the cups on the table.

'Tea!' Josie exclaimed. 'How lovely!'

Well done, Mum, Elliot thought. *Just keep it together for a bit longer.*

'So, who would like—'

A flash of green shot past the window, followed by a large bronze axe. Elliot froze.

'Elliot?' said Ms Givings.

'Dude?' said Mr Trick.

'That tour!' Elliot said, plonking everything back on the tray. 'Let's go upstairs!'

'But I thought you . . .' said Mr Trick, looking helplessly at Ms Givings.

'It's fine if we go together!' said Elliot, his voice far too high. 'I mean – Ms Givings is the school welfare officer!'

'True,' she said, with a nervous laugh. 'Let's go, then. Josie?'

'Oh, let's leave Mum here to enjoy the tea,' said Elliot, gesturing towards the door. 'It's not like she hasn't seen upstairs! Come on!'

He ushered Ms Givings and Mr Trick out of the room. He risked a glance out of the window on the stairs. Hephaestus was looking blankly around the paddock. Where was Gorgy?

'On the left we have the bathroom,' he said, seeing the blacksmith dart off, 'then Mum's room is there, mine is here and Vir . . . Anna's is over there.'

'Yes – where is Anna today?' said Ms Givings. 'I was hoping to see her.'

'Really?' frowned Elliot.

'Really,' said Ms Givings.

Elliot wracked his brain for another lie. Even he was struggling at this pace.

'She's got . . . a piano lesson. She sends her apologies. You did say it was an informal chat . . .'

'Absolutely,' said Ms Givings reassuringly. 'We can catch up another time. It must be fun having a cousin your own age around. Who's the eldest?'

'Oh, she is,' said Elliot, thinking of his 1,964–year-old housemate. 'And every day's certainly an experience with her. Is there anywhere else you'd like to see?'

'Would you mind if we had a peek at your room?' asked Ms Givings. 'Just being nosy, really . . .'

'Sure,' said Elliot. 'I should warn you, though – it's a bit messy . . .'

'I'd be concerned if it wasn't!' laughed Ms

43

Givings. 'A tidy thirteen-year-old boy? That would be something to worry about!'

'Oh, you'll be really happy, then!' said Elliot, trying to open his door against the wall of belongings he'd stuffed in there.

'This is so cool, dude!' said Mr Trick, walking around Elliot's unremarkable bedroom as if he'd stepped on to the moon. 'I bet you get up to all kinds of—'

'Owwweeeeeee!' came a pained squeal from beneath his left shoe.

'What was that?' said a startled Mr Trick. 'And what's this?' He peeled his foot off the floor, leaving a trail of green slime.

Elliot spotted Gorgy's bottom poking out beneath a discarded jumper.

'I, er, have a . . . paper cut,' said Elliot, snatching his finger to his mouth. 'You know how they are – always stinging. And I'm really sorry, I've had a stinking cold . . . I warned you it was a mess. Am I in trouble?'

'No, Elliot, not at all,' said Ms Givings, putting a comforting hand on his shoulder. Elliot thought she gave Mr Trick a warning stare.

'Er, yeah – my room was just the same,' said Mr Trick, bending to pick up the jumper.

'Bad plop man!' squealed the jumper, as Gorgy

pulled it out of Mr Trick's hands.

'What did you say?' asked Ms Givings.

'Sorry,' said Elliot, dropping a pillow on Gorgy. 'I just don't like people touching my stuff.'

He sighed. This was exhausting. He needed to get these people out of his house.

'Well – that's all there is to see here,' he said, ushering the two adults out on to the landing. 'I'm sorry there's not much more to show you. We don't have a big house . . .'

'It's lovely,' said Ms Givings, her eyes full of reassurance. 'I can see why you love it so much.'

Elliot sneaked a quick look out of the window. No sign of Hephaestus. Time for the welfare officers to leave.

'Let's go back downstairs,' he said brightly. 'Don't want your tea to get cold.'

'Of course,' agreed Ms Givings. Elliot tried to analyse her again. She wasn't giving anything away.

'So as you can see, we're really boring,' Elliot said, as he followed Ms Givings and Mr Trick down the stairs. 'Aren't we, Mum?'

Josie didn't reply.

'Don't go all shy on us again, Mum!' called Elliot nervously.

His blood froze at the empty chair in the front room. Where had Josie gone?

'Ah – Mum must have nipped down to the shops,' he said quickly. 'We're all out of . . . milk!'

At his command, the fridge door flew open, revealing a door full of semi-skimmed.

'Oh,' he said, feeling the dread creep up his chest. 'Must get that fridge door fixed.'

Ms Givings nodded to Mr Trick.

'Elliot, thank you so much for having us today,' she said. 'We've taken up quite enough of your time.'

Elliot hesitated. They were leaving voluntarily. Was that a good thing?

'Oh, OK,' he mumbled. 'Thanks for coming to see us. Do come . . . again.'

'We will,' said Ms Givings, giving him another inscrutable smile. 'See you soo—'

The door flew open. In the doorway was a soaking wet Josie. And wrapping his coat around her was Dave.

'Get off me!' Josie shrieked, clawing at him. 'You monster!'

'I'm so sorry, Elliot,' said Dave, looking grimly at the welfare officers. 'I had no choice. I heard her shout from the field – she fell in the pond.'

'You pushed me! You pushed me, you evil—'

'Mum!' Elliot cried, taking her into his arms. 'Calm down, no one pushed anyone, you just had an accident . . .'

'And you are?' Ms Givings asked.

Dave gave Elliot an apologetic look.

'I'm David Hooper,' he said. 'Elliot's father.'

'I see,' said Ms Givings, consulting her notes. Elliot felt the world grow heavier around him.

'Forget him,' exclaimed Josie angrily, shrugging off the coat and grabbing Mr Trick by his collar. 'Who are you? GET OUT OF MY HOUSE!'

4. Oh, Brother

The past two months had given Thanatos little to smile about. The boy still had the Earth and Air Stones. The Daemon of Death had no idea where the Water and Fire Stones were. His faith in his mother's plan was fading by the hour. And he was still in a foul mood.

But as he sat upon his throne of bones in the Cave of Sleep and Death, the front page of the *Daily Argus*, the immortal newspaper, brought a long-awaited smile to his lips.

WISE COUNCIL
BY PLINY, POLITICAL EDITOR

At a time when the good news is sadly elusive
The *Argus* has landed a great big exclusive
This story is massive! A journalist coup!
(The bloke down the pub told my mate it was true)
The Zodiac Council has said that it's time
To step up their efforts to minimize crime
There's no need to panic, it's nothing too drastic
(Although Elementals might feel less fantastic)
Just raise the alarm if they're being suspicious
(Those Unicorns always look mighty malicious)
And they'll be invited to have a brief stay
In Tartarus, where they are out of harm's way
And if they require a little assistance
The Titans are free to prevent their resistance
So try not to worry, whatever you do
(But if you're Elemental, we're all watching you . . .)

'Excellent,' Thanatos murmured to himself, a new plan forming in his mind as Nyx swept into the cave in a plume of black smoke. 'Hello, Mother. Long time no see.'

'I can't stay long. Some of us are busy retrieving our Chaos Stones,' said the Goddess of the Night. 'How delightful it must be to have the luxury of time to sit around reading the paper.'

'Help yourself,' said Thanatos, tossing it towards her.

Thanatos looked over at his brother, Hypnos, Daemon of Sleep, who had been in an enchanted slumber ever since Nyx turned his own sleep trumpet on him.

'I still say we should finish him,' said Thanatos. 'You're getting soft in your old age, Mother . . .'

The Goddess of the Night flashed a look that warned her son not to try her patience. Thanatos knew he'd be wise to heed it. She turned her attention to the newspaper.

'The Titans?' said Nyx slowly. 'Haven't seen them in a while.'

'My thoughts entirely,' said Thanatos. 'We're long overdue a catch-up.'

'Indeed,' said Nyx.

'I've decided to take an extended break in Tartarus,' said Thanatos.

'To do what?' asked Nyx.

'Rally the troops,' said Thanatos. 'War is coming. We need to be ready.'

'What can you do?' Nyx objected. 'Without your Chaos Stones, the Daemon Army is trapped. What use are you there?'

'Oh, you'll see,' smiled Thanatos. 'But this does mean I'll be unavailable to babysit my dear brother.'

'Well, what do you propose?' said Nyx. 'I can't

be here. I'm busy.'

'You know my thoughts. He won't stay like this for ever. More's the pity,' sneered Thanatos. 'His Daemon strength will fight the magic. He will awaken. And soon.'

'I know this,' hissed Nyx, following Thanatos towards his throne of bones. 'But he's still—'

'My brother,' yawned Thanatos. 'Don't I know it.'

'I was going to say, "potentially useful".' Nyx glowered. 'For our plans to succeed, we need as much help as possible. Hypnos is still virtually unknown on Earth; he could be an asset. If you're going to be in Tartarus and I'm going to be—'

'What was that?' said Thanatos, interrupting his mother as a noise from the next chamber pricked his senses.

'Nothing,' said Nyx. 'Just the wind. You're getting paranoid in your old age . . .'

Thanatos raised a lone eyebrow at his mother's gleeful grimace.

'My brother cannot be trusted,' he said. 'How much more proof do you need? He betrayed me to Zeus. He lost us our Chaos Stones. And he told the boy where to find them. He is a liability.'

'Maybe he's learnt his lesson,' said Nyx.

'Or maybe he'll wake up seeking revenge,' said Thanatos. 'Face it, Mother: the stakes are too high now – there is no place for a treacherous fool.'

Nyx's black wings fluttered in a sudden breeze. She wrapped them around her and stood as still as a tomb while she thought.

'Who's going to do it?' she said at last.

'Oh, please let me have the pleasure,' said Thanatos, rising happily from his throne. 'Don't get me wrong – it's a much easier death than I'd hoped for my evil twin, but taking his kardia will have to do. Let's get on with it—'

'Wait!' said Nyx, holding up a talon. 'He's still my son. He deserves a final farewell from his mother.'

'If you must,' sighed Thanatos, slumping back on his throne. 'But make it quick.'

Nyx walked nervously to the dark corner of the cave where Hypnos's sable-covered bed lay in the shadows. The black curtains wafted in the dank air. Nyx took one in her talons and slowly drew it back.

Thanatos cracked his knuckles. He'd been looking forward to this for centuries.

'THANATOS!' cried Nyx. 'He's . . . he's—'

'He's what?' snapped Thanatos impatiently. He strode over and snatched back the curtains. He stared down at Hypnos's bed with a horrified gasp.

'He's gone!' screeched Nyx.

5. Bottoms Up

Being headmaster of Brysmore School was very stressful. But then, for Graham Sopweed, lots of things were. Most aspects of daily life caused Call Me Graham untold stress. Maybe the weather forecast had predicted light drizzle when it was actually moderate. Maybe he'd left his favourite biro in his other cardigan. Or maybe Friday just didn't feel . . . Fridayish enough. Every day brought unique challenges for Graham as he navigated life's path. A path that, for Graham, was beset with uneven paving stones, sharp thorns and dog mess.

But no more. A month ago, Graham had

decided it was time to seek help for his dreadful nerves. His wife Lilith had reported great results with hypnotherapy – she was losing over thirty pounds a week! And, as she kept insisting, it was only a matter of time before she shed some weight too. Lilith said her hypnotherapist made her feel like 'a different woman' – and made her realize how much she wished Graham were 'a different man'. So Graham decided to take the plunge and booked his first hypnotherapy session.

It was the best decision he'd ever made. As Lilith pointed out, he had been lucky to get an appointment – Dr C. U. Cumming was much in demand. His hourly rate was a steal – and as he only accepted cash, Graham didn't have to worry about card fraud (just to be sure, the hypnotherapist kept his wallet for the whole time Graham was in a trance). And to top it all, Dr Cumming's practice couldn't be more convenient, located in a gazebo in the supermarket car park.

Dr Cumming had given Graham techniques that had changed his life. He had taught Graham to clap his hands three times every time he got stressed. For the following few seconds, Graham would enter a deep hypnotic trance that completely cleared his mind. He had no idea what happened in these brief absences, but when he emerged, he was as calm as a vegan's pet pig. Dr Cumming had spent hours perfecting this technique and it had proved invaluable. Graham was a fortress. Graham was a rock. Graham was a . . .

'PATHETIC LITTLE SLACKER!' roared Mr Boil, storming into the office without an invitation.

Graham felt his heart quake.

'I want a word!' demanded his deputy.

'Yes, of c-course, Mr B-boil,' stammered Call Me Graham. 'Just one moment.'

He quietly turned away and clapped his hands three times.

'My PIN number is 2679,' he chanted, quite unaware he was doing so.

'What are you . . . ?' Boil spluttered. 'Who cares . . . It's about Hooper.'

'Which one?' sighed Graham. 'Elliot or Anna?'

'Both,' glowered Boil. 'They've been playing truant.'

'Really?' said Graham. 'When?'

'This morning,' leered Boil. 'While I was having my . . . procedure.'

'Yes – how did that go?' whispered Call Me Graham. 'All sounded very . . . personal.'

'The doctors say I should make a full recovery,' said Boil. 'But I'm to avoid putting undue pressure on the affected area.'

'You have to admit,' laughed Graham nervously, 'it is rather ironic that you of all people should get a boil on your—'

'Bottom!' pronounced Boil, thrusting a register in Call Me Graham's face.

'I didn't know it was common knowledge . . .' murmured Graham.

'The register!' snapped Boil. 'Look at the bottom. Hooper times two. My substitute noted them down as absent! Expulsion is the only way forward!'

'Ah – not to worry, Mr Boil,' said Call Me Graham. 'Their absence was fully authorized. Today was their inspection by the school welfare team.'

'It was?' asked Boil, with something the headmaster thought might be a smile. 'What happened?'

'I'm about to find out – Ms Givings should be here any moment,' said Graham, putting a folder on his desk. 'So, if you'll excuse me . . .'

'No, no, no, headmaster,' smiled Boil. 'I am your deputy. I should be aware of any issues regarding my students – especially one as . . . special as Hooper. I'll stay.'

'I'm not sure that's—' Graham began.

'Worth my time?' Boil cut in. 'I know, but I do

57

like to go the extra mile for my students.'

'I thought you liked to run a mile from your students,' said Graham.

'Enough!' roared Boil, making Graham jump. 'I am staying and that is final.'

Graham clapped his hands beneath the desk.

'My bank account is 21369743, sort code 39-42-06,' he chimed.

'What are you blithering about?' asked Boil.

'Sorry?' said Graham serenely. 'I didn't say anything.'

'Yes, you did,' snapped Boil, plumping down in the nearest chair. 'Owwweeeeee!'

'Ah, yes,' winced Graham as Boil leapt into the air. 'Your . . . affected area. Perhaps you put undue pressure on it?'

There was a gentle tap on the open office door.

'Hello, Mr Sopweed,' said Ms Givings. 'Is now a good time?'

'Of course – do come in. You'll have to excuse Mr Boil, he's just recovering from surgery.'

'Nothing serious, I hope,' said Ms Givings.

'Just a . . . routine procedure,' groaned Boil.

'Well, I hope they get to the bottom of it,' said Ms Givings, pulling a chair up to Graham's desk. 'So, I wanted to get my findings back to you immediately. I'm afraid it's not good news.'

'Really?' Graham shivered. This sounded stress-ful. He kept his hands at the ready.

'I'm afraid so. I'll email my full report, but I'm sorry to say that my initial assessment is . . . that Josie Hooper is sadly not capable of caring for Elliot.'

A fleeting movement caught the corner of Graham's eye. Surely Mr Boil hadn't just fist-pumped?

'Oh, no!' Graham exclaimed. 'What's the problem?'

'During our visit, Mrs Hooper was variously unresponsive, confused, vacant and finally very aggressive. From what I observed – and I'm no doctor – I think that she is in an advanced state of mental deterioration. I believe Josie Hooper to be suffering from some form of dementia.'

'No!' gasped Graham. 'That's awful! Dementia? But she's not old enough, surely?'

'Some people can develop it as early as their forties,' explained Ms Givings. 'It's called "early-onset dementia". It's rare, but very serious. And, sadly, it will only get worse.'

'That poor, poor boy,' whispered Graham, clapping his hands. 'The spare key to my house is under the gnome with the pink spotty hat.'

'What was that?' asked Ms Givings.

59

'Nothing,' said Graham, exhaling deeply. 'It's just so—'

'Yes, yes, all very sad,' grinned Boil. 'So what are you going to do about Hoop . . . young Elliot and Anna?'

'That's where it gets a bit complicated,' sighed Ms Givings, consulting her notes. 'Anna has her parents – Brad and Bridget, I believe? Although neither of them was there during our visit. But we did discover another adult residing in the house. David Hooper, Elliot's father.'

'The criminal!' cried Boil.

'The ex-offender,' Ms Givings corrected. 'Elliot's been hiding him.'

'Oh, Elliot,' sighed Graham. 'Can his father take care of him?'

'That's what I'm trying to establish,' said Ms Givings. 'But I'm having trouble tracking down Mr Hooper's parole officer. Obviously, I need to know a great deal more about his situation. Especially as Josie may need to be removed from their home.'

'Removed?' trembled Graham.

'Removed!' sang Boil.

'I'm afraid so,' said Ms Givings grimly. 'Josie's going to need specialist care as her mental and physical state deteriorates. What I now need to find out is if she appointed a legal guardian for Elliot.'

'Who cares about that?' asked Boil.

'We do, Mr Boil,' said Ms Givings firmly. 'We need to know if Josie has chosen someone to take care of Elliot if she can't. It's very important.'

'Won't it be her husband?' suggested Graham.

'Maybe,' said Ms Givings. 'But if David Hooper has been in prison for ten years, he may no longer be Elliot's legal guardian. We don't even know if they are still married – many couples divorce and change custody arrangements when one partner is imprisoned. Unfortunately, Josie couldn't answer my questions.'

'So Hooper's legal guardian gets to decide where he goes?' leered Boil.

'Potentially, yes,' said Ms Givings guardedly. 'If David Hooper isn't responsible for Elliot, then we need to find out who is. They could hold his future in their hands.'

'This is all so dr-dreadful,' stammered Call Me Graham, clapping again. 'I'll be out of town for three days next week. The combination to my private safe is in my sock drawer.'

'Er – thank you, Mr Sopweed. We're already working on it,' said a confused Ms Givings, rising to leave. 'I wondered if the neighbour might have some insight – Mrs Horse's—'

'Porshley-Plum,' grinned Boil. 'Oh, yes. I think Patricia's going to want to do everything she can to help.'

'For the last time, I'm telling you – I locked Gorgy in his cage!'

Elliot glowered at Virgo as they walked to their maths lesson. They'd been having the same argument the whole way to school.

'Then how did he get out?' snapped Elliot.

'I do not know!' said Virgo. 'Before I left for the Council, I put Gorgy in his cage, gave him a book, he wiped his nose on it and I locked the door. I remember it precisely.'

'A lot of people seem to be remembering a lot of things that didn't actually happen,' scowled Elliot. 'It was a total disaster.'

'You cannot presume this,' said Virgo. 'Surely it would be optimal to save your foul mood for when you know you have something to be foul about?'

'Just . . . shut up,' huffed Elliot as he stormed past Call Me Graham's office.

'Hooper?' an unwelcome voice called behind him.

Elliot charged on. He seriously wasn't in the

mood for Mr Boil.

'HOOPER!' yelled the history teacher. 'Come here, I want to talk to you.'

Elliot stopped and clenched his fists. This was the last thing he needed right now. He turned to face his nemesis.

'What?'

'You are addressing a teacher!' cried Boil.

'What – sir?' sulked Elliot.

Mr Boil's face lit up with a horrifying grimace. What was he up to?

'I've just been hearing about your house guest,' whispered Boil. 'So Daddy's home?'

Elliot could feel his fingernails digging into the palms of his hands.

'So?' he said.

'Must be nice for you, that's all,' said Boil. 'Having some help. With your mother.'

'How do you know—' gasped Elliot.

'Oh, I know everything, Hooper,' hissed Boil. 'Everything.'

'Come along, Elliot,' said Virgo, tugging at his blazer. 'We need to get to maths . . .'

'What do you mean?' demanded Elliot. He wasn't in the mood for Boil's games.

'I mean,' said Boil, bringing his flabby face far too close to Elliot's, 'that my days of looking at

63

your insolent, disrespectful, horrible little face are numbered. I wonder where your new family will send you to school. Let's hope it's a long, long way away . . .'

Elliot's heart raced. New family? What did Boil know?

'I'm not going anywhere. Sir,' he said, as firmly as he was able.

'Oh, yes you are!' Boil winked. 'And so's Mummy. I knew you were trouble the first moment I laid eyes on you. You're a rotten seed, Elliot Hooper. Rotten to the core.'

'No, I'm not. Sir,' seethed Elliot.

'Oh, yes you are,' said Boil, bringing his bloated face even closer. 'Rotten. Just like your criminal father.'

'He isn't a criminal,' hissed Elliot, 'he was—'

'Just like your failure grandparents.'

'You leave them out of this—'

'Just – ' Boil paused to lower his face still closer to Elliot's – 'just like your dotty mother—'

SMACK!

It happened before Elliot had the slightest awareness he was going to do it. One minute his right fist was clenched by his side. The next, it had flown through the air – and hit Mr Boil square in the face.

'Elliot!' cried Virgo, as Mr Boil crumpled to the floor.

But Elliot was ablaze with white-hot anger. His hand instinctively went to the hole-free pocket where he always kept his father's watch containing the Earth and Air Stones. He yanked the watch out and felt the stones' power start to surge through his body as the elements awaited his command.

'Rotten?' he roared at Boil's hunched figure on the floor. 'See how rotten you find this ...'

He raised the watch above his head. The school hallway filled with the mingled glow of the diamond and emerald within the watch, bursting to unleash their power.

Suddenly, he felt his arm wrenched back down.

'Elliot!' Virgo cried. 'What on *Earth* are you thinking? Put them away before someone gets killed ...'

The shock snapped Elliot back to the present. He looked at the unopened watch in his hand. What had just happened? He nearly ... he could have ... he'd wanted to ...

'Elliot!' gasped Call Me Graham, tripping over Mr Boil's body, writhing on the floor outside his office. 'Whatever have you done?!'

Elliot looked at the horrified faces all around

him. He dropped his fist slowly to his side, scooped his bag off the floor – and ran as fast as his faltering feet could carry him towards the open door.

6. Fight or Flight

Elliot's heart pounded as he raced across the fields away from Brysmore. He heard Virgo calling his name, but all he knew was that he needed to get away. He didn't know where he was going and he didn't care. He ran for ages, miles, hours – he had no idea. He ran until his legs burned and his heart buzzed. He ran as the rain lashed down around him, until his clothes clung to his body and water streamed down his face, mingling with his angry tears. He ran until he collapsed breathlessly next to a stone wall. He slumped to the grass and beat the jagged stones with his fists until they bled. He couldn't feel a thing.

It was happening. It was really happening. They were going to take Mum away. Elliot buried his head in his knees and wept.

He had no idea how long he sat sobbing in that field. All the pain, frustration and fear he had corked up for so long came pouring out. He was going to lose her. His mum. His world. Where would they take her? Where would they take him?

Wave after wave of tears ebbed and flowed as Elliot felt his world collapse.

But by the time his tears had run dry, the sky had grown darker. And so had his thoughts.

He didn't care what it took. He didn't care what he had to do. He wasn't going to let this happen. He had to save his mum.

Elliot yanked open his school bag and pulled out the *What's What* Virgo had given him for Christmas. It was one of the few magical possessions he still had since Nyx stole his bottomless satchel at Stonehenge. He kept this one in his school bag – it came in pretty handy for cheating on tests.

'Panacea's potion,' he yelled into it, as he had done so many times since Hercules had blurted it out weeks ago. The medicine that could cure everything – it had to exist. It just had to.

The scrawl started magically to appear across the page. Maybe this time . . .

No matches, it said. *Do you mean Pants of the Ocean?*

'Aaaaaaargh!' Elliot threw the scroll across the grass and slammed his head back against the wall. Again. And again. And ag . . .

Elliot felt a hand cushion his blurry head from another blow.

'So, it's none of my business, but whatever's troubling you will be easier to solve with your brains inside your head? Yesssss?'

Elliot looked up groggily. The figures swimming before his eyes started to form a single image with a winged head and a wild grin . . .

'Hypnos?' he mumbled. 'Get lost.'

'Missed you too, buddy!' squealed the Daemon of Sleep, dropping down on the grass next to him. 'So what's new?'

'I mean it,' said Elliot through clenched teeth. 'Leave me alone.'

'One of those, huh?' said Hypnos, extending one of his feathered wings from the side of his head to form an umbrella over Elliot. 'Not that you asked, but I'm having a terrible day too.'

'I don't care.'

'No one does,' pouted Hypnos. 'My brother

hates me. I had to run for my life, without my beautiful trumpet. Even my own mumsie wants to kill me.'

'Good for her,' said Elliot, putting a hand to his bruised head. 'Listen – you've sworn on the Styx not to hurt me, but I'm seriously tempted to hurt you. So do me a favour and go away.'

Hypnos frowned, but didn't leave. 'So what do you want with Panacea's potion?' he asked.

Elliot's head drooped. 'Mind your own business.'

'OK,' said the Daemon. 'I just thought you might be looking for it, s'all.'

'It doesn't exist,' growled Elliot.

'Like fun it doesn't.'

'What do you mean?'

'The potion – it's as real as taxes. Seen it with my own eyes.'

'Where is it?' cried Elliot. 'Tell me! Now!'

'Well, now,' said Hypnos slowly. 'There's the rub. I don't know ...'

'I knew it,' Elliot huffed, standing to leave. 'You're just full of—'

'But I know a man who can tell you,' said Hypnos, leaping up to hover right in Elliot's way.

'You're lying,' said Elliot uncertainly.

'Where's the trust?!' squealed Hypnos. 'What have I ever done to you?'

'Tried to kill me on a speeding train. And at Buckingham Palace . . .'

'OK, so maybe I tried to kill you a teensy bit,' Hypnos conceded. 'But name a time I've lied to you?'

Elliot's mind struggled against itself. He hated to admit it – but Hypnos had a point.

'I'm telling you,' Hypnos said slowly, 'the potion exists. And there's only one person who can tell us how to find it.'

'Right,' said Elliot forcefully. 'You need to take me to them. Now!'

'Whoa there, stable the horses! If I'm going to help you, I need two things. Firstly, old man Zeus. You need him to agree to look for it – and then you need to get him into the sea. There's no way he'll do it voluntarily, so you'll have to trick him. And, believe me, it won't be easy . . .'

'What?!' said Elliot. 'Trick him how? Why wouldn't he go in the sea? What are you talking about?'

'Uh, uh, uh,' said Hypnos, waggling a finger. 'No more spoilers. If I tell you everything, you'll have no reason to give me the second thing I need.'

'What's that?' said Elliot impatiently.

'Your protection,' whispered Hypnos. 'Thanatos

wants me dead. You're the only person he can't touch, so you're the only one who can keep me safe. I need to stay with you.'

'I don't trust you,' said Elliot. 'And neither do the Gods. They'd never allow it.'

'You leave the Gods to me,' said Hypnos. 'I know precisely how to get them onside. I will help you find Panacea's potion. In exchange for your protection.'

Elliot turned his options over in his mind. It didn't take long.

'Done,' he said, striding off over the field. 'Let's go.'

'Yippeeee!' said Hypnos, flying into the air and grabbing Elliot. 'Where to, boss?'

'Home,' said Elliot. 'Then we're going to the sea. Whether Zeus likes it or not.'

7. Home Truths

Not for the first time since she became mortal, Virgo couldn't understand what was happening to her. Ever since the vote at the Zodiac Council that morning, she had been troubled by an unpleasant sensation within her body. It reminded her slightly of the time she'd tried ice cream with gravy, but that wasn't it.

This feeling wasn't just in her stomach. It sort of . . . swirled around her insides, churning around her heart and into her throat every time she thought back to the vote. She was under strict instructions not to discuss the Council's plans if she wished to see her kardia returned. But whatever this new sensation was, it made ice cream and gravy seem like a good idea.

'Any sign?' called Zeus, as Athene and Aphrodite bustled back into the kitchen.

The Goddesses shook their heads. They had been searching for Elliot ever since he'd bolted from Brysmore. Virgo felt conflicted about Elliot's actions. Punching anyone, particularly someone in authority, was wrong. But she couldn't help but feel that Mr Boil sort of . . . deserved it. Mr Sopweed had prevented her – rather feebly, she thought – from chasing after Elliot, but the moment she could, she'd raced home to alert his father and the Gods.

And yet Dave seemed curiously calm.

'Stop fretting,' he'd said, as the Gods sprang into action to scour the Wiltshire countryside for Elliot. 'The boy's just blowing off a bit of steam. He'll come home when he's hungry. Relax . . .'

But several hours later, there was still no sign of Elliot.

'Father, I really think we should alert the mortal authorities,' said Athene anxiously. 'It's been too long.'

'Great idea, genius,' snapped Aphrodite. 'The school welfare officer is already suspicious – telling the police that Elly is missing will really help.'

Athene glowered at her sister, but said nothing. This was highly irregular. She must be very worried indeed.

'Elly!' Josie-Mum cried suddenly, racing into the kitchen. 'Elly, where are you?'

'It's all right, Jo,' said Dave calmly, reaching for Josie-Mum's hand and receiving a slap in return. 'Everyone just chill . . .'

'Don't worry, Josie,' said Athene, giving Dave a sub-optimal look. 'Let me make you some tea.'

'Elly!' murmured Josie-Mum more feebly. Aphrodite helped her into a chair. Virgo felt the same heavy sensation she experienced every time she looked at this fading mortal. Josie-Mum was becoming more sub-optimal by the day.

'Been all over,' huffed Hephaestus, limping into the kitchen. 'Can't see the boy nowhere.'

'I'm telling you,' said Dave casually, making himself a cup of tea. 'He'll be back when it gets cold and dark. He's just a kid . . .'

Virgo felt the air in the kitchen grow uncomfortable. She had yet to conclusively analyse Elliot's father. When Elliot was present, he seemed very amiable. But away from his son, somehow he was — different. She had tried to engage him in conversation several times, but he never seemed especially interested in what she had to say. She had raised this with Elliot, but he believed it was because her conversation was 'a load of bum'. Elliot had certainly been more optimal since his father returned, which was a positive. And yet . . .

She looked at the King of the Gods' dark face. Zeus clearly *had* concluded his analysis of David Hooper. It wasn't good.

'Oh, Elliot,' cried Zeus in frustration. 'Where are you?'

'Here,' said a familiar voice behind them.

Virgo immediately found that her breathing was more optimal. There in the doorway was Elliot, safe and well.

'Elly!' screamed Aphrodite, running over to gather Elliot in her arms. 'You're – you're bleeding . . .'

'I'm fine,' said Elliot, holding his hand to his head. 'Listen, there's something I need to—'

'You must be starving,' panted Athene, running over to the stove as Aphrodite tended to Elliot's head with some ice. 'Let's get you some supper . . .'

'Here – I'll do it,' said Dave, barging Aphrodite out of the way. 'It's just a scratch – stop fussing around the boy, he said he's fine . . .'

'We're not fussing,' Athene said tersely. 'He needs to eat.'

'Sounds suuuuuper!' screeched an owl above

them. 'What's on the menu?'

That didn't sound like an owl . . .

Within a second, Zeus had thunderbolts in both hands, Aphrodite had her crossbow aimed straight at the owl, and Athene had drawn her sword.

'Hypnos!' boomed Zeus. 'Show yourself!'

'Well, this is the worst game of hide-and-seek ever!' grinned the Daemon of Sleep as he dissembled back into his customary feathered form. 'Oh, this house is *daaarling* – so shabby chic . . .'

'Stay back, Elliot!' Athene commanded, bustling Elliot behind her. 'We've got you.'

'How did you get past me fence?' Hephaestus demanded, with his axe above his head.

'Because he's invited,' said Elliot quietly, raising his hand to their weapons. 'He's with me.'

'He's what?' said Zeus. 'Elliot, what on Earth . . . ?'

'You'd better all sit down,' said Elliot 'There's something we need to discuss.'

'I'm telling you, Elliot, it's a fool's errand!' roared Zeus five minutes later. 'Hypnos – he can't be trusted as far as we can spit him!'

'I agree,' said Dave, who, Elliot noticed, seemed weirdly on edge since he got home. 'I don't trust him.'

'What choice do we have?' insisted Elliot. 'They're going to take her – I have to cure her, I just have to!'

'Who's going to be taken?' said Josie anxiously. 'We must keep you safe . . .'

'Dad?' said Elliot, nodding at Josie in frustration. 'Can you just—'

'I think I need to stay here,' said Dave, eyeing Hypnos suspiciously.

'Please,' said Elliot.

With a heavy sigh, Dave took Josie's arm.

'Get off me!' she hissed.

'It's OK, Jo,' said Aphrodite soothingly. 'You go, I'll be up in a minute.'

'Come on,' Dave said impatiently, as Josie resisted his attempts to lead her upstairs.

'Elliot . . .' The King of the Gods sighed, momentarily lost for words.

Elliot tried to calm his racing heart. He had to persuade Zeus. This was going to be a tough sell.

'It's not just about Mum,' he said slowly. 'If – when – we find the potion, she's not the only person we can help. We could cure Hermes . . .'

The Goddess of Love gave a small gasp.

'Daddy – he's right,' she whispered. 'Our powers never could help Josie – but they're not helping Hermes either. We've tried everything –

my potions, Athene's medicines, Now That's What I Call a Tuuuuuune 867 . . . Nothing is working. He's fading. This could be our only chance.'

'Panacea's potion doesn't exist!' cried an exasperated Athene. 'There's no record of it anywhere – I've searched. How do you know about something I do not?'

'Simple,' gloated Hypnos. 'Because Panacea wanted me to know about it. And she didn't want you to know about it.'

'Don't be ridiculous,' snorted Zeus. 'Why on Earth would she tell you and not us?'

'Oooooh – let's review your track record with immortals who tried to help the mortals,' said Hypnos. 'Prometheus – ring a bell? He gave the mortals fire. You gave him an eagle to eat his internal organs every day . . .'

'Yes, well, we all have our off days,' mumbled Zeus. 'Besides, he made a fortune when he claimed through EternalPunishments4U . . .'

'And then there's Panacea's own father, Asclepius,' Hypnos went on. 'He was such an incredible doctor, he could bring mortals back from the dead! You killed him with a thunderbolt!'

'He wasn't that good a doctor, then,' burbled Zeus uncomfortably.

'So you can hardly blame Panacea for keeping

her potion on the down-low, can you? But I've seen it with my own eyes. She was so terrified of what you might do to her for creating it, she took refuge with the Daemons for a while. She feared she'd be hounded until the Gods made her hand it over.'

'So the Daemons have it?' asked Elliot keenly.

'No. *We* hounded her to try to make her hand it over,' said Hypnos. 'So she ran away. But I was there. I saw it. It's real. So we can find it.'

'All we have to do,' Elliot gabbled to Zeus, 'is look for it. And you can start by getting in the s—'

'Same mindset!' Hypnos interrupted, pulling Elliot into a hug that covered his mouth with his arm. 'Positive thinking, that's what we need!'

Elliot looked up at the Daemon. Hypnos imperceptibly shook his head. Elliot took the hint.

'Look at it this way, chief,' whispered Hypnos. 'What if the potion is real? What if you could cure your son? What if the answer to all of Elliot's problems really does exist? And what if you're stopping him from finding it? Are you prepared to take that risk?'

'It would be like looking for a needle in a haystack!' roared Zeus. 'No. Not a chance. It's out of the question . . .'

'What did you just say?' Elliot whispered.

'I'm just . . .' Zeus burbled.

'Out of the question?' Elliot repeated quietly. 'You said that it's "out of the question"?'

'Elliot, I didn't mean—' Zeus began.

'OUT OF THE QUESTION?!' Elliot shouted. 'Getting the Earth Stone from the Queen was "out of the question". Stealing the Air Stone from the Natural History Museum was "out of the question". Facing down a Death Daemon trying to kill me was "out of the question". But I still did them. In fact, whenever you've needed my help, I've risked my life to do whatever stupid thing was "out of the question"! You live in my home, you mess up the one chance I had to get the welfare officer off my back, and now I need your help it's "out of the question"?!'

'All I'm trying to say is—' Zeus pleaded.

'Oh, I hear what you're saying,' said Elliot. 'I hear it loud and clear. You're not prepared to help me. And if that's how it's going to be, then it works both ways.'

'Elly, you don't mean . . .' said Aphrodite, coming to take Elliot in her arms. He roughly shrugged her off.

'Yes, I do,' said Elliot. 'If you won't help me, you

can forget about it. Everything. The Chaos Stones. Thanatos. Living here. It's over.'

'Elliot,' gasped Athene. 'That's blackmail. That's not you.'

'Well, maybe you don't know me as well as you think you do,' Elliot glowered.

He stared at the King of the Gods. They were both trembling.

'You'd really risk us losing to Thanatos?' said Zeus incredulously.

'You'd really risk me losing my mum?' Elliot replied.

Zeus's eyes went straight through Elliot's soul, as they had done so many times before. But this time, Elliot wasn't budging.

'So, what will it be?' he said, his fingers encircling the watch in his pocket. He felt the power of the Chaos Stones giving him the strength he needed. He fought the urge to get them out. That would bring the conversation to a quick end.

Zeus bowed his head and sighed deeply.

'I'll help you look for it,' he said quietly. 'I'm only trying to protect you.'

'And I'm only trying to protect Mum,' said Elliot. 'Swear it.'

'Elliot, you know I'd never—' Zeus began.

'Swear it,' Elliot repeated more firmly. 'Swear

on the Styx you will help me find Panacea's potion.'

The King of the Gods stared deep into Elliot's eyes.

'I swear it,' he whispered. 'I swear on the Styx, I will help you find Panacea's potion.'

'Whatever it takes?' Elliot insisted.

'Whatever it takes,' Zeus repeated reluctantly.

The King of the Gods stared at Elliot as if seeing him for the first time. Elliot felt himself soften – these were his friends. An apology bloomed in his heart. But he refused to let it out of his mouth.

'Well played,' whispered Hypnos. 'Show 'em who's boss.'

But as Elliot released his grip on the Chaos Stones, he didn't feel like the boss. He felt horrible.

For a few moments, no one spoke. Eventually, the house phone broke the tense silence in the kitchen.

'I'd better get that – it's been ringing all afternoon,' said Athene. 'I'll be straight back.'

'You,' Zeus growled at the Daemon. 'What do you want?'

'Before big bro came back, I was a gambler, I was lazy, I was deceitful,' said Hypnos wistfully. 'It was wonderful. I just want my old life back. With Thanatos on the loose, I'll never have that. He won't rest until I'm gone. And I can't rest until he's gone. You're the only people who can get rid of him. And I'm the only person who can help you do it.'

'And in return?' said Zeus in a menacing whisper.

'Think not what you can do for your Daemon – think what your Daemon can do for you,' grinned Hypnos, waggling his eyebrows. 'How are you getting on with those Chaos Stones?'

'You lied to Elliot,' Zeus glowered. 'Poloformous doesn't exist.'

It was true. Elliot and the Gods had poured over maps of the mortal and immortal realms for hours, searching for the place where Hypnos had told Elliot he had hidden the Water Stone – Poloformous. It was nowhere to be found.

'Oh, yes he does,' sang Hypnos.

'He?' said Elliot, ignoring memories of all the school reports that insisted he listen more carefully. 'You mean . . .'

'Yup!' chirped Hypnos. 'It's not a place, it's a person. And it's not Poloformous. It's Polyphemus.'

'Told you your hearing was sub-optimal,' Virgo sighed.

84

'Polyphemus!' bellowed Zeus. 'As in—'

'You got it, grandad!' said Hypnos, taking off around the kitchen. 'He's got his eye on the prize . . . it's Polyphemus the Cyclops!'

'Why in the name of a Nereid's knickers would you give a Chaos Stone to a Cyclops?' roared Zeus.

'Why not?' shrugged Hypnos. 'Like all the Cyclopes, Polyphemus is terrified of water. I felt sorry for him – with the Water Stone, he could protect himself from it. You told me to hide them where no one could find them. Who's going to go to the Island of the Cyclopes?'

'I am,' said Zeus darkly. 'We need to get that stone before your brother does. Peg!'

'Not so fast,' whispered Hypnos. 'He'll never give it to you.'

'He won't have a bally choice!' yelled Zeus, putting his hand to his thunderbolts.

'Er, yeah, he will,' said Hypnos. 'Since his run-in with Odysseus, he's become kinda . . . paranoid. Even if you blast him back to the Hellenistic period, you won't get past his security system to get the stone. For that, you'll need me.'

'Fine,' glowered Zeus. 'You and I leave at first light.'

'And Elliot,' said Hypnos.

Zeus laughed a laugh that Elliot knew wasn't funny.

'Don't be so ridiculous!' cried the King of the Gods. 'I'm not letting Elliot go on such a perilous journey! You're even crazier than you look!'

'I'm telling you – you won't get the Water Stone without him,' whispered Hypnos. 'We need someone Polyphemus doesn't know. And Elliot has the Earth and Air Stones for protection.'

'And you. And Hypnos. And Dad,' Elliot chimed in. 'I'm going.'

'You've let him before . . .' Hypnos hissed.

'Taking a stone from mortal buildings is one thing,' hissed Zeus. 'Stealing it from one of the most ferocious creatures in the immortal world is quite another! We are invulnerable. Elliot is not, even with the Chaos Stones. Besides, there's too much going on here. He has school . . .'

'No, he doesn't,' sighed Athene, walking slowly back into the room.

'What?' said Elliot.

'That was Mr Sopweed,' said Athene. 'From what I could gather through the sobbing, in light of today's . . . incident, you are suspended until further notice.'

'Good,' said Elliot, feeling a surge of angry pride. 'I hate that place anyway. I'm going with you.'

'Well, that's settled then,' said Hypnos, winking at Elliot. 'Boys' road trip! Trust me, we need him. We'll pick up the Water Stone – and who knows? It just might lead us to Panacea's potion. When you're looking for one thing, another always turns up ...'

'If you're lying to us—' said Zeus menacingly.

'Then you'll fry me with a thousand thunderbolts, blah, blah, blah,' said Hypnos, pinching his thumb and fingers together. 'Listen, chief – if I am lying, you get to pull me apart like yesterday's roast chicken.'

'You can count on it,' growled Zeus.

'Good to know,' said Hypnos. 'But if I'm not, you can get your hands on the Water Stone. And I'm telling you now – if you don't get it, Thanatos will. If you'd rather waste time chatting, however ...'

Zeus stared angrily at the Daemon.

'So be it,' Zeus hissed. 'We leave at dawn.'

'I'm coming too!' said Virgo.

'No, you're not,' said Athene and Zeus together.

'You still have school,' said Athene.

'Temporarily,' said Virgo. 'Tell them I have acquired the vomiting bug that the dinner lady so kindly served with her spaghetti bolognese. That'll give me a few days.'

'You're not coming,' Zeus insisted.

'Zeus, if I may,' Virgo began in a whisper that everyone could hear. 'I will be invaluable on this mission. I am the only one who is able to force some sense into Elliot's head. Unless it's regarding his personal hygiene – or total absence thereof – he listens to me. I can help.'

Zeus considered her point. He nodded reluctantly.

'Excellent,' said Virgo. 'Besides, soon I'll have my kardia back and will be returning to the Council.'

'You're very confident all of a sudden,' said Aphrodite. 'Did they say something to you up there?'

'No,' said Virgo quietly. 'I just have an optimal feeling.'

With the Gods busy quizzing Virgo, Hypnos whispered into Elliot's ear.

'Right,' he hissed, 'now we've got Zeus on the loose, we need to get him in the sea if you want to find your potion. Follow my lead . . .'

'OK,' said Elliot uncertainly.

'Hmmmmm,' mused Hypnos loudly, nudging Elliot unsubtly in the ribs. 'How to get to the Island of the Cyclopes?'

'Uh – we could sail there,' said Elliot. 'Perhaps

Charon could take us on his ship—'

'NOOOOOOOOOOOO!' roared Zeus, making the kitchen tremble.

Everyone was stunned into silence.

'Told you,' Hypnos whispered to Elliot.

'Er, I just mean . . . I hate travelling by sea. Makes me, er . . . terribly queasy. We'll go by plane. I know just the chap.'

Dave strolled back into the kitchen.

'So, about school,' he said severely, taking Elliot by the shoulders. 'I'm not gonna lie, I'm disappointed in you, son.'

Elliot looked down at his feet.

'I'm disappointed it's taken you this long to smack that idiot in the face.' Dave smiled. 'Sounds like he had it coming.'

Elliot accepted his dad's high-five, ignoring the disapproving looks of the Gods.

'Listen, we'd better pack,' said Elliot. 'We're going to need . . .'

'Er, son – I think I'd better sit this one out,' Dave said quietly.

'What?' said Elliot. 'You're . . . you're not going to come?'

'Think about it, mate,' said Dave. 'You don't need me – you've got the King of the Gods and the Daemon of Sleep on your side!'

'How do you know he's the Daemon of Sleep?' said Athene darkly. 'He never said.'

'Oh, come on!' Dave laughed. 'Like I haven't heard you lot banging on about Hypnos enough . . . ! And anyway – Josie needs me.'

'Josie has us,' said Aphrodite, standing next to her sister.

'Yeah, but – no disrespect – it's not the same, is it, girls?' shrugged Dave. 'I'm better off taking care of everything here.'

'Elliot?' said Zeus quietly. 'What do you want?'

Elliot was getting tired of making impossible decisions. Of course he wanted his dad to come with him. They'd missed out on so much together. And however dangerous the journey, he would feel a lot better with his dad along for company.

But if Mum needed him . . .

'You'd better stay here,' he said quietly to the floor. 'With Mum.'

'Excellent,' said Dave, rubbing his hands together. 'There's plenty to be getting on with here. You do what you've got to do. I'll take care of everything.'

Elliot smiled weakly at his dad. This was for the best. Of course it was.

'You'd better get some rest,' said Athene,

putting her hand gently on Elliot's arm.

'We all had,' said Zeus. 'Hypnos, you're coming with us to the shed. I don't want you out of my sight.'

'I'm flattered,' said Hypnos with a wink. 'Nighty-night.'

'Goodnight, Elliot,' said Zeus, not turning to look at him as he left.

As the kitchen door closed, Elliot released the breath he'd been holding.

On the one hand, he felt awful. The Gods were his friends. And he'd just threatened them. He felt the Chaos Stones in his pocket. Zeus had warned him of their corrupting power. Were they starting to work their dark magic on him?

But on the other hand, he had no choice. He didn't care who he had to threaten, or what he had to do. He was going to find Mum that potion if it was the last thing he ever did.

8. Millionaires' Row

'. . . and then he swung at me with a huge left hook, but I dodged beneath it, grabbing his other arm and pinning it behind his back,' panted Boil, as he struggled to keep up with the brisk pace. 'Of course, I could have put him out cold, but these bleeding-heart liberals and their precious rules about beating children . . . Anyway, another student came down the hall and – without a thought for my own safety – I went to protect her. Little blighter landed a lucky punch. I barely noticed it, but Sopweed insisted I take the day off . . .'

His companion stared at him suspiciously in

the dying light of the day.

'I see,' said Patricia Porshley-Plum slowly, trying not to look at Mr Boil's revoltingly bruised eye. She hadn't seen one that swollen since she'd defended herself from that man who demanded her money in the street. And she'd do it again – those charity collectors were a menace.

With a perfectly judged sneer, she turned her attention to her latest purchase. Auld Manor: her new house.

Patricia had snapped up this stately home for a bargain after the previous owner, Lord Farmer, was sent to prison for robbery. Yes, she'd have to maintain the thirty-six-bedroom house and 143-acre estate, but that was the burden she would have to bear as a multi-millionaire lottery winner. And faking that robbery had saved her a fortune. She allowed herself a small smile. Patricia Porshley-Plum was back.

'Tell me more about this welfare visit to the Hoopers,' she said, opening the vast oak door to her new home.

'Total disaster,' Boil crowed, his voice echoing around the great entrance hall and up the twin staircases ahead. 'They want to move the mother out.'

Patricia's blackened soul belched with delight.

'Indeed? Josie's being moved on? The boy will be shipped off. Home Farm will be up for sale. And I'll be there to snap it up in cash. I think this calls for champagne,' she drawled. 'Dawson!'

An aged butler shuffled out from behind a nearby door.

'GOOD AFTERNOON, MRS NAUSEOUS-THUMB,' he shouted cordially. 'LOVELY TO SEE YOU AGAIN.'

'It's Porshley-Plum!' snapped Patricia, her anger reverberating off the cracked walls.

'BEG YOUR PARDON?' shouted Dawson. 'I'M A TOUCH DEAF IN ONE EAR.'

'You're a touch stupid in half a brain,' muttered Patricia. 'We'll have two glasses of champagne.'

'TWO VASES OF LAMB MAIN COMING UP,' said Dawson. He was about to shuffle away when a lady in an ageing cook's outfit bustled over.

'SHE SAID CHAMPAGNE, YOU DOLT!' she shouted in his ear. 'Go fetch – and don't be long about it.'

Dawson moved as fast as he could – which, Patricia observed, wasn't nearly fast enough.

'You'll have to excuse my husband,' said the cook, performing a small curtsey. 'He's a touch deaf in one ear.'

'So he shouted,' said Patricia. 'What do you want?'

'Well, you see, m-ma'am,' Mrs Dawson stuttered. 'Me and the other staff, well, we were wondering, see – now the old master has gone – what your plans are for us?'

'You want to know about your jobs?' said Patricia.

'Please, ma'am,' said Mrs Dawson. 'You see, most of us were born and bred here. We ain't never worked nowhere but Auld Manor. We don't know any other way of life ...'

'Layabouts,' grunted Boil beneath his breath.

'And you see, we love it here. It's our home. So we were hoping—'

'Oh, muffin,' Patricia said with a smile, taking Mrs Dawson's hand in hers. 'Of course I want to keep you all on. What kind of person do you think I am?!'

'Well,' said Mrs Dawson uncertainly, 'I'd heard the rumours ...'

'Pish!' laughed Patricia. 'Like you say, who else would employ you?'

'That's right, ma'am,' said Mrs Dawson sadly. 'Don't think we're no good to no one no more!'

'Hush now!' trilled Patricia. 'After all – where

would you all live? If you didn't work here, you'd all be out on the street.'

'Can't begin to imagine,' said Mrs Dawson, allowing herself a small sob. 'Me and Mr Dawson have lived here all our lives – met and married here, raised our kids on the estate – our Polly is a maid. And now we're in our autumn years, the thought of moving on . . .'

'Shhhhhh,' Patricia said softly. 'Let's have no more talk of that. We all know you must stay . . .'

'Oh, thank you! Thank you, ma'am,' cried Mrs Dawson. 'You have no idea—'

'On half your current wages,' Patricia added.

Mrs Dawson paused and put a finger in her ear. 'Lord – I think *my* hearing's going now – I thought you just said—'

'I did,' said Patricia, dropping the cook's hand like a soiled lace handkerchief. 'You said it yourself. You're all over the hill and far away. You're not fit for purpose – frankly, you're lucky I'm keeping you.'

'B-but . . . but . . .' stammered Mrs Dawson.

'Of course, if you'd like to seek alternative employment,' Patricia mused. 'Remind me how many other stately homes there are within a hundred miles that need domestic staff . . .'

'There ain't none,' said Mrs Dawson quietly.

'Oh, dear. Then there's my offer,' said Patricia, turning away to look at the grand staircases. 'Take it or leave it.'

Mrs Dawson's face soured into a dark, dark scowl.

'Thank you, ma'am,' she said quietly. 'Will there be anything else?'

'Hurry that husband of yours along with my champagne,' said Patricia. 'He might be deaf as a doorpost, but he still has the use of his legs.'

'As you wish,' said Mrs Dawson, turning angrily back towards her kitchen.

'Superbly handled,' said Mr Boil, breaking into a small round of applause. 'You can't afford hangers-on who are only after you for your wealth. Speaking of which, you couldn't lend me—'

'No,' said Patricia firmly. 'Is that everything?'

'Not quite,' said Boil excitedly, his multiple chins wobbling with anticipation. 'The welfare woman found something else at Home Farm . . .'

He paused for dramatic effect.

'Well? Get on with it,' snapped Patricia. 'You're about as enthralling as an aid appeal.'

'It's the boy's father,' grinned Boil. 'He's back.'

'So. The jailbird flies home,' said Patricia

thoughtfully. 'How inconvenient. David Hooper always was a horrible do-gooder. So he'll be at the house taking care of the brat . . .'

'Not necessarily,' wobbled Boil gleefully. 'The welfare officer is trying to find out if he's Hooper's legal guardian – they don't even know if the Hooper parents are still married. If not, this guardian will get to decide what happens to Hooper.'

'Will they, now?'

'They're hoping you might be able to shed some light.'

'Oh, I can do more than that.' Patricia smiled. 'I can switch on a search beam. Thank you, Mr Boil. You've proved most useful.'

Boil clapped his hands gleefully. 'Marvellous. So what's next?'

'I'm sorry?' said Patricia, imagining how elegant her new lounge would look draped in endangered-animal fur.

'What's next?' Boil repeated. 'What are we going to do?'

'We?' said Patricia absently.

'Er, yes.' Boil laughed nervously. 'You and me. Us.'

'Oh dear, dumpling,' pouted Patricia. 'How awkward. There is no "us". In fact, I find the thought rather nauseating . . .'

'B-b-but — we're in this together!' Boil spluttered. 'I've risked everything for you! I've been complicit in lottery fraud! I've shared confidential information about a pupil! I could lose my job . . .'

'Something you might want to bear in mind if you ever decide to grow a conscience,' said Patricia, as Dawson stumbled over with her champagne. 'Breathe a word of this to anyone and I'll bring your pathetic little world crashing down around your flabby ears. You have served your purpose. I can't imagine you hear that very often. Goodbye, Mr Boil. Dawson will show you out.'

'Just you wait,' glowered Boil, his chins wobbling in outraged unison as Dawson led him towards the door. 'I'll get you for this. You'd better sleep with one eye open, Horse's-Bum!'

'I sleep with both eyes open, you cretinous moron,' muttered Patricia. 'Dawson — pack my bags for a couple of nights away. I'm going on a trip.'

'VERY GOOD, M'LADY,' Dawson bellowed. 'OFF ANYWHERE NICE?'

'Not really,' said Patricia. 'I need to see an old acquaintance.'

'FRIEND OF YOURS?'

'Far from it,' scowled Patricia, picking up the phone. 'He's the most despicable human being I've ever known.'

'THEN WHY GO SEE HIM?' yelled Dawson.

'Because,' sighed Patricia, 'he's still my husband.'

9. The Odyssey

There was a moment every morning, just before he fully woke, where everything in Elliot's life was perfect. Before the bad thoughts flooded his mind like vinegar through oil, there was a blissful second where he lived the life of a normal thirteen-year-old boy . . .

The flying horse tapping at his window brought that moment to an abrupt end on Saturday morning.

'Rise and shine,' said Pegasus. 'Time to shake your tail feathers.'

Elliot groaned as the weight of the world returned his shoulders. His mum was ill. His future was uncertain. And today he was off to find another mythical Chaos Stone that would almost certainly put his life in jeopardy. Again. Great.

But a hopeful thought leapt into his mind as well. Today they were setting off on the journey that might find his mum's cure. The next time he was in this bed, he could be that normal kid. Hopefully.

Pegasus tapped impatiently again.

'Hurry up,' he said. 'Everyone's waiting downstairs.'

Elliot pulled on some clothes and shuffled downstairs to where the Gods were assembled around the kitchen table. He smiled as he saw his dad sitting to one side, swathed in a black hoodie, sipping a hot coffee. So that's where his own dislike of early mornings came from. He waved a greeting to a yawning Virgo, who waved sleepily back.

'So, we're all agreed?' said Zeus, as his daughters and Hephaestus nodded solemnly.

'Agreed on what?' asked Elliot, accepting the plate of breakfast that Athene magically summoned from the stove.

'We're making a battle plan,' said Zeus.

'Literally,' said Athene, tossing the *Daily Argus* over to Elliot. 'In all the drama yesterday, we missed this.'

'What does it mean?' Elliot muttered, his brain not nearly awake enough to process the immortal news – in rhyme.

'Those nappy-heads on the Zodiac Council have really done it this time,' said Aphrodite. 'Suspending basic immortal rights *and* releasing the Titans. They have completely lost it! Did they really not mention any of this yesterday, V?'

Virgo shook her head and stuffed her bacon sandwich in her mouth.

'You're being very quiet,' said Elliot.

'No, I'm not,' snapped Virgo. 'Are you suggesting I'm acting suspiciously? Because that would be ridiculous! I haven't done anything! What are you accusing me of?'

'Nothing,' said Elliot. 'It's brilliant. Carry on.'

'They're playing right into Thanatos's hands,' scowled Zeus. 'Division, hatred, lies – he draws his power from these. Evil always does. If we didn't have to go, I'd be up there right now, giving them a good old-fashioned—'

'But you do have to go,' said Athene. 'The Chaos Stones are still our best defence against Thanatos. Without them, he's just talk . . .'

'With them, he'll be unstoppable. That's what you need to worry about,' trilled Hypnos, flying over and helping himself to Zeus's toast. 'He won't stop until the mortals are all but wiped out and we are all his slaves. With the power of the Earth, Air, Water and Fire Stones, he'll have the whole of nature at his command. If it wasn't for me handing them to you, he would have beaten you last time . . .'

'We're painfully aware of that, thank you,' said Zeus, snatching his toast back. 'Heffer – are you all set?'

'Just say the word, boss,' said Hephaestus with a small incline of his head. 'Got the boy all loaded up and ready to go outside.'

'I still say Hermy should stay here with us,' pouted Aphrodite. 'We can take perfectly good care of him.'

'What?' said Elliot, suddenly waking up. 'Where are you taking Hermes?'

'It's OK, old boy – just a precaution,' said Zeus. 'I need Heffer to . . . catch up with some old friends for me – he can watch over Hermes while he's doing it. Let's get you on the road, old chap.'

Still not entirely sure what was going on, Elliot followed the procession of immortals out to the paddock.

'Let's make this quick,' winced Dave, scowling at the ascending sun. Elliot knew that feeling –

he'd often hated the sunrise after a bad night with Josie. He watched Zeus stride towards Aphrodite's car, which had transformed into a pink minibus for their journey.

'You will look after her, won't you?' said Elliot to his father.

'Course I will,' said Dave, pulling his hoodie tighter around him.

'Don't let the welfare people anywhere near here until I'm back. And be on your guard for Horse's-Bum, I know she's still sniffing around somewhere . . .'

'Relax!' Dave muttered, putting his hands firmly on Elliot's shoulders. 'By the time you get back, I'll have everything sorted. I swear it.'

A low snort from Pegasus drew Elliot's attention to the other side of the paddock.

'Aren't you ready yet?' huffed the magnificent winged stallion. 'I want to get this done in the daylight. I hate flying at night. Straining my eyes is disastrous for my crow's feet.'

'Hold yer horses,' Hephaestus grumbled, as he tinkered with the litter attached to Pegasus's harness. Elliot peered inside. There, deathly still, lay Hermes. He reached through the window and gave the comatose Messenger God a gentle fist-bump.

'See you soon, mate,' he said quietly. 'Not even joking.'

'All right there, young fella,' said Hephaestus, placing his grimy hand tenderly on top of Hermes's. I've got you all tucked up, snug as a bug in a rug, never you mind.'

The blacksmith winked at Elliot and shuffled away.

'Where are you taking him?' Elliot asked.

Hephaestus paused and looked nervously at Zeus.

'I'll keep that on the q.t. for now – the walls have ears,' said Zeus, glowering at Hypnos. 'But he'll be safe, don't you worry.'

'Bye-bye, Hermy,' said Aphrodite, kissing her brother's limp hand. 'See you soon.'

'We'd better be off too,' said Zeus. 'Long journey ahead.'

'Hello?' said Josie, coming out into the paddock in her nightgown. 'Who are all these people? What are you doing on my farm?'

Elliot released a quivering breath. Mum never got up this early. Why did she have to choose now?

'It's OK, Mum – I'm just going on a quick trip – nothing to worry about . . .'

'Don't go!' Josie cried, clinging to his arm. 'We

must keep you safe!'

'I have to do this, Mum,' Elliot mumbled, struggling to meet his mother's tear-filled eyes. 'I'm sorry.'

'I'll look after you, love,' said Dave, giving her a friendly squeeze.

'Get off me!' shouted Josie, shoving Dave away.

'Suit yourself,' said Dave, walking off towards the farmhouse. 'Good luck, son.'

'OK . . . bye, Dad,' Elliot called after his father. He looked at Josie, fighting in Athene's strong grasp.

'You'd better just get on your way,' said the Goddess of Wisdom. 'Once you're out of sight, she'll calm down.'

'Leave me alone!' Josie screamed, with Aphrodite trying to soothe her. 'Elliot – please don't go!'

Elliot bit back the tears as he watched the two Goddesses try to calm his mother, who lashed at them like a wild animal. He hated leaving her like this. Should he stay?

But he couldn't. If he found Panacea's potion, he could cure her and she'd never feel like this again. It was worth it. It really was.

'Bye, Mum,' he choked, heading for the minibus.

107

'Don't go!' Josie shrieked while Athene and Aphrodite held her back gently. 'Don't leave me! Don't leave me with him!'

'I have to,' Elliot cried through the lump in his throat. 'I'll be back soon. I promise.'

He scrambled into the minibus and shut the door. Virgo looked at him strangely. After a few seconds, she took her second bacon sandwich from her mouth and silently offered him the rest of it. He shook his head with a weak smile.

'Are you ready?' said Zeus softly.

'I guess,' replied Elliot, pulling his hood over his face as the car drove him away from Home Farm and the haunting sound of his mother's screams.

After a fitful sleep in the back of the minibus, Elliot awoke to find it had stopped outside a large, rundown office block.

'Where are we?' he mumbled sleepily.

'Here to see our old pal Odysseus,' said Zeus brightly. 'He's taken the immortal travel world by storm with Don'tcAIR, his "no frills, more thrills" approach to travel – and bally good luck to him. He's become quite the business leader.'

'I heard he's going to star in the new series of *Dragons' Dungeon*,' said Hypnos, fluttering out of the minibus. 'It's been so much more exciting since they started actually flame-roasting the rubbish entrepreneurs!'

Elliot looked out of the window.

'We're on an industrial estate in Slough,' he said, spotting a sign.

'This is the address on the website,' said Virgo. 'Funny site – it charged me twenty-seven obals just for looking at it.'

'This can't be right,' scowled Zeus, pulling the remains of a plastic bag off his shoe.

'What a dump,' snorted Hypnos. 'Are you sure this is—'

'GREETINGS, MY GOOD FRIENDS!' bellowed an almighty Greek voice behind them. 'Welcome to Don'tcAIR: you cut prices, we cut corners!'

Odysseus was what Elliot's nan would have politely called 'big-boned'. He had a face and belly bigger than his legendary adventures. With a huge smile, he opened his arms, offering a hug as warm and fragrant as a falafel.

'Hello, Odysseus,' smiled Zeus, crushing the hero's hand with his handshake. 'Elliot, this is Odysseus, travel agent extraordinaire!'

'You're crazy!' guffawed the hero. 'But it's going great. I have a fleet of over two thousand and sixty-two aeroplanes, most of which work nearly all the time. I've just won a contract from Helios, the Sun God, to replace the chariot he uses to pull the sun with my budget planes. OK, so sometimes the sun will be three days late and sometimes it won't arrive at all, but it's saved him a fortune!'

Elliot looked up at the ramshackle offices. This place was a dump.

'Odysseus, old boy. We really need your help,' said Zeus.

'But of course!' yelled Odysseus. 'I can get you wherever you want to go. We fly somewhere close to a hundred and fifty-seven nearly top destinations.'

'Can we come inside?' asked Virgo, turning her nose up as an empty tin of beans rolled past, complete with a dead rat inside.

'Ay – where are my manners!' laughed Odysseus. 'Here – let me help you with your bags.'

'Oh, thank you,' said Virgo, handing over her suitcase.

Odysseus lifted the bag up and down several times to gauge its weight.

'That'll be five obals to bring the bag into my office,' he said. 'I'll let you bring your handbag as hand luggage.'

'Thanks,' said Virgo warily. She reluctantly

handed over her money and they made their way through the deserted building to Odysseus's office. Elliot had seen better-furnished cardboard boxes – everywhere was barren and coin-operated. Even the water cooler charged twenty-three obals for people to stand there and chat.

'Here, here – come in.' Odysseus gestured to his office, a tiny space with a low ceiling, with rows of three chairs on either side of a tiny aisle. In order to reach the desk at the front, everyone had to turn sideways, leading to much treading on toes and bashing of elbows.

'Ow!' said Virgo, as Elliot attempted to put his bag in one of the overhead lockers, releasing an avalanche of sick bags.

'So what can I do for you?' Odysseus asked, taking his place behind his desk. 'Can I get you a coffee? Something to eat maybe?'

'Yes, please – I'd love some tea and biscuits,' said Virgo as she slumped into a chair at the front.

'Of course,' said Odysseus. 'That'll be six obals. And that seat is extra legroom. There's a surcharge of fifteen obals.'

'Where is everyone?' asked Elliot, thinking of the unoccupied offices they had passed.

'Cost-saving measures,' said Odysseus. 'If I'm gonna offer flights to the Arctic tundra for seven

111

obals, I need to make some efficiencies. That's my job as Chief Executive Officer. And Accounts Manager. And Head of Human Resources. And Senior Toilet Cleaner . . .'

'Listen,' said Elliot. 'We need to get to the Island of the Cyclopes.'

'Island of the Cyclopes, eh?' said Odysseus. 'A great choice for the adventurous traveller. Beautiful sea views, idyllic country setting, away from the hustle and bustle . . .'

'Not according to this review on Odyssey-Advisor,' said Hypnos, craning his neck to read from Odysseus's computer screen. '*Went to the Island of the Cyclopes on a coach trip. Enjoyed the local cuisine. But then so did the Cyclopes, who ate our tour guide and everyone sitting in rows 1–15.* Oh, dear. Says she wouldn't recommend it for a business trip either.'

'There's always one fusspot,' sighed Odysseus. 'Those review sites will be the death of me . . .'

'And half of your customers,' said Elliot. 'So the Cyclopes eat people?'

'Listen, no holiday is perfect,' said Odysseus, angling his computer screen away from Hypnos. 'People are always complaining about things beyond my control. "Ewwww, the weather wasn't as good as you said . . . Ewwww, the food wasn't as good as you said . . . Ewwww, the flesh-eating Cyclopes ate more people than you said . . . There is no pleasing some people!'

'Ooooh – what's this?' said Hypnos, picking up a brochure with a picture of a ship from Odysseus's desk.

'Ah, yes – my new budget cruise line, FLOATERZ. Forty-seven countries in three days. Two if you help with the rowing . . .'

'Sounds wonderful,' said Hypnos, nodding significantly at Elliot.

'Great idea,' said Elliot quickly. 'Let's sail to the Island of the Cyclopes.'

'NOOOOOOOO!' Zeus roared, inciting another downpour of sick bags from the overhead lockers. 'NO SAILING!'

Hypnos shrugged at Elliot. Elliot shrugged back. How were they ever going to get Zeus into the sea when he wouldn't even go on a boat?

'Er, OK then,' said Odysseus. 'You'll have to fly – and you're in luck, we just made that route even faster. You'll only have to change five times . . . That'll be 2,786 obals for your whole party. And I'll even throw in express check-in.'

'What's that?' asked Virgo.

'We throw your bags out of the terminal window to the plane,' said Odysseus. 'Saves time *and* money.'

'C'mon, old boy, can't you do us some mates' rates?' said Zeus. 'This is a matter of world security – we're getting the Water Stone to defeat Thanatos.'

'Thanatos?' said Odysseus. 'That wooden-horse dropping has raised his head again?'

Zeus nodded grimly.

'It's going to be a teensy bit tricky to sell holidays when he's destroyed the Earth with earthquakes and tsunamis,' chirped Hypnos.

'You'd be surprised,' Odysseus mused. 'I once sold a detox holiday to Pompeii – two weeks after Vesuvius had erupted . . . But I want to help. I'll tell you what I'm gonna do for you. Not only am I going to give you the flights – excluding airport taxes and fuel duty – I'm going to upgrade you to Nearly Economy *and* offer you half-price life jackets! Whaddya say?'

'Gee, thanks,' said Elliot unenthusiastically.

Odysseus smiled and looked closely at Elliot.

'I recognize a fellow reluctant hero,' he said. 'All I ever wanted was my home.'

'Me too,' said Elliot softly.

Odysseus opened a drawer in his desk.

'Take this,' he said, pulling out a small metal disc and handing it to Elliot.

'Wow – thanks!' said Elliot, turning it over in his hands. It was a silver compass, exquisitely engraved on the outside with waves and on the inside with the four points of the compass: N, S, E and W.

'This will help you find your way,' said Odysseus. 'I hope you get home soon.'

'How much is it?' asked Elliot cautiously, turning the compass over in his hands.

Odysseus laughed. 'This is a gift, my friend. I know how hard it can be for the wandering hero. That's why I'm only charging you two obals if you want a carrier bag.'

'Appreciate it,' smiled Elliot, putting the compass in his pocket. It immediately fell through the hole. He picked it up sheepishly and was grateful Athene wasn't there to see that he'd neither fixed, nor washed, those trousers.

'Right – we'd best be on our way to the airport,' said Zeus, rising to shake Odysseus's hand and bumping his head on the low ceiling. 'Thanks, old bean.'

'Before we go, can I use your lavatory, please?' said Virgo. 'Or is that going to cost money too?'

'You crazy!' laughed Odysseus, slapping the desk so hard it bent. 'At Don'tcAIR, you don't have to spend a penny to spend a penny!'

115

'Phew, that's a relief!' sighed Virgo.

'But if you need toilet paper, it'll be one obal a sheet,' said Odysseus. 'This isn't a charity, y'know.'

10. Your Daemon Needs You

There were few things Thanatos enjoyed more than a stroll through the fiery wastelands of Tartarus. The tortured souls, the screams of anguish, the scent of despair – it was truly one of his favourite places.

But today he was here on business. His first appointment had gone exceptionally well – better than he'd dared hope. A thin smile twisted his lips. Now for phase two.

He arrived at the foot of a scorching valley. On one side, Asteria and her forty-eight sisters were trying to fill their almighty bronze urn, using only their hands and the water from the pool below. In the centre of the pool was Tantalus, hungrily eyeing the luscious fruit that hung just out of his reach. And on the other, Sisyphus was trying to push his boulder up the hill.

'Greetings friends!' Thanatos called. 'How are you this fine day?'

'Today thuckth!' shouted Sisyphus from his hill. 'Every thingle day ith thuckier than the latht – no thankth to THOME people!'

'Oh, thop your thulking,' came a new voice from beneath a nearby rock. 'Thuck it up, thunshine.'

'Salmoneus? Is that you?' smiled Thanatos. 'I hadn't spotted you there.'

'It thertainly ith,' said Salmoneus, looking anxiously at the rock that eternally teetered above his head as if it were about to fall. 'Thorry about my thtupid thibling. Thithyphuth alwayth wath a thimpering little thithy . . . whoa!'

At his slightest movement, the rock wobbled precariously, forcing Salmoneus into absolute stillness.

'Thilenth Thalmoneuth!' cried Sisyphus. 'It'th thankth to you that I'm thtuck in thith thoulleth thtink-hole!'

'That'th thuch a thlander!' Salmoneus cried back. 'You tried to thlaughter me!'

'At leatht I'm here for thomething theriouth!' laughed Sisyphus. 'You were thent for imperthonating Zeuth! How thilly is that!'

'Now be nice, boys,' drawled Thanatos. 'Trust me, I know how irksome brothers can be. But siblings should stick together. Isn't that right, ladies?'

'Oh, sure,' scoffed Asteria. '"You must all kill your husband on your wedding night," Dad said. We all stuck together – now we're all stuck here ...'

'Quite right,' snarled Tantalus from his pool. 'Children should obey their parents. You let one of your sisters disobey your father. Serves you right.'

'Serves us right!' shrieked Asteria. 'You cooked your own son for a banquet! That didn't serve him right! That served him with chips!'

'Calm yourself, Asteria,' said Thanatos. 'I am here to make you an offer.'

'Unless it's for an industrial hosepipe and some hand cream, I'm not interested!'

'Shame,' said Thanatos. 'I always had you down as more of a "the urn is half-full" kind of a girl ...'

'Don't lithen to him!' shouted Sisyphus. 'He'th a thlippery thnake ...'

119

'You thound abthurd,' said Salmoneus. 'Lithen to what the man hath to thay.'

'Thank you, Salmoneus,' said Thanatos. 'My friends – you were placed here by the Gods for your crimes on Earth. You have all proven that you are murderous, untrustworthy, deceitful and evil.'

'Tho what?' snarled Sisyphus.

'So, I want you to come and work for me.'

'Oh, wow, thanks,' said Tantalus. 'Great offer, boss – let me think it over. Hmmm – holiday, sick pay, pension scheme . . . Oh, yes, that's right – just a shame we're all SENTENCED TO STAY HERE FOR ETERNITY, YOU MORON!'

'Maybe. Maybe not,' said Thanatos. 'War is coming. It is time the Gods paid for their treatment of us all. I have experienced the pain of unjust captivity. I have suffered the centuries of solitude. I have felt the rage of the righteous. Join me and I will free you from this place. Tantalus – for years you have been denied food and drink. Imagine how it will feel to feast on the sweet taste of freedom!'

'I'd rather have a kebab, if it's all the same to you,' said Tantalus, reaching for the fruit, which immediately swayed out of his reach.

'Daughters of Danaus!' Thanatos roared. 'Don't

you want justice? For hundreds of years you have toiled fruitlessly, working endlessly on a thankless task because of what a man told you to do!'

'We know,' snapped Asteria. 'We might as well have stayed married.'

'And Sisyphus,' pleaded the Daemon of Death. 'My old friend Sisyphus. Don't you want peace from your back-breaking toils? Don't you want to rest your weary limbs? Don't you want to ease your bodily pains?'

'Then I'll get a mathage!' shouted Sisyphus. 'I wouldn't trutht you ath far ath I could thpit you!'

'Put a thock in it!' Salmoneus shouted. 'Count me in, Thantatoth! Where do I thign?'

'Excellent,' drawled Thanatos. 'Then I appoint you the first general in my army!'

Thanatos's voice echoed around the silent valley.

'Sorry to be a pedant – what army would that be?' sneered Tantalus. 'All your Daemons are locked away.'

'Patience, my friend,' said Thanatos. 'My troops will be here shortly.'

'Well, in that case, why not?' said Tantalus. 'It's not like I have anything more to lose.'

'Delighted to have you on board,' said Thanatos. 'Ladies?'

'Whatever,' said Asteria, scooping water from the pool and trudging back up the hill. 'Can't be any worse than sharing a bedroom with forty-eight sisters. When I find out who took my favourite earrings . . .'

'A wise decision,' nodded Thanatos. 'Come on, Sisyphus. You don't want to be left out, do you? I'm going to rule the world. Surely you'd like to join the winning team?'

'Pah! I'll believe that when I thee it,' scoffed Sisyphus, returning to his rock. 'You're a trickthter and a thcammer and a thcemer and I wouldn't thide with you if you were the latht thoul on the fathe of the Earth!'

'I'll put you down as a maybe,' said Thanatos. 'Good luck with that.'

'Er, ith that it?' said Sisyphus.

'What more is there to say?' said Thanatos. 'And for the record, I'd like to apologize for my . . . interference with your task. It was childish and petty.'

'Yeah right!' scoffed Sisyphus. 'I wathn't born yethterday . . .'

'I mean it,' said Thanatos. 'I am truly sorry.'

'You're theriouthly not going to thtop me rolling my boulder?'

'Absolutely,' said Thanatos.

'No trickth?'

'Never.'

'No thilly thennaniganth?'

'I swear it on the Styx! I will never touch your boulder again.'

Sisyphus paused for a moment. 'Then I acthept your apology. Let uth theparate ath friendth.'

'That's all I ever wanted,' said Thanatos, putting his long fingers over his heart. 'Because I know what's coming. And when it does, trust me. No one will want to be my enemy.'

11. Don'tcAIR

'**W**e have begun our descent into the Island of the Cyclopes. Please ensure you have all your belongings before disembarking the aircraft. Thank you for choosing Don'tcAIR: you cut prices, we cut corners.'

'Well, that was highly sub-optimal,' groaned Virgo as she attempted to free her knees from the seat in front of her. As something of an expert in air travel, she had never been forced to travel with only enough belongings to last her until lunchtime, nor flown to her destination via six different stops. Oh, to have her star-ball – *Constellation* – powers returned. And they would be. Soon.

'Get me off this bally contraption!' shouted Zeus from further down the plane. Despite the flight being virtually empty, their group had been dotted all around the aircraft, after Zeus refused to pay the seventy-four obals per person to sit together. 'And for the last time, I do not want to buy an infernal scratch card!'

Virgo looked at Elliot in the opposite row. He had been unusually quiet on this journey. And yet this didn't please her. Elliot being quiet meant one of two things: he was harbouring a secret, or he had in fact 'dropped one'.

For the purposes of the journey, Virgo under-stood why Hypnos had dissembled into a Satyr to avoid suspicion. She just wished he hadn't chosen such a large Satyr, as he was squashed in the seat next to her.

'No one's watching,' she whispered. 'Perhaps you could lose a few pounds?'

'I *beg* your pardon?' he said. 'How dare you!'

'Highly amusing,' said Virgo. 'But seriously, your thighs have been encroaching upon my personal space for the entire flight. It's like sharing a seat with two sacks of hairy jelly!'

'Why you horrible little . . .'

Virgo felt a tap on her shoulder. She turned to

see Hypnos sitting in the row behind, with a hat hiding his feathered head.

'Hiya, superstar!' he trilled.

Virgo turned back to the irate Satyr to her right. She experienced a burning sensation similar to the time she had realized that wearing headphones did not stop passers-by from hearing your singing.

'Er, safe travels!' she smiled, hurriedly slipping into the row behind to sit next to the Daemon of Sleep.

'Told you we should have sailed,' smirked Hypnos.

'You heard Zeus,' said Virgo. 'He has forbidden travel by water.'

'And you always do as you're told?'

'Don't you?' said Virgo, wrinkling her nose.

Hypnos smiled. 'Never.'

'Why not?' Virgo asked. This was highly irrational.

'Listen, toots,' said Hypnos, reclining the centimetre his seat would allow. 'When the centaur dung hits the hurricane – and you can bet your starry socks that it will – there is only one thing I can rely on.'

'What's that?'

'Number one,' grinned Hypnos.

Virgo paused to consider this. 'I don't under-stand. How is passing urine going to help?'

The Daemon rolled his eyes.

'*Me*, darling,' he said, 'along with myself and I. We're the only people I trust. So why would I listen to anyone else?'

'Because there are people who know better than you. People who know what's best for you.'

'Oh, yeah? So who's looking out for you?'

'Many people,' said Virgo, stiffening. 'There's . . . the Council . . .'

'You think they care about you!' laughed Hypnos. 'They suspended you! They could give back your kardia and your life in Elysium right now if they wanted to. So ask yourself – why don't they want you?'

'Well,' said Virgo, refusing to answer such a ridiculous suggestion. Especially given the uncomfortable sensation in her stomach. 'I have the Gods.'

'Ha!' squealed Hypnos. 'Those doddery old deities? They just want the Chaos Stones. If they get them, you won't see them for dusty drachma, mark my words.'

'Elliot!' said Virgo at considerable volume. 'I have Elliot!'

'And if he cures his mother, do you really think

they'll want you hanging around?' whispered the Daemon. 'None of my business, but I'd start seriously considering your options. At the end of the day, who really cares about you – except you?'

Virgo had a quite brilliant argument against all of Hypnos's points. It was just evading her presently.

'Excuse me, Galatea,' drawled Zeus as the plane bumped down on to the runway, his mood improved significantly by the attractiveness of the air stewardess before him. 'What time does this tin can leave for home?'

'I'm sorry, sir – I don't understand,' smiled Galatea.

'How you're so beautiful?' Zeus flirted. 'Me neither. But I need to know our return flight time so I can book dinner tonight. Where shall we go?'

'I'm afraid that won't be possible.' Galatea smiled again. Virgo started to become concerned that the stewardess's face was in fact unable to move.

'Urgh – boyfriend?' muttered Zeus.

'Not any more,' chirped Galatea. 'My boyfriend Acis was killed by a jealous Polyphemus dropping a boulder on him.'

'That's awful!' cried Virgo.

'Oh, it was OK,' Galatea said cheerfully. 'I turned him into a river spirit so we could share immortality. Didn't work out though. I found him a bit of a drip. So I left the heating on and he evaporated.'

'Beautiful story,' laughed Hypnos.

'But as for your return flight, I'm afraid that Don'tcAIR no longer offers the route back to England.'

'Since when?' roared Zeus.

'Since about forty-five minutes ago.'

'But how are we supposed to get home?' cried Zeus, thrusting a ticket in Galatea's face.

The air stewardess examined the ticket, then looked up, her face quite unchanged.

'I'm afraid you have only been issued with a one-way ticket,' said Galatea. 'I suggest you refer to the full terms and conditions on our website. They are eight obals each.'

'Wait till I get my hands on that cheapskate Odysseus!' thundered Zeus.

'I'm going to have to ask you to move along now, sir, as you are blocking an exit aisle,' smiled Galatea, turning her white teeth away.

'Um, excuse me – where do we collect our luggage?' Virgo asked politely. Her suitcase was stuffed with essential items, including Zeus's thunderbolts, Hermes's iGod and all the other things they'd not been allowed to take into the cabin because they hadn't paid to have more than five personal belongings within ten metres. All Virgo was carrying was her small handbag, which was entirely insufficient for their journey.

'May I see your luggage receipts?' said Galatea.

'Receipts?' said Virgo. 'But we had the express check-in. I saw the bags thrown into the plane myself.'

'Ah,' said Galatea. 'But did you pay the surcharge to guarantee they went on the plane you were travelling on?'

'No, we bally well did not!' shouted Zeus. 'We were all skint from paying rent in the waiting room! We need that luggage, it's got all my thunder . . . underpants in.'

'I'm afraid I am unable to help you,' smiled Galatea.

'So, our luggage could be on any plane, anywhere in the world?' said Virgo. 'But we were told that Don'tcAIR promises that all luggage will arrive safely.'

'Absolutely,' beamed Galatea. 'We just don't promise where. Now, if you'd kindly disembark . . .'

Virgo couldn't believe it. All of their possessions were gone, including any means of communicating with the Goddesses back home. She walked down the steps on to the lush green grass of the Island of the Cyclopes. It was a very pleasing scene – rolling green meadows with wild flowers bringing splashes of colour like fireworks to the verdant pastures. The question was, how were they going to leave it again?

'This is absurd!' she said to Elliot. 'Now we can't change our clothes, bathe or clean our teeth!'

'So what?' he said.

The boy was revolting.

'Well, this is a bally rum deal!' glowered Zeus. 'I'm going to throttle that . . . But first, the Water Stone. I'll go to Polyphemus and sort that out. You all find a way off this island.'

'Just a thought, boss,' said Hypnos. 'You appear to be a couple of thunderbolts short. We're on the Island of the Cyclopes. Who make thunderbolts. Hashtag – just saying . . .'

'Yes, well . . . I suppose that might work,' mumbled Zeus. 'Then if Polyphemus won't play ball, I'll bally well blast him until he does.'

'Excellent!' squealed Hypnos. 'Except for one teeny tiny problem.'

'What's that?' huffed Zeus.

'Polyphemus won't talk to you,' said Hypnos. 'Like I said. He's a little . . . paranoid.'

'We'll soon see about that!' grumbled Zeus. 'He'd better talk to me, or I'll give him something to be paranoid about . . .'

'Juicy Zeusy, this is your picnic and the sand-wiches are divine,' sang Hypnos, throwing his arm around the King of the Gods. 'I have a plan B. All you need to do is follow my lead. Not that we'll need to, of course. You have this under control, natch.'

Hypnos winked at Elliot.

'Too bally right I do,' said Zeus. 'Right, then – Virgo, you find us a way out of here.'

'Well, we're on an island,' said Elliot. 'We're going to have to go by sea . . .'

'NO!' roared Zeus. 'Absolutely no sea! Let's go. Elliot and Hypnos, you're with me.'

'Laters!' said Hypnos, waggling his fingers at Virgo as he followed Zeus and Elliot across the meadow.

Virgo watched them go.

'Right,' she said. 'I'm sure if I just reason with the airline staff – after all, the plane has to go back anyway, and if they would just—'

The rest of her idea was lost to the roar of an engine as their plane took off into the sunshine.

She looked helplessly up at the sky.

'Snordlesnot,' she muttered under her breath.

12. Keeping an Eye Out . . .

Elliot's mind hadn't stopped whirring for the twenty-four hours they'd been travelling. How did he know that Panacea's potion actually existed? And how was he going to persuade Zeus to get in the sea? Zeus trusted Hypnos about as far as he could throw him – which, in fairness, would be pretty far – but Elliot believed the Daemon of Sleep. Hypnos had no reason to lie. Did he? Or was Elliot just hearing what he wanted to believe from a Daemon? It wouldn't be the first time.

But no potion would be any use if Thanatos destroyed humanity with the Chaos Stones, so

Elliot tried to focus his mind on the task ahead – getting the Water Stone. He'd read up on the Cyclops Polyphemus in *What's What* on the way – he was the one-eyed monster that Odysseus had tricked on his voyage. He was a vicious, violent giant who loathed Gods, mortals and water.

So Elliot was feeling super-confident about rocking up at his cave with the King of the Gods . . .

But, to give the Cyclopes their due, they knew a pretty place to live. The sun-drenched island was idyllic, with flocks of sheep and cows feeding on the lush grass and fragrant flowers of the verdant rolling pastures. It was warm without being hot, and breezy without being cold. If it weren't for the flesh-eating giants, Elliot reflected, it would be a nice place to live.

'Just a jiffy,' said Zeus, as they passed a hut with a sign saying Maro's. 'Need to nip in here for a pressie – won't be a second.'

'Take all the time you need, big guy,' said Hypnos.

'Hmmmm,' growled Zeus.

The moment Zeus disappeared into the shop, Hypnos grabbed Elliot's shoulders and started chattering at top speed.

'Right – listen to me. You are a security expert

called Mypu.'

'What?' said Elliot.

'Go with me on this,' said the Daemon. 'You've come here to install an update for Polyphemus's security systems.'

'But I haven't got a clue about . . . whatever you just said,' said Elliot. 'You do it – you can dissemble.'

'Our survey said uh-uh,' said Hypnos. 'After he was blinded by Odysseus, Polyphemus had a top-of-the-range digital eye installed. It can see through dissemblers – I told you, paranoid . . .'

'But I can't—'

'Shhhh. Grandad's back.'

'Top-hole,' said Zeus, winking and shaking a brown paper bag. 'I've got everything we need. Let's go!'

They made their way through the bucolic landscape until they came to a cave in the nook of a hillside. It was a simple dwelling, covered in grass and flowers, with a small wooden door. Elliot was reminded of a picture from a sappy fairy book. Not that he'd ever read one.

'Some security,' muttered Elliot, as Zeus raised a fist to bang on the door.

'I really think you should let me try—' said Hypnos.

'Stand aside,' said Zeus. 'Leave this to the professional.'

'Suit yourself,' said Hypnos, leaning against the hillside as Zeus pounded on the wooden door.

At Zeus's touch, all the flowers surrounding the cave's entrance swung around to reveal small eye-shaped cameras at the centre of their petals. A nearby toadstool opened up to reveal a screen inside.

'No junk mail,' growled a voice over the intercom.

'Polyphemus!' boomed Zeus. 'It's me, Uncle Zeus. I was just in the neighbourhood and thought I'd pay you a visit! Look – I bought a bottle of Maro's finest nectar. Thought we could pop it open, chat about the good old days!'

'I don't drink any more,' said the voice. 'Nectar impairs judgement, damages the organs and puts drinkers at severe risk of karaoke. Stand on the X, please.'

Elliot now noticed a dusty X scratched into the path. Zeus took a step backwards until he was in the centre.

'*Initiating full body scan*,' intoned a computer voice.

'What the—?'

But before the King of the Gods could object

further, a wreath of spring flowers flew overhead and encircled his body. A computer-generated image appeared on the toadstool screen.

Status: Immortal, God
Weaponry: Thunderbolts – not detected
Body mass: Ample – mostly fat

'How dare you!' roared Zeus. 'It's all muscle . . .'

Predicted threat level: 164 per cent
ACCESS DENIED

And with that, the X upon which Zeus stood shot out of the ground, propelling him across the meadow until he landed in large pile of animal droppings.

'Very professional,' giggled Hypnos, approaching the door. 'Listen, Zeusy – why don't you go and get your thunderbolts sorted – if this goes south, we might need them . . .'

'I'm not leaving Elliot with you!' said Zeus. 'How do I know he's safe?'

'I'll be fine,' said Elliot. 'And I'd feel a lot safer knowing you had your thunderbolts handy . . .'

'All right,' sighed Zeus. 'But first we need to get you inside.'

'Watch and learn, old-timer,' said Hypnos, standing on the X. 'Oh, Polyphemus! It's your old buddy Hypnos!'

Once again, the wreath of flowers encircled the intruder.

Status: Immortal, Daemon
Weaponry: Sleep trumpet – not detected
But as trustworthy as a second-hand
chariot salesman
Body mass: Lean – well-suited for
quick escapes

'Too kind!' winked Hypnos, taking a small bow.

Predicted threat level: 2,673 per cent
ACCESS DENIED

Hypnos leapt elegantly off the X before it had time to fire him over to Zeus.

'Hypnos!' said the voice more pleasantly. 'So good to see you!'

'You too, Polyphemus, me old mucker!' squealed Hypnos. 'You gonna let in an old friend?'

'Ha – we do go way back,' laughed the Cyclops. 'Which is precisely why you're staying out there, you old devil!'

'Listen – I've brought someone you must meet,' said Hypnos, pushing Elliot forward. 'This guy is the world's foremost authority on security. He's protected all the world's most important treasures. The *Mona Lisa*. Fort Knox. The Colonel's secret recipe . . .'

'Er, I'm here to update your security systems,' said Elliot uncertainly, as Hypnos had instructed. 'I'm . . . Mypu.'

'On the X, please.'

Elliot looked over at Zeus, who was cursing and wiping the dung from his Hawaiian shirt. Elliot had already endured one uncomfortable flight today. He seriously didn't feel like a second.

Hypnos winked and Elliot cautiously stood on the X as the floral wreath scanned his body.

Status: Mortal, child
Weaponry: Negative
Body mass: Puny
Predicted threat level: 7.6 per cent
ACCESS GRANTED

Elliot breathed a sigh of relief. He heard a series of locks clunk open from within the cave – he lost count as the endless symphony of metal clanked from inside the door. How could such a tiny door need so many locks?

His question was answered as the entire side of the hill slowly slid open.

'I dread to think what'll happen when he tries to sell the place,' Hypnos tutted. 'It's got zero kerb appeal . . .'

Elliot looked into the mouth of the massive dark cavern. Now he felt that Zeus had got the better end of the deal.

'Go on, Mypu,' said Hypnos a little too loudly. 'Get to it!'

Elliot nodded his head slowly as he remembered Hypnos's instructions. He was Mypu, the world's foremost security expert, who could protect anything. Not Elliot Hooper, who lost his entire PE kit six months ago.

He took a tentative step into the dark cave. With all the chaos at Home Farm, he often longed to be alone. But now felt like a bad time to start. He looked back at Hypnos.

'You'll be fine,' whispered the Daemon. 'He's a pussycat really.'

'Right,' said Elliot uncertainly, looking at the huge footprints in the dirt beneath his feet.

'I'm going to find us some weapons – I'll be straight back with a pocket full of thunderbolts,' Zeus said nervously. 'Be careful, Elliot!'

'And just make sure you don't disturb the others,' said Hypnos quickly, as the door started to close behind him. 'They'd gobble you up like a teenage tasting platter. See ya!'

'Wait a minute!' cried Elliot, trying to stop the door. 'What do you mean—?'

The hillside slammed back into place, leaving the King of the Gods in a cloud of 'Snordlesnot's outside.

'Great,' said Elliot.

'SHOW YOURSELF!' roared a voice in the darkness. Elliot's breath caught as the ground shook slightly beneath him. A tiny red dot was coming towards him, growing with every thundering footstep. Elliot could hear a mechanical sound, like a robot moving its arms, as the light got closer and higher, flitting around the cave. Suddenly, it shone directly down on him, blinding him with its fierce red glare.

'Are you alone?' whispered a voice.

Elliot put his hand up to shield himself from the light. As his eyes adjusted, he could just make out the figure standing before him. He was a giant – not Jack and the Beanstalk league, but a solid three metres tall. At first he appeared to be very bulky, covered in bulging muscles. But as his eyesight sharpened, Elliot could see that the Cyclops's natural bulk was enhanced by substantial padding all around him – knee pads, elbow pads, shin pads – even a nose pad. A helmet protected his massive head, which was dominated by a single digital eye in the centre.

'Er, yeah,' Elliot replied, moving out of the eye's beam.

'And you're not carrying anything?' said the voice nervously.

'No – you scanned me, remember?'

'I mean, like germs – you haven't got a cold?'

'Nope,' Elliot sniffed.

'Any rashes?'

'Not that I'm aware of,' said Elliot honestly. It had been a while since he'd showered.

'You're up to date on all your vaccinations?'

'Absolutely,' said Elliot, wondering what they were.

'OK, good,' said the Cyclops. 'I'm Polyphemus.'

'Nice to meet you,' said Elliot, holding out his hand.

'Oh . . . let's not,' said Polyphemus, squirting some antibacterial spray on Elliot's hands before pulling his own out of reach. 'You can't be too careful. Around seventy per cent of common illnesses are spread through hands that have touched everyday surfaces. Come on through.'

He led Elliot through the darkness, until they came to a small door at the back of the vast cave. Elliot worried about what would be on the other side. What kind of dark, skeleton-filled dwelling would a Cyclops inhabit? The door creaked open. He shut his eyes and walked through.

But when he opened them, he found himself in a quaint cottage kitchen.

'Would you like a vegetable smoothie?' said Polyphemus, gesturing to a blender. 'You could have a coffee, but I gave up caffeine when I discovered that drinking four cups a day increases your chances of all-round mortality by twenty-one per cent, with side effects including insomnia, nervousness, restlessness, irritability, an upset stomach and breath like a Satyr's sewer system.'

'Smoothie sounds . . . great,' said Elliot, looking glumly at the green sludge Polyphemus poured into a glass. 'So I'm here to—'

He was interrupted by a loud bleep from Polyphemus's eye.

'Take medication,' it droned.

Elliot, startled, slopped green sludge all over his hand.

'Bum,' he grumbled. He looked over at the sink. 'I'll just wash my hands.'

'NOOOOOOOO!' screamed the Cyclops. 'Not the – wet stuff. I'm acutely hydrophobic!'

'Hydro-what-now?' Elliot asked, before his

own memory answered the question. Hypnos had mentioned this – Polyphemus was afraid of water.

He looked at the quivering Cyclops. Imagine a life without water! No cooking. No cleaning. No washing.

It sounded epic.

'It's OK,' he said. 'No wet stuff.'

'You promise?' trembled Polyphemus, pulling a small disc out of his pocket and spinning the outer ring.

'What's that for?' Elliot asked.

'This? Oh, this is my fidget spinner. My therapist recommended it for alleviating stress, but I read that they carry a forty-two per cent chance of fingernail breakage, a twenty-one per cent chance of repetitive strain injury and a ninety-seven per cent chance of irritating nearby teachers. Actually, I don't want it any more . . . Here – you take it.'

'Oh, thanks!' said Elliot, giving it a spin. He'd wanted one of these for ages. Still wasn't sure why. He stuffed it in his good pocket.

'OK,' said Polyphemus, opening a cupboard filled with bottles. 'Medicine time.'

'Wow,' said Elliot. 'Are you unwell?'

'No,' said Polyphemus proudly, lining up the bottles on the counter. 'Because I take my medicine to prevent everything. Right – antihistamines, anti–inflammatories, antifreeze . . . Oh, these childproof caps are very sensible, but they make it a bit tricky to—'

'Here you go,' said Elliot, removing all the lids in seconds. 'Listen, I really need to—'

A deafening alarm suddenly blasted throughout the cave.

'What's that?' shouted Elliot, clamping his hands over his ears.

'It's my . . .' Polyphemus shouted back.

'What?' Elliot yelled.

'Polyphemus?' a gruff voice boomed over a speaker. 'Come in, Polyphemus?'

'Hang on!' cried Polyphemus, pressing an intercom by the toaster and silencing the alarm. 'Stand down, boys – all's well.'

'Who's in there with you?' said the voice. 'It's not a mortal, is it?'

'Noooooo,' said Polyphemus, winking at Elliot. 'You know I gave up mortal flesh when I discovered it's full of saturated fat and filled with artificial additives, making you twice as likely to experience poor cardiac health and troublesome wind.'

'Shame,' said the voice. 'I fancy a snack. Laters.'

'Sorry about that,' said Polyphemus to Elliot.

145

'It's the neighbours. I installed intercoms in every room. They check in every ten minutes to make sure I'm not the victim of a domestic accident, an acute medical emergency, fire, flood, robbery or door-to-door salesmen . . . Although they're getting so cheesed off with it, I'm probably more likely to get attacked by them. So, you can upgrade my security?'

'What? I mean, yeah, yeah – that's me,' said Elliot.

'I'm sorry – totally forgotten your name,' said Polyphemus. 'I hope it's not a sign of premature ageing. Must take more vitamin D . . .'

'It's El— Mypu,' said Elliot. 'So I understand you have a safe? Can you show it to me?'

'Follow me,' said Polyphemus. 'I was going to check my pulse, blood oxygen and blood pressure, but you can worry too much. You haven't finished your smoothie – why don't you bring it with you?'

Reluctantly clutching the glass of green sludge, Elliot kept up with the Cyclops as he unlocked doors, deactivated alarms and slathered himself in antibacterial gel. Next to the guest bedroom (where the bed linen was synthetic to reduce the risk of allergies by twenty-three per cent), there was a huge set of steel doors.

'What's that?' asked Elliot.

'My panic room,' said Polyphemus. 'In case of a meteor hitting the Earth. It's totally secure – nothing and no one can get in and I have everything I need to live in there until the doors automatically release after six months.'

'You really have thought of everything, haven't you?' said Elliot, who hadn't made any plans for a meteor hitting the Earth. Or for what he was going to have for tea.

'You can't be too careful,' said Polyphemus, coming to a huge black door. 'Here we are. My safe.'

'Ah, yes,' sighed Elliot. 'Very out of date. I see this a lot.'

'Really?' said Polyphemus anxiously. 'I thought it had been made just for me. If there are others, then other people can get in and take my lovely . . . Wet Stuff Stone!'

Elliot's mind hummed. Behind this door was the third Chaos Stone. Imagine how powerful that would make him . . .

'Yes, I'm afraid to say that this safe is yesterday's news,' said Elliot, snapping himself back to the moment. 'You need our recent model, the . . . XF3900.'

'Really? OK,' said Polyphemus, taking some long, slow breaths. 'So where can I get—'

'First I'll need to take a look inside,' said Elliot.

'No,' said Polyphemus quickly. 'No one goes in but me. I've been tricked before.'

Elliot looked at the vast black door with a massive combination lock in the centre. How was he going to break into that?

A wicked thought crept into his mind.

'Oh, it's up to you, of course,' he said casually. 'It's just that we've had reports of . . . leaks in these safes. And with a Water Stone inside . . .'

Polyphemus gasped.

'Leaks!' he whispered. 'You mean – the wet stuff?'

Elliot nodded his head.

'Could – be in there?'

'Uh-huh,' said Elliot grimly. 'Just imagine it, pouring out of the door, seeping into your home, drenching everything you touch . . .'

Polyphemus started to shake uncontrollably.

'I mean, personally, I love the idea of water running between my toes, sloshing around the floor, making everything lovely and . . . wet,' Elliot said to the hyperventilating Cyclops. 'All that water flowing through your cave, gushing and slopping and pouring . . . But, like I say, it's up to you.'

'OK!' squealed Polyphemus. 'But you'll have to

go in by yourself. I can't run the risk of touching any—'

'Wet stuff,' said Elliot. 'That's absolutely fine, that's what I'm here for. I just want to take a quick look.'

'You won't touch anything?'

'Wouldn't dream of it,' said Elliot, with as sincere a smile as he could manage.

'OK,' said the Cyclops. 'This is going to take a minute, as I specifically requested the most secure system money could buy. So, first of all, we need a retina scan from my eye. It's totally unique and the only thing that can open the door from the outside.'

'Very sensible,' said Elliot, as Polyphemus held his eye to the red pad near the door. A ray of light shone from the pad and scanned his eye up and down, then turned green. The door clicked open.

'You go in,' said Polyphemus, moving cautiously away from the door. 'I'll talk you through it.'

Elliot peered into the dark safe that contained a mystical Chaos Stone hidden in a Cyclops's cave. His life was truly weird.

He took a step inside, just as Polyphemus slammed the door behind him. And then it hit him. Sitting on a plinth in the centre of the room was a vast red ruby. The Water Stone. He took a step towards it. Immediately, the room filled with strings of red lasers.

'Be careful, or you'll trip the lasers,' Polyphemus shouted from outside.

Elliot swallowed down a swear word.

'Er, I need to make sure they are operative,' he said. 'How do you shut them off?'

'There's a button,' said Polyphemus.

'Where?' said Elliot, peering through the labyrinth of red light.

'On the far side of the lasers.'

'Great,' Elliot sighed.

'So – how is it?'

'Soaking,' said Elliot quickly. 'I'm going to have to take a look around. How do I get through them?'

'There is a path,' said Polyphemus. 'I can talk you through it, but anyone would be crazy to try it.'

'Will it set off another alarm?'

'No. The lasers slice through whatever touches them like a thunderbolt through butter. They can cut through anything. They could chop you up like an overripe banana! Seemed more effective than an alarm. You listening?'

'Sure,' said Elliot. It had been weeks since his life had been in danger. Why not risk it again?

'So, firstly, take two steps to the left,' said Polyphemus.

Elliot took two tentative steps to his left. He felt something wet and slimy slop on to his hand. He'd forgotten he was still holding the vegetable smoothie. He bent down to put it on the floor, but a laser running dangerously close to his chest prevented him. He was stuck with it.

'Then you'll have to lift your left leg in front and stretch out your left arm above your head,' said Polyphemus.

'Why?' asked Elliot.

'Because any second now, there will be—'

A huge burst of flames shot across the floor, precisely where Elliot's left leg and arm would have been.

'A huge burst of flames shooting across the floor, precisely where your left leg and arm would have been.'

'Thanks,' said Elliot, extinguishing the end of a scorched shoelace. This was going to be fun.

Carefully following Polyphemus's instructions, Elliot made his way cautiously through the room. Twice his hair was singed by lasers overhead, he melted the sole of his left shoe when he didn't pick his foot up high enough, and he nudged a laser with his bottom.

Eventually, with a sigh of extreme relief and rather singed trousers, he reached the plinth. He saw the red button and shut off the lasers. There, before him, was the Water Stone.

Elliot immediately experienced the power surge he always felt in the presence of the Chaos Stones. His whole body tingled at the prospect of the command he could have over three elements: Earth, Air and now Water. Zeus had warned him never to use the stones – but he could do so much good with them. There were so many places in the world that needed water – or had too much. Imagine if he could help them. Imagine if he had that much power. Imagine . . . He reached his hand towards it. It was so close. So very, very close . . .

'And then the pressure pad ensures that, even if someone gets through all of that, the moment the stone is moved by anyone but me, a big boulder will fall from the ceiling and smash their head in.'

'I thought you didn't kill mortals any more?' said Elliot nervously, looking at the massive boulder suspended from the ceiling.

'Oh, I don't *eat* them – they clog up your colon like nobody's business,' shuddered Polyphemus. 'But if any of them tried to steal something from me, I'd kill them until they were dead.'

'Good to know,' Elliot whispered. A pressure pad. He'd seen a film with one of these once – the Water Stone would need to be replaced with something else of equal weight, or he'd be squished like a fly on a windscreen. He looked at the stone. It was pretty substantial. He needed something small but heavy to take its place. Something like . . .

His eyes lit on the glass of green sludge in his hand. Something exactly like that.

Elliot weighed up the glass of smoothie, which by now had slightly congealed and smelt even more like it had already cleansed someone's colon.

He raised it to the plinth and held his breath. He'd have to do this quickly but perfectly, first time. He steadied his hands, held the glass above the Water Stone and let out a long, slow breath. He was going to do it in one . . . two . . . thr—

'Everything OK in there?' yelled Polyphemus.

Elliot jumped. The smoothie slipped from his hand. Everything seemed to drop into slow motion. He watched aghast as the glass fell, nearer, nearer, nearer . . . It was going to hit the Water Stone in three – two – one . . .

But before his body and brain had time to discuss it, Elliot's right hand whipped the Water

Stone away. A nanosecond later, the glass of smoothie landed squarely on the pressure pad. Had he been quick enough? Clutching the ruby, he flung his arms over his head in a futile attempt to protect himself from the boulder.

It didn't fall. He had done it.

Elliot allowed himself a few silent fist pumps to celebrate his sheer epicness.

'Yeah, it's drenched in here,' he called back. 'I'm coming out.'

He swaggered over to the door, looked at the glass of green sludge sitting on the plinth and congratulated himself on a job well done.

'I'll have to send my team over to dry it out,' he said, emerging back into the cave and slamming the door safely behind him. 'Don't go in there, whatever you do.'

'Oh, thank goodness,' said Polyphemus, breathing a sigh of relief. 'Do you need anything else? Another smoothie, perhaps? I do a wonderful cauliflower and frogspawn kidney cleanser . . .'

'No, I'll be on my way,' said Elliot, hastily shoving the ruby into his pocket as they passed the panic room. 'I'll just . . .'

CLUNK!

The Water Stone, falling through the hole in his pocket, hit the floor and rolled endlessly across the floor, coming to an incriminating halt by Polyphemus's big toe.

'What's this?' roared the Cyclops. 'Wait a minute! You're not a security expert! You're not interested in cleansing your colon! You're nothing more than a dirty thief – come here, you little—'

And the Cyclops lunged at Elliot, both of his massive hands outstretched to wring his neck. Elliot backed up against the panic-room doors, but there was nowhere to go. He looked from side to side, what could he—

SMACK!

Before he even registered what he was doing, Elliot hit the pad that activated the panic-room doors. As they slid open, he dived forward, sending Polyphemus flying straight over his head and into the panic room, landing with a thud on the floor. Elliot and Polyphemus both struggled to their feet and charged towards the door pad . . .

Elliot reached it first. He slammed his palm down and the doors locked tight, just in time.

'Wait until I get my hands on you!' the Cyclops screamed from inside.

'I'll see you in six months!' Elliot shouted back, picking up the Water Stone. He pulled out his dad's pocket watch and opened it. The diamond Earth Stone and emerald Air Stone sparkled invitingly. He held the enchanted ruby to the watch, and, just as the others had done, it immediately shrank to fill a quadrant of the inside. He'd done it! Three Chaos Stones. And they looked incredible.

Reluctantly, Elliot closed the lid of the watch. He looked around with satisfaction. Now all he had to do was get out of here. Shouldn't be too—

The deafening alarm filled the cave once more.

'Polyphemus!' came the gruff voice. 'Come in, Polyphemus!'

Polyphemus shouted from inside the panic room, but it was to no avail. The thick doors prevented the sound from reaching the intercom.

'Polyphemus!' the gruff voice bellowed. 'Do you copy?'

Elliot considered trying to impersonate the Cyclops, but decided that this would simply tell the other giants he was there. The silence was as heavy as Elliot's thundering heart. He held his breath, lest the crackling intercom picked up the movement of air. Perhaps the other Cyclopes would think it was another false alarm ...

'I'm coming over,' said the voice at last. 'But I'm warning you. If this is just you meditating again, I'll smash your skull in.'

Or maybe not.

Elliot opened the kitchen door and peered into the darkness of the vast cave – did he have time to get out before they arrived?

The hillside sliding open gave him his answer. A huge lumbering figure appeared at the mouth of the cave. Another Cyclops. The entrance slammed shut behind him with a sickening crash. Elliot looked all around, but it was no use.

He was trapped.

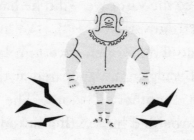

13. A Friend in Need

'Right, then,' Virgo said to herself as she came to the island's glistening coastline. 'How to get off the island . . .'

She reflected that on the Zodiac Council there were many perfect ways to come up with ideas. Should she try some free-thinking brain-storming? Or role-playing seminars? Or perhaps produce a twenty-page flow chart?

Yet as she looked out over the ocean, none of these seemed as optimal as building a floating device that could travel across water. Zeus had banned travel by sea. But Virgo reasoned that, as there was no alternative, he'd be delighted with her problem-solving genius. And, of course, Virgo was always right.

She looked around for some raw material. A short walk across the island, she saw a small copse. Wood – that was just what she needed. She made a note to put it in her flow chart.

Walking towards the trees, she found her mind awash with the conversation with Hypnos back on the plane. *At the end of the day, who really cares about you – except you?* The Daemon's arguments were ill-considered and incorrect. Not to mention, as Elliot might put it, stupid, pants and bum. She was just going to ignore it. It wasn't worth another thought. She wouldn't allow herself to waste another second on it. Wood. That was what she needed now. She would give that her entire focus.

In any case, Hypnos's argument was clearly sub-optimal. Elliot needed her – the boy couldn't be trusted to change his underwear without her. Not that he changed it frequently enough anyway. He needed a female companion to guide him through life. All right, so that could be Josie-Mum, were she well again, and maybe at that point Elliot wouldn't need her any more and would throw her out into the world all alone . . .

But it was nonsense anyway. The Zodiac

Council would welcome her back with open arms once she proved herself a hero and regained her kardia. Then her life would resume – all the administration and paperwork and . . . stationery. OK, so there was a remote possibility she might not get her kardia nor her job back . . .

So then the Gods would take care of her. They had expressed a sincere degree of affection for her. She was one of them – an immortal. They were in this together. For ever. So, she might be an immortal who had agreed to the imprisonment of other immortals without trial for an indefinite period of time in order to secure her own kardia, but the Gods would understand. Probably. Maybe. Perhaps . . .

Virgo dismissed the unpleasant sensations swirling around her stomach. She had done absolutely the right thing in supporting her colleagues on the Council. She was ensuring the safety of the Earth. Everything was going to be perfectly fine.

What she needed to do now was get away from this island. She slipped her bag off her shoulder. She had discovered that a handbag was a highly optimal accessory favoured by female mortals for carrying all the things you didn't even realize you needed. She rifled through the contents: lip balm (three), pencil (blunt), tissues (unused: four), more tissues (used: three), a plastic keyring that had seemed an excellent investment at the time. But nothing of immediate use. She dropped the bag in exasperation. If only she had a—

'Plop!'

Virgo put her finger to her ear. That beetle in her brain really was causing havoc. She thought she could hear—

'Plop!'

There it was again! She looked down at her bag, which was twitching curiously. She opened it cautiously and observed a large green mass inside. Either those dirty tissues had leaked or this was . . .

'Gorgy!' she cried, trying hard to be displeased at her pet gorgon. 'Whatever are you doing here?'

Gorgy bounced out of the bag and into her arms.

'Mama,' he cooed up at her. A weaker individual might have found him quite irresistible.

'Well,' she smiled, putting the gorgon on her shoulder, 'it seems I have no choice but to keep you with me. How very inconvenient . . .'

Virgo set off towards the sun-dappled trees. A small group of Dryads were making daisy chains in the grass and throwing them gleefully over each other's heads. Virgo watched the wood nymphs from a distance. What a ridiculous waste of time to sit around laughing with your friends all day! There must be so many better things to do than languishing in the warm sun, having a joyful time and talking and playing and . . . being with other people. It must feel futile, she thought, as the Dryads burst into peels of happy laughter. Ridiculous! Absurd! Perhaps she should go over and join them for a moment, just to fully understand how pointless it must be . . .

A massive shadow fell across the copse. Virgo looked up at the sky. That was strange. It was still perfectly blue — the sun was shining down as it had been all day. So what was blocking it out?

The ground beneath Virgo's feet began to tremble with rhythmic thuds. The Dryads reached out to hold each other's hands. Virgo instinctively ducked behind a tree as leaves rained down from the shaking branches.

The copse grew dark and the Dryads clung to one another, quivering. Shafts of sunlight broke the gigantic shadow apart, revealing that it was not one dark mass, but two.

''Ello girls,' said a voice Virgo had heard before.

The nymphs trembled in their terrified huddle.

'Who are you?' one of them asked shakily.

'Bad plop man,' whispered Gorgy. Virgo nodded dumbly.

'Don't matter who I am,' said The Ram, stepping into the light. 'It's you who's the problem. The Zodiac Council says you're a security risk. You're coming with us.'

The nymphs started to wail and sob.

'No, please, sir – you don't understand!' cried one. 'We mean no harm – here, have one of these.'

She plucked a daisy chain from her hair and threw it at the Titan. The Ram swatted it away with one of his massive hands.

'You saw them, brother – they just tried to attack me!' He grinned. 'They're resisting arrest ...'

'Actually, I think they're daisies, bruv,' said The Brain.

'You're a melon,' said The Ram, clipping his brother's ear. 'If you won't come quietly, ladies, you leave us no choice ...'

'Quick – run!' screamed one of the nymphs and the group scattered among the trees.

'Come on, bruv,' gloated The Ram, pulling an enormous net and a sack from his back pocket. 'Let's make a citizen's arrest.'

Virgo stood pressed against the tree, her heart pounding. She felt the cold gust as the Titans swept past her, squeezing her eyes shut in the irrational hope it made her invisible. When she dared to open one, she saw the Titans lumbering after their screaming prey. Surely this wasn't what the Council intended? The Titans were supposed to be rounding up immortals who posed a security risk. Not ones peacefully living their lives. What should she do? She quickly assessed the situation: what were her optimal chances of rescuing the Dryads while evading capture herself? She came immediately to a sound and logical conclusion.

She gathered Gorgy into her arms – and ran.

Trying to block out the screams of the nymphs echoing around the wood, she pelted as fast as her stumbling legs could carry her, until the sea shimmered ahead once more. Her chest felt as if it might explode, but she kept running until she felt the sand beneath her feet. Then, and only then, did she sink breathlessly to her knees.

'This is a necessary measure, this is a necessary measure,' she repeated under her breath.

'What's a necessary measure?' trilled Hypnos at the top of his voice. 'A straitjacket?'

'Argh!' yelled Virgo, startled. She tried to gather herself.

'Some . . . different wood,' she panted eventually. 'What I found was sub-optimal. I'll search closer to the beach.'

'Just thought I'd check in.' Hypnos narrowed his eyes. 'You look like you've seen a ghost.'

A gigantic bellow went up from the other side of the island.

'Ooooh – that's my cue. Back in a jiffy.'

Virgo watched Hypnos hurtle across the sky. A ghost she could handle. What she had just witnessed – that was going to haunt her for much, much longer.

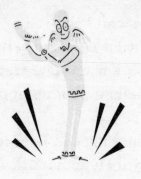

14. Beware Mypu

'Polyphemus!' roared the new Cyclops. 'It's me, Argos. Came as soon as I could. I've called for backup too. Where are you?'

'I'm in here!' yelled Polyphemus, banging on the panic-room door.

The Cyclops followed the sound of the hammering until he came to the steel doors. He was centimetres from Elliot's hiding place. And he smelt really bad.

'What are you doing in there, you fool?' asked Argos.

'I'm stuck!' shrieked Polyphemus.

'How did you manage that?'

'It wasn't me,' said Polyphemus. 'It was Mypu.'

'You what?' said Argos, answering the doorbell with a thud on a nearby button. Elliot saw the light pierce the cave once again. The door was open. Perhaps he could just ...

Two more gigantic Cyclopes lumbered into the cavern. Perhaps not.

'Brontos, Steropes,' said Argos. 'He's finally cracked. Listen to this ... Say that again, mate. What's the problem?'

'Mypu!' yelled Polyphemus.

'What?' said Steropes. 'Your what?'

'Mypu!' screamed Polyphemus. 'It's all Mypu's fault. Mypu has trapped me!'

The three Cyclopes looked at each other in awkward bewilderment.

'Listen, mate,' said Argos. 'What you do on the lav is your business, don't go involving us ...'

'No – you don't understand!' cried Polyphemus. 'You need to search everywhere! You need to sniff him out! You need to find Mypu!'

'That's disgusting!' scoffed Brontos. 'We're not going anywhere near your poo!'

'No, no, no!' shouted Polyphemus. 'Listen to me. Look outside. Look everywhere.'

'Like where?' puzzled Argos.

'I dunno!' squealed Polyphemus. 'Could be

anywhere. Maybe . . . maybe Mypu is in your cave?'

The Cyclopes gagged.

'It had better not be, you dirty doughnut!' thundered Steropes. 'All those vegetable smoothies have gone to your nut, mate. You've finally lost it – c'mon boys.'

Elliot finally let out his breath. They were leaving.

'Wait a minute,' said Argos, holding the other two Cyclopes back. 'Can you smell that?'

'Smell what?' said Brontos, sniffing the air. 'Not his poo . . .'

'No. That,' said Argos. 'Smells just like . . .'

'Mortal flesh,' grinned Steropes. 'Oh, boys. I think dinner has been delivered.'

Elliot looked for any possible escape route as the Cyclopes sniffed around. It was no use. He was completely trapped. He closed his eyes and wished for two things: firstly that the Cyclopes didn't find him, and secondly that he'd had a shower at least once that week.

But he was out of luck on both.

'Found it!' cried Argos, throwing aside the sofa with a massive arm and grabbing Elliot with a giant hand. 'Dinner is served.'

'Don't come crying to me with your clogged

colon,' sang Polyphemus from inside the panic room.

Elliot struggled against the iron fist imprisoning him, but it held fast.

'Let me take the first bite,' said Steropes. 'I let you have that backpacker last summer. You remember? The one who was trying to "find himself".'

'He found himself all right,' laughed Argos. 'Inside my belly! OK. But don't leave me the rump. It's so chewy . . .'

'I'm having him first,' slavered Brontos, grabbing Elliot. 'I'll start with the legs. I love a mortal drumstick.'

'Well, hurry up – I'm starving,' grumbled Argos.

'Are you ready?' said Brontos, holding Elliot up to his uneven yellow teeth.

Elliot gulped. He was going to end his days in a Cyclops's colon. What a lame way to die.

'Then let's get outta here!' screamed Brontos, two feathered wings sprouting from the side of his head.

'Hypnos!' cried Elliot. He'd never been so pleased to see a Daemon in his life.

'I got my eye on you!' said Hypnos, blasting past Argos and Steropes and whizzing Elliot back

169

towards the cave's entrance.

'Oi!' said Argos, lumbering after him. 'Bring us back our dinner!'

'Come back here!' said Steropes, charging behind his friend. 'I'm starving!'

'Let's go!' cried Elliot.

Elliot felt a blast of acceleration as Hypnos zoomed out of the open cave mouth into the evening air.

'Look out!' yelled the Daemon, charging straight into Zeus struggling with armfuls of thunderbolts.

'What the devil—?' said Zeus.

'Quick!' said Hypnos. 'Blast them, big boy!'

The second the Cyclopes emerged from the cave, Zeus took aim and launched a thunderbolt at Argos. But when the thunderbolt left his hand, there was no flash, no lightning – it just bounced off the Cyclops like a ping-pong ball.

'Wh–what the . . .' Zeus stuttered. 'They're not working. I don't understand . . .'

'Let's get out of here!' cried Elliot.

With the earth-shuddering footsteps of the Cyclopes behind them, Hypnos flew towards the azure coastline, struggling to bear the weight of his two passengers.

'When we get home, I'm giving that bally

Don'tcAIR an OdysseyAdvisor review they'll never forget,' Zeus blustered, looking behind to see the Cyclopes gaining on them with each thundering step.

'It's no good – you're too heavy,' puffed Hypnos, dropping Elliot and Zeus to the ground. 'I can't fly with more than one person. What now?'

'We fight them,' said Zeus, putting up his fists. 'And, failing that, we run very fast.'

'I've got a better idea,' said Elliot.

He put his hand in his pocket and gripped his watch. The stones glowed in his palm and their magic surged through his body. He yanked the watch out of his pocket and held it above his head.

'Elliot – no!' cried Zeus. The ruby cast its ethereal red light into the darkening sky. He was too late. With the authority of three stones empowering every atom of his being, Elliot roared his command at the Water Stone.

'RAIN!'

At once, the clear evening sky darkened with black clouds, chasing every last chink of light from the heavens. A low rumble sounded overhead as the Water Stone obeyed its new master. Elliot felt the first drops start to run down his face, but they did nothing to cool the raging fire that the Chaos Stones always awoke within him.

'Wh–what is this?' yelled Argos, coming to a grinding halt.

'It . . . it . . . it's . . . WET STUFF!' whimpered Steropes, covering his head with his arms. 'Aaaaaaaaargh!'

The two massive Cyclopes jumped about on the spot, trying to avoid getting their feet wet with their hands, then whipping their hands back to their heads to keep those dry. Elliot laughed and laughed as he watched them dance around, terrified of the water cascading from the sky. He looked out to sea and wondered how they'd feel about a tsunami. He raised the Water Stone higher . . .

'Elliot – ENOUGH!' roared Zeus. 'Let's get out of here.'

Elliot dropped his arm to his side and the rain immediately stopped. He startled slightly as his mind and body cooled. He'd nearly gone too far. Again.

'There she is!' cried Hypnos, pointing towards Virgo in the distance.

They continued to pelt towards the seashore, where Virgo was waiting for them.

'Quick,' panted Elliot. 'How do we get off the island?'

'On my raft,' said Virgo proudly.

'Well, where is it?!'

Virgo held up two sticks tied together with seaweed.

'Under construction,' she said, defensively.

'No – absolutely no travel by water!' Zeus shouted. 'There has to be another way . . .'

'Elliot,' said Hypnos, pointing towards a shadow looming over the shore. 'Look!'

An enormous T-shape appeared at the crest of the hill. The ground started to shake once more as Argos, holding a struggling Steropes over his head, lurched forward.

'New invention,' he called. 'Keeps off the wet stuff. I'm calling it . . . Bumbrella!'

And with that, he hurled his companion towards the group.

'There isn't another way,' Elliot shouted at Zeus. 'Everyone – SWIM!'

'No!' roared Zeus. 'We mustn't go in the—'

The rest of his objection was lost as Elliot shoved the King of the Gods into the sea before a Cyclops could land on his head.

'Nice one,' said Hypnos. 'Now it gets interesting.'

But Elliot had no breath to answer him, swimming his fastest front crawl out to sea, until the roars of the Cyclopes were washed away by

173

the waves.

'Is everyone OK?' he yelled, pausing to tread water.

'Pleurgh!' spat Virgo, emerging centimetres from his face.

'We need to find land – quickly,' said Zeus, looking anxiously at the darkening waters. 'We mustn't stay in the sea.'

'Why?' said Virgo. 'Apart from the fact that it's wet and cold and full of seasoning, I fail to see the—' A sudden current dragged her around in a circle. 'Why am I—'

The sea around them began to swirl, as if someone were stirring it with a giant teaspoon.

'What's happening?' Virgo yelled.

'Hold on,' shouted Elliot, pulling the watch out of his pocket. 'I'll use the—'

But no sooner had the words left his lips than a fist of sea-spray fingers grabbed the Chaos Stones from his hand.

'Hey!' he shouted. 'Someone help me! I'm being sucked under!'

'So am—' was Virgo's last remark before the sea swallowed her.

'Oh, crumbs,' groaned Zeus, his silver head sinking beneath the surface.

'Trust me,' shouted Hypnos, fluttering overhead.

'It's all going perfectly to plan.'

But Elliot's plan didn't involve drowning. He used every shred of his strength to fight the water, frantically paddling his arms and legs against the powerful current. But it was no use. He was no match for the might of the sea.

As Hypnos made an elegant dive beneath the surface, the sea pulled and pulled at Elliot's feet – until, with one gigantic suck, he was dragged deep beneath the waves.

15. Parental Controls

Josie Hooper was so very, very tired. For months now, her body had been battling her mind – and it didn't feel like either was winning the war.

Her mind had become like a tangled necklace. On days when she felt calm, she could work steadily through the knots. It took time and patience, but eventually she could unpick the knots and link the chain smoothly together.

But on other days, panic and frustration claimed her mind. The knots stuck to one another until they were one big jumble and the necklace was good for nothing. Her body no longer obeyed her mind and her mind no longer gave clear commands. With each day that passed, she longed to be free from both.

Elliot had gone. She couldn't remember where and she didn't know why – but she needed him safe at Home Farm with her. That was all she had ever needed. That, and her husband home again.

Or at least so she had thought.

Josie wasn't sure whether it was time or her mind that had changed Dave Hooper. He wasn't the man she remembered and he wasn't the man she had loved. At night, when her mind was at its most tangled, she was haunted by visions of him hounding her, getting angry when she couldn't answer the questions he screamed. But by day he seemed to be a different man. Which one was real? Josie had learnt to trust neither her mind nor her memories. But she didn't trust Dave either.

A voice woke her from her dozing. It was a different voice, but not new. She had heard this woman before. Josie looked for the sisters who always took such good care of her. But there was only Dave.

'Thank you so much for inviting me over again, Mr Hooper.'

'Please, do come through, Ms Givings,' said Dave. 'I'm sorry our last meeting was so dramatic.'

Ms Givings? Josie knew that name. Who was she?

'I quite understand, Mr Hooper,' the young woman said, giving Josie a sympathetic smile as she passed her chair. 'It must be a very confusing time for you all.'

'It is,' sighed Dave with a saintly look. Josie wished she could give his face a hard slap with a wet fish. 'But we try to muddle through . . .'

'Of course,' said Ms Givings with a compassionate nod.

'I'm just trying to do my best,' said Dave. 'It's so tough . . .'

'It really must be,' she agreed. 'And all anyone wants from this situation is what's best for everyone. You, Mrs Hooper and, of course, young Elliot.'

Dave pursed his lips and nodded. Everyone had told Josie not to marry him, that he was no good and would never change. How Josie wished she'd listened.

'That's what I want too,' he said quietly. Josie just hoped that Ms Givings wasn't buying this complete pile of steaming . . .

'First things first – I'm struggling to get in contact with your parole officer,' said Ms Givings. 'Could you give me their details, please?'

'Of course,' Dave replied with a smile. 'If you leave me an email address, I'll get them straight over to you.'

'Thank you,' she said, with a pause that invited further conversation. Dave made her wait for it.

'So, the reason I called you over was to discuss my Elliot,' said Dave. 'He's very worried about what the future holds. For all of us.'

Ms Givings took a deep breath. That's never good, Josie thought. Happy news never needs oxygen. It breathes on its own.

'I often find it's best in these situations to be completely open,' Ms Givings continued. 'This is no reflection on you or Elliot – clearly you are both doing your very best to look after Mrs Hooper.'

'That's all we can do,' whispered Dave weakly. Josie commanded her legs to give him a swift kick. They didn't listen.

'And I must say, I am amazed at how Elliot has carried this burden alone while you were . . . away,' said Ms Givings. 'He is a remarkable young man.'

'He's quite something,' nodded Dave.

'But . . .' Ms Givings faltered. 'You are in a huge period of transition yourself. Adjusting to life outside prison takes time. There's no shame in finding it hard. Even without the additional . . . issues that you have here at home.'

'I know,' said Dave. Josie watched him muster up a tear from somewhere in his dark soul.

'So – we were wondering if it might all be a little too much,' said Ms Givings.

Dave pursed his lips and hung his head.

'I agree,' he said eventually. 'That's why I wanted to meet today. Things can't carry on as they are.'

Josie tried to tell her body to toss this man out of their lives, for her lips to let out the scream inside her soul. She willed every atom of her being to do something, to do anything, to stop this deceitful charade.

'Obviously, there is a huge amount to discuss,' Ms Givings said slowly, 'but we feel that Josie might benefit from some more . . . specialized care. Somewhere that has experience of dealing with her condition. Somewhere she can be safe and well looked after.'

Dave looked at Josie mournfully.

Don't you do it, David Hooper, Josie thought. *Don't you dare . . .*

She awaited his words, like a convict awaiting a sentence.

'You're right,' he said, allowing a fake tear to roll down his fake face. 'I wish you weren't . . . but you're right. I've known it since I came home. I can't take care of her. It's just too much.'

Josie watched, empty inside, as this devil cried his false tears. If only her body were her own. She would have given him something to cry about.

But she could do nothing. All she could do was sit and watch as this monster destroyed everything Elly had worked so hard to protect. Josie Hooper had never thought she was capable of the hatred she felt at that moment.

'We will refer you to a specialist team who can make all the necessary arrangements,' said Ms Givings. 'And you will be able to visit her whenever you like.'

And with a silent nod, Dave Hooper sentenced Josie to her imprisonment.

'OK,' he said. 'When were you thinking?'

'We feel it's better not to delay these things. Where is Elliot today, by the way?'

'He's visiting my aunt,' Dave lied. Josie knew he didn't have an aunt. He didn't have a heart.

'Are you expecting him back soon?'

'Anytime now,' said Dave. 'You really think this is for the best?'

'We do. Josie has very specific needs at the moment. Perhaps you all just need a bit of space to get the support you deserve?'

Josie tried to move again, if only this one time. But all that came out was a low moan.

'Are you OK, Mrs Hooper?' said Ms Givings. At least she had the decency to look genuinely concerned. 'Perhaps we should have this conversation elsewhere . . .'

'She's fine,' said Dave. 'She gets hungry around this time – I'll sort her out in a minute.'

Josie raged within. *Sort her out?* She was his wife, not the laundry.

'Besides, you're right,' he said. 'Do what you think is right. You know best.'

Ms Givings nodded. 'If you could just send me those parole officer details as soon as possible. And let's meet again soon. There's still a lot to discuss. But I think that's enough for today.'

She rose to leave.

'Goodbye, Mrs Hooper.' She looked at Josie with genuine apology in her eyes. Josie still hated her.

But not as much as she hated him.

She sent up a silent prayer. Wherever Elliot was, whoever he was with, he needed to stay there.

Because Home Farm was no longer safe. Not for either of them.

16. Under the Sea

Elliot woke up with a splutter. What had just happened? He remembered being sucked beneath the surface of the sea and then . . . nothing. Had he drowned? Was he dead? Was this . . . heaven?

As his senses awoke, it certainly sounded like everyone was having a good time in heaven. He could hear laughing, singing, glasses clinking and . . . was that – an accordion?

Elliot slowly sat up and shook the water from his ears. He was inside a cage within some kind of giant dome. He walked over to the wall to take a closer look. It was a bubble, the rainbow colours

shimmering across its surface. Through the irides-
cence he could just see that the sea surrounded
the dome, save for the sandy surface he was standing on. He poked the wall with his finger. It gave
and gave, until his finger poked through into the
water beyond. But the bubble didn't burst. Which,
Elliot realized, surveying the millions of gallons of
water above him, was kinda lucky. He dusted the
sand off. He hated sand. Trust him to land in a
heaven full of it.

He took a deep breath – which struck him as
odd if he were dead – and squinted towards the
light coming from the barred door of his cage. He
walked over to see what was happening outside,
quickly withdrawing his hands from the sharp
coral bars.

Elliot was greeted by what looked like a great
big pub. He remembered how Grandad used to
take him to the Dog and Dolphin in Little
Motbury for a bag of crisps and a glass of
lemonade.

'Where have you been?' Nan would say when
they got home, slapping her spatula menacingly
on her hand.

'Church.' Grandad would wink at Elliot who
would try not to giggle. He'd loved those secret
trips to the cosy village tavern.

But this place was huge, with a vast bar running the length of the bubble, lined with wooden barrels from which the customers were filling stone flagons with golden nectar. It was standing room only in the packed tavern, and it was stuffed with every imaginable sea creature – nymphs, mermaids, mermen, half-human–half-fish . . . things.

Elliot's eye was drawn by some frantically waving arms. Virgo and Hypnos were locked up in cages alongside his.

'About time too,' said Virgo. 'You've been asleep for hours.'

'Plop!' squealed Gorgy.

'What's that doing here?' Elliot demanded. 'Get rid of it.'

'I will not,' huffed Virgo. 'Besides, we have bigger things to worry about.'

'Are we dead?' Elliot asked.

'Not yet,' grinned Hypnos. 'Welcome to the Coral Cove, the pub that brings new meaning to the phrase "watering hole".'

'What are we doing here?' asked Elliot. 'And where's Zeus?'

'Oh,' said Virgo. 'He's . . . over there.'

Virgo pointed to a very grumpy Zeus bound with seaweed at the foot of a huge throne made of shells. Sprawled across the throne, swigging from a golden tankard, was a man of not dissimilar age and build to Zeus, right down to the big belly and white beard. He was dressed in a long blue coat, like the kind Elliot had seen in pictures of old naval officers, with a frilly white shirt sticking out at the chest and cuffs. His trousers were cut off at the knee, as apparently was his left leg, which had been replaced by a coral stump. He wore a golden eyepatch over his left eye and a black pirate hat with a whale skeleton pictured on the front. On his left shoulder perched a colourful parrot; in his right hand was an enormous golden trident. It was weird – the more Elliot looked at this pirate guy, the more he looked like Zeus. They could almost be—

'Brothers!' roared the pirate, raising his flagon to the crowd. 'And sisters of the sea! Ahoy there! Welcome to the Coral Cove!'

A huge roar greeted him, and nectar slopped from the flagons raised in salute.

'As ye know, all o'ye are always me special guests,' said the pirate. 'But tonight we have an extra-special visitor. Raise yer tankards to me brother – Zeus!'

Another huge roar went up from the crowd and tankards clashed together in a toast.

'Brother?' said Elliot. 'So this must be—'

'Poseidon!' shouted Zeus. 'This is ridiculous. Release me at once, you scurvy knave!'

An amused gasp went up from the crowd.

'Ye wound me,' whispered Poseidon with a grin, clutching his hand to his heart. 'Is that any way to talk to the brother ye've not seen for so long?'

'You told me you never wanted to see me again!' shouted Zeus. 'I have simply agreed to your conditions.'

'And why be that, landlubber?' said Poseidon. 'Why did yer baby brother never want to see ye again? Tell all our friends.'

'You're not still going on about that?' sighed Zeus. 'It was *one* date . . .'

'WITH ME WOIFE!' barked Poseidon. 'You went out to dinner with me Amphitrite!'

'Your *ex*-wife! I left it a perfectly respectful amount of time before asking her out!' Zeus shouted back. 'You had already separated!'

'At breakfast time!' yelled Poseidon. 'Her toast hadn't separated from the jam before ye pounced on her, ye scurvy dog!'

'You've been divorced for centuries,' grumbled Zeus. 'And besides, it didn't work out between us.'

'Not surprised,' said Poseidon, winking at

the crowd. 'Who wants shrimp when ye're used to lobster!'

A riotous cheer went up in the tavern.

'Siblings are so sub-optimal,' sighed Virgo. 'I'm relieved I don't have any.'

'Me too,' said Elliot. 'Hypnos – why are we here?'

'Wait and see . . .' Hypnos grinned.

'But I—'

'Shhhhh,' hissed Virgo.

'You shhhhh,' Elliot hissed back.

'Ye don't go fishing in yer brother's pond. I made meself very clear,' said Poseidon as the crowd settled back to their drinks. 'The sea is my kingdom and I told ye *never* to set foot in it again. If ye did, ye'd be me prisoner. The sea is mine! And now, ye great landlubber, so are you! Avast behind!'

'What . . . where . . . who's there?' said Zeus, trying to turn around in his binding.

'No one,' said Poseidon more clearly. 'I'm just saying – ye've got a vast behind!'

The crowd fell about laughing.

'Now listen here, you stupid old salt,' growled Zeus. 'We were on an important mission to reclaim the Water Stone and now thanks to your petty grudge, three Chaos Stones are floating around the ocean!'

'Are they now?' said Poseidon, pulling Elliot's watch from his coat and throwing it up and down in his hand.

Elliot's heart pounded as he saw his Chaos Stones carelessly tossed in the air. They were *his*.

'I thought you said this was going to help me find the potion?' Elliot hissed at Hypnos. 'All you've done is lost the Chaos Stones!'

'Where's the trust?' squealed Hypnos, feigning hurt. 'Give it a minute . . .'

'Will you shhhhh!' said Virgo.

'*Will you shhhh*,' Elliot mimicked.

'Bad plop man,' whispered Gorgy, sticking his green tongue out at Elliot.

Elliot returned his gaze to the squabbling brothers.

'Those aren't yours,' Zeus growled at the God of the Sea.

'Me woife wasn't *yours*!' shouted Poseidon. 'Finders keepers. Huge booty.'

'That's *not* booty,' scowled Zeus.

'Never said it was,' said Poseidon. 'I'm just saying – ye've got a huge booty!'

The crowd roared again.

'This goes far beyond our petty squabble,' said Zeus. 'We need to protect the Earth from

Thanatos. Those Chaos Stones are our best hope.'

'Ye see – there ye go again,' sighed Poseidon, still throwing the watch up and down. Elliot's heart pulsated and he gripped the bars, ignoring the pain from the coral. He wanted his Chaos Stones back.

'Always with the Earth. That's all ye ever cared about. Never gave a thought to us down here below . . .'

'That's simply not true,' said Zeus. 'I have always—'

'Looked out for yerself,' said Poseidon, thrusting the watch in Zeus's face. 'Well, two can play at that game. You do what ye've got to do. If Thanatos shows his bony britches down here, we'll be ready for him . . . Besides – I told ye that anything ye took on the water would be mine to keep. That includes this, you and all yer scurvy crew.'

He gestured at the row of cages and the crowd raised their flagons in mock salute.

'Er – excuse me?' squawked the parrot on Poseidon's shoulder.

'Who's there?' snapped Poseidon, leaping out of his throne with his trident aloft.

The parrot took off into the air with its wings outstretched. With a gentle pop, it transformed into a . . . Elliot didn't really know what it was. A man from the navel up to his long black hair and beard, his bottom half was coiled like a giant snake. He folded his arms and let out a huge sigh next to Poseidon.

'Thought that was strange,' said Poseidon. 'Never had a parrot before. Hello there, Proteus.'

'And . . . voila,' said Hypnos, folding his arms and winking at Elliot.

'I don't get it,' said Elliot. 'How's he going to help?'

'Watch and learn,' said Hypnos quietly.

Poseidon slumped back down on his throne.

'What are ye doing here?'

'You hired me to give you guidance,' said Proteus. 'So that is what I will do. You need to let Zeus and his friends go and give them every assistance in their quest.'

'What?!' roared Poseidon. 'I'd rather boil me backside in barnacles.'

'Remind me again,' said Proteus, stroking his beard. 'Which one of us is the All-Knowing Shepherd of the Sea, who has the gift of knowing all things, past, present and future?'

Poseidon rolled his eyes.

'That be ye.'

'I know,' said Proteus. 'So you employ me to tell

you anything you need to know.'

'That be right,' said Poseidon.

'I know!' said Proteus. 'So when I say that you're going to let your brother go and help him, it's not because I want to see his holiday snaps, it's because—'

'Ye know,' sighed Poseidon.

'I KNOW,' shouted Proteus. 'They have an important journey ahead and you aren't going to stop them – it is destined. Incidentally, it is also destined that you burn your tongue today, so be careful.'

Elliot's heart was racing. He looked over at Hypnos, who smiled at him smugly. If this Proteus knew everything, he must know where to find Panacea's potion. Elliot had to talk to him.

'Honestly,' scoffed Virgo. 'Someone who thinks they know everything. How insufferable . . .'

'Ah – go on, then,' said Poseidon, using his trident to unbind Zeus. 'Ye're no fun.'

'I know,' said Proteus sadly.

'Release the prisoners!' Poseidon commanded, and immediately Elliot's cage door swung open.

'Proteus!' Elliot cried, struggling to reach him through the crowds. 'I need to—'

'You one-eyed wally,' Zeus shouted at Poseidon, unsheathing a thunderbolt. 'You've always been a jealous little baby. Take this!'

The King of the Gods hurled a thunderbolt at his brother. But, as with the Cyclopes, it simply bounced harmlessly off the God of the Sea.

'What is going on with these?!' muttered Zeus. 'They're useless. And I have no idea where I put the receipt . . .'

'Attack a man when he's down, would ye, brother?' bellowed Poseidon, rising angrily from his throne. 'Well, then – have some of this!'

And, with a great roar, he struck his golden trident on the ground.

'Duck!' cried Virgo, shielding Gorgy in her arms. 'Poseidon's trident commands the sea and everyone in it. It can create seaquakes, tsunamis, tidal waves. This is going to be immense . . .'

Elliot ducked. There was no time for this – he needed to get to Proteus.

But nothing happened.

'Plop,' squeaked Gorgy from inside Virgo's jacket.

'Barnacle bum!' growled Poseidon, banging his trident on the floor again. 'Proteus! Why won't me trident work?!'

'Well,' said Proteus, 'it didn't help that you dropped it in the bath yesterday. You must stop playing with your trident in the tub . . .'

193

'How do ye know . . . Oh,' said Poseidon sheepishly.

Zeus nearly doubled over laughing.

'Y-you-you . . .' he stuttered, the tears rolling down his face. 'You, the God of the Sea, have a weapon that . . . that . . . ISN'T WATERPROOF?! PWAHAHAHAHAHA!'

'It can still give you a right good hiding,' said Poseidon. 'See . . .'

And he poked the prongs of his trident straight into Zeus's backside.

'Owwwwweeeeeee!' howled Zeus, clutching his bottom. 'How dare you! Here – take that!'

Zeus threw another redundant thunderbolt at Poseidon, who retaliated by trying to poke his brother again with his trident.

'You stop that!' huffed Zeus.

'No, you stop it,' Poseidon snapped back.

'But mainly,' Proteus continued, 'it's because of Zeus's new thunderbolts. Your weapons need to be reunited.'

'Ye what?' said Poseidon.

'Beg pardon?' said Zeus.

'Your trident and Zeus's thunderbolts were both crafted from the same labrys, a double-headed axe,' Proteus explained. 'They are two halves of the same whole – brothers, if you like. If one isn't right, the other won't be either. They need to be brought together to empower each other. They must be reunited with the words:

I give you my power and I accept yours.

Together we're stronger to win any wars.'

The two ancient Gods sneered at each other.

'Well, go then,' said Poseidon, holding out his trident. 'Ye first.'

'After you,' said Zeus, proffering a thunderbolt. 'I insist.'

'No.'

'Fine.'

'Then I'm not doing it.'

'Me neither.'

'This reminds me of the time Daisy Collins and Lily Smith had a disagreement in the Brysmore playground over whose dad would win a fight,' Virgo mused as they finally made it to the throne.

'STOP IT!' shouted Elliot, shocking both Gods into silence. 'Can't you see there are more important things?'

'Welcome, child,' said Proteus thoughtfully. 'I knew you'd come. Ask me. I know you want to.'

Elliot's breath caught in his throat. This man – or whatever he was – could tell him everything he needed to know. He readied himself to ask the question.

'You're right,' said Virgo. 'There is something I want to know.'

'Virgo, he didn't mean—' Elliot began.

'Please,' smiled Proteus. 'Ask me anything.'

'Do I get my kardia back?' said Virgo. 'Will I ever be immortal again?'

Proteus said nothing.

'Er, did you hear me?' said Virgo. 'I asked you a question.'

'And if you want the answer, you need to hold on to me,' said Proteus.

'I need to what?' said Virgo.

'You need to hold on to me,' said Proteus. 'That's the deal. If you want an answer, you need to hold on to me for one minute while I change shape. I have to have some boundaries, or people would be asking me stupid questions all the time. I'm the All-Knowing Shepherd of the Sea. Not Siri.'

'OK,' said Virgo, taking Proteus's extended hand. 'So that's all I have to do? I just have to hold on to you?'

'That's all,' said Proteus. 'But I know you'll fail.'

'No, I will not,' huffed Virgo. 'I have the heart of a lion. I have the courage of a warrior. I have the . . . Aaaaaaarrrrrgh!'

Virgo screamed as Proteus transformed.

'Argh, argh, argh!' she said, running squealing into Zeus's arms. 'Save me from this hideous beast!'

'It's just a spider,' said Elliot, walking over to Proteus, who turned back into the Shepherd of the Sea with a grin. 'You're right, there is something I need to know.'

'I know,' said Proteus. 'You want to know where to find Panacea's potion.'

Elliot nodded. His heart thundered in his chest. 'Does it exist?'

'Let's find out,' said Proteus, holding out his hand again.

Elliot took the Sea Shepherd's hand with his firmest grip.

'Are you ready?' smiled Proteus.

Elliot nodded again.

'Then let's do this!' cried Proteus, immediately transforming into a massive eagle, flapping its wings and yanking Elliot's arm into the air.

'Hold on, Elliot!' cried Zeus. 'You've got this.'

Elliot clung desperately on to the eagle's talon as the bird flapped around with all its might.

'You're strong,' said Proteus. 'But I'm a slippery customer.'

Elliot resisted every urge in his body to let go as Proteus transformed into a slimy snake, slithering and snaking up Elliot's wrist. But Elliot held on.

'Ssssso, jussssst how brave are you?' said Proteus. 'Braver than—'

The rest of his sentence was lost to an almighty roar as he turned into a lion. It gnashed its teeth and threatened to tear Elliot's face with its claws, but every time he wanted to let go, he thought of Mum, cured and back to her old self. The image of Josie's smile burned into his mind and made his fingers like steel.

Proteus changed again and again, taking a new form every second. One moment he was a huge fish, swiping his powerful tail, the next a tiny frog, trying to leap from Elliot's hand. As Poseidon counted down the final seconds, Proteus turned from a cat to a wolf to a bear and then ...

'Time's up!' cried Poseidon, as a steaming bowl of clam chowder was set before him. 'You did it, landlubber! Ow – that's hot! Burnt me tongue!'

'I know,' sighed Proteus, returning to himself.

'You knew I'd win,' grinned Elliot, feeling as if he could take on the world.

'I know,' said Proteus again. 'It's a curse. And it takes all the fun out of watching *Immortals' Got Talent* – watch out for Mike the Magic Minotaur in the next series, by the way. But now I have to truthfully answer any questions you ask me. Starting with the whereabouts of Panacea's potion.'

'So it exists?' whispered Elliot, not daring to believe it could be true.

'It does,' said Proteus quietly.

'Told you so, told you so, told you, told you, told you so,' chanted Hypnos, doing a little victory dance in Zeus's face.

'How do we know you're not lying?' growled Zeus, belting the Daemon away.

'I can't lie,' said Proteus plainly. 'It comes with the job. I know everything that has been and that will ever happen, yet I cannot tell even the teensiest white lie. It makes updating my CV a real chore.'

'But Athene said that no one has seen Panacea for centuries,' said Virgo. 'So where is she?'

'The Isles of the Blessed,' said Proteus. 'She knew that while she remained on Earth she would be hounded for her cure, so she took her leave.'

'So how do we get there?' said Elliot, his mind pulsing. There was a cure for his mum. He was going to save her.

'You can't,' said Hypnos. 'Only the purest and most perfect can access the Isles of the Blessed after seven lifetimes of heroism. It's so exclusive hardly anyone knows where it is or how to get there. A bit like Monaco . . .'

'Besides, only Gods and Heroes can go to the Isles of the Blessed and only then if they surrender their kardia,' said Virgo. 'How will we get the potion from her?'

'She didn't take it with her,' Proteus explained, looking straight at Elliot. 'She knew that what she had created had enormous importance. Someday someone would need it so desperately they would be prepared to undergo the unthinkable to get it.'

'I'll do it,' said Elliot quietly. 'Whatever it is. I'll do it.'

Proteus smiled and put his hand on Elliot's shoulder.

'I know,' he whispered.

'So where the bally heck is it?' said Zeus.

'The one place where Panacea knew it was safe from mortal hands,' said Proteus. 'She left it with Tiresias.'

'The prophet?' said Virgo. 'But Tiresias is—'

'What?' shouted Elliot. 'Dangerous? Far away? Hiding? I don't care, I'll find him.'

'Dead,' said Virgo bluntly.

Elliot's heart fell a thousand metres as his last ray of hope was extinguished.

'Technically, yes,' said Proteus.

'Technically?' Elliot asked. 'Doesn't sound that

technical to me. Is he dead or isn't he?'

'Yes,' said Proteus. 'And no. Tiresias is in the Afterlife.'

'So how do we get there?' said Elliot. 'Can we fly . . . sail . . . crawl?'

'I'm afraid not,' said Proteus. 'There is only one way to get to the Afterlife.'

There was a heavy silence as all the immortals looked at one another.

'Well!' shouted Elliot in exasperation. 'What is it?'

Proteus looked uneasily at Zeus. The King of the Gods gave him a reassuring nod and put both his hands on Elliot's shoulders.

'Elliot,' said Zeus. 'It's impossible.'

'No, it's not!' Elliot cried. 'We've come this far, we're so nearly there – I can do it, I can do whatever it is! You swore to me – you swore you'd do whatever it took . . .'

'I can't help you with this,' said Zeus, boring his kindly eyes into Elliot's soul. 'You can't go there.'

'Why not?!' Elliot shouted, his voice broken by the sobs rising from his chest.

'Because, my dearest boy, to get to the Afterlife,' Zeus whispered, 'you'd have to die.'

17. Marriage Guidance

Charles Equinas was a happy man. After all, why wouldn't he be? He had everything a man could want. Money? Charles had plenty. A beautiful girlfriend? Charles had several. Good looks? Charles paid people to tell him so.

The past five years had been everything he could have dreamt of and so much more. Throughout his career as a lawyer, he had helped clients to make their wills and dispose of their money after their deaths. And Charles had found an entirely safe place for it – his own bank account. For decades he had been leaving himself money in other people's wills and had amassed a significant fortune. As he stood on the veranda of his villa in the south of France, he raised a glass to all the people whose money had put him there. The idiots.

Charles was just deciding whether to play golf or take the yacht for a spin when he heard a commotion downstairs. He wasn't expecting anyone, but nor was he unduly worried. He had hired the best security team money could buy to protect him. Nothing and no one could get past his guys.

'Hello, Charles.'

Every nerve ending in Charles's body signalled Code Red. That voice. He hadn't heard it for years. Five, to be precise.

'Long time no see,' said the woman. Charles would normally refer to all females as ladies. But not this one. He knew her too well.

'Not long enough, it seems,' he said drily.

'Aren't you going to offer me a drink? I've had a long, long journey. You're not an easy man to find.'

Charles's mind raced to cover all the angles. If she'd found him, others could. Everything he had let other people work so hard for was at risk. This was more dangerous than a game of Russian roulette atop an icy clifftop in roller skates. And he knew his visitor to be the most dangerous opponent on Earth. He had to play this one as if his life depended on it. Because it did.

He turned around and walked slowly to greet his ex-wife.

'You're looking well,' he said, 'for a middle-aged woman.'

'You too,' said Patricia Porshley-Plum, 'for a dead man.'

'Too kind,' said Charles with a slight smile. He'd forgotten how delightfully chilly she could be. The air around them froze as they smiled icily at one another. 'Let me get you that drink. My staff will fetch whatever you want.'

'Ah – they're my staff now. I only had to offer them double the pay to come and work for me too. There's no loyalty these days. Besides, we have business to discuss.'

'We do?' said Charles, hoping his eyes didn't betray the terror pumping around his heart. 'Then let's go into my office.'

Charles ushered his ex-wife into a large leather chair on the other side of his desk.

'What can I do for you?' he asked.

'I want a divorce,' said Patricia plainly.

Charles wrinkled his brow.

'Er – dear heart, as far as the world is

concerned, I've been dead for five years. Why would you want—'

'Not ours,' said Patricia, 'although I can think of several good reasons. Let me see now – you used to leave your wet towels on the floor for the housemaids to pick up, you never remembered to tell the butler to take the bins out and . . . ah, yes, you cleared all our joint bank accounts into a new identity then faked your own death.'

'I'm so sorry,' said Charles gravely. 'Sincerely. That towel thing must have been most annoying . . .'

The corner of Patricia's mouth twitched. Charles allowed a smile to colour his lips.

'I need divorce papers for Josie and David Hooper,' said Patricia. 'David is out of prison. I need to be named as the Hooper child's legal guardian.'

'You never struck me as the maternal type,' queried Charles. 'That was why we never had children.'

'We never had children because there was a fifty per cent chance they might turn out like you. And because they are repulsive.'

Charles sat back in his chair. So Patricia needed him. That was interesting.

'Why would I do this?' he said.

'You've done it before,' shrugged Patricia.

'Charles Porshley-Plum was the most corrupt solicitor in the country!'

'Charles Porshley-Plum is dead,' said Charles. 'I wrote his death certificate myself. Besides, I only help people I like. And I don't like you, Patricia. Not one little bit.'

Patricia's lip twitched again. This was almost fun.

'Don't you want to know how I found you?' she whispered.

'No,' Charles lied.

'Trust is priceless,' sighed Patricia. 'I'm not sure we ever had it. But you and your brother did – that must be why you left him everything in your will.'

'That is correct,' said Charles. 'Because I knew that James would give it all back.'

'Most of it,' Patricia corrected.

'I'm sorry?' said Charles, a shard of fear piercing his heart.

'He gave most of it back,' Patricia said plainly. 'Didn't he tell you about the bit he kept for himself?'

'No,' said Charles darkly. 'He did not.'

'Oopsie!' giggled Patricia. 'How careless of me. Yes, poor James. He is so terrible with money – even what he kept didn't last him – all those holidays and fast cars gobbled it up. Then there was that doomed marriage to the model ...'

'James married a model?' scoffed Charles. 'What did she model? Clay?'

'Footwear,' said Patricia. 'But she absolutely cleaned him out. He had credit cards, loans, debts coming out of his ears . . . He was quite destitute when I called on him over the weekend.'

'Is that so?' said Charles.

'Oh, but no need to worry,' winked Patricia. 'I made everything better and now he's right back on his . . . feet. As I said, trust is priceless. Or at least – not nearly as expensive as I'd feared.'

'What if I refuse to help you?' said Charles, not really wanting to hear the answer.

'Oh, pudding,' pouted Patricia. 'I think we both know the answer to that. I'd have no choice but to tell the police exactly where you are. You robbed a lot of people. I'm sure the authorities would be very interested to know that you're living it up in the south of France.'

'You were equally involved,' said Charles. 'You'd be put behind bars as quickly as I would. You're bluffing.'

'Try me,' said Patricia, stone-faced. 'I've already convinced the authorities that I was an innocent victim. The brainless morons.'

If Charles had learnt two things in his business dealings, one was to know when you were beaten.

And the other was that you never, ever messed with a dangerous woman.

'If I do this, I never want to see or hear from you again,' said Charles.

'Sweetums, I didn't want to see or hear from you while we were married,' said Patricia. 'You're quite safe from me now.'

Charles smiled and walked over to his filing cabinet.

'So, I'm guessing you're still trying to get your hands on Home Farm?' he said, pulling the relevant documents out of a folder. 'It's been years, Patricia. You must be losing your edge.'

'A foolproof plan takes time,' said Patricia, her eyes following his every move as he forged the necessary dates and signatures on the relevant papers. 'You of all people should know that. I must say, your death was most convincing. You fooled everyone with that "boating accident".'

'Thank you,' said Charles, putting the documents in an envelope. 'But how did you know I hadn't drowned? The water is a treacherous place.'

'Two things really,' mused Patricia. 'Firstly, I didn't feel nearly happy enough. And secondly, you went sailing on a boating lake. Your biggest threat was being hit by a swan-shaped pedalo.'

'It worked, though,' smiled Charles, handing

the envelope to his ex-wife. 'Don't let me keep you.'

'Of course, pumpkin,' said Patricia, putting the documents into her handbag. 'I'll be on my merry way.'

She walked to the door, but stopped before opening it.

'Before I go, I do have a teensy, tiny confession to make,' she whispered. 'I was bluffing. I was never going to go to the authorities.'

'I know,' said Charles. 'But a few fake documents to get rid of you is a small price.'

'Indeed,' said Patricia. 'But when are you going to pay your price, Charles?'

'What?'

'After all, you've been very naughty. And there are lots of people who want to see you pay.'

'Patricia, if you say one word . . .' Charles threatened.

'Oops, me and my big mouth,' chimed Patricia, opening the door to reveal two large men in black overcoats standing in the doorway. 'You must remember the Preston twins, Donny and Digby? They just wanted a quick chat about what happened to their late mother's life savings – I'm sure you can help them find some answers . . .'

The two men stepped menacingly into the room.

'Gentlemen!' laughed Charles nervously. 'I thought you were in prison! Actual bodily harm, wasn't it?'

'Mrs Porshley-Plum just paid our bail,' said Donny. 'And we didn't do it.'

'No, no – of course not,' stuttered Charles.

'It was attempted murder,' said Digby, cracking his knuckles. 'Now, about our mum ...'

'Patricia,' said Charles, running back out on to the veranda. 'Patricia, you've made your point. Don't leave me here ...'

'Have fun, Charles,' trilled Patricia. 'Oooh, and by the way – my edge?'

'No, please ...' said Charles as the Preston twins each took an arm and dragged him back into the office.

'It's sharper than ever,' snapped Patricia, slamming the door on his screams.

18. Those in Peril on the Sea

'Here, sprat,' said Poseidon, plopping a huge, writhing sack down at Elliot's feet. 'I like the cut of yer jib. Now not only can ye have the use of me beauty, *The Pearl*, to get ye where ye need to go, but here's a little bonus.'

Poseidon's chariot had carried them up from the Coral Cove and they were on the tiny island where he moored *The Pearl* – a classic galleon, straight from the pages of any pirate adventure, with its high mast, billowing sails, wooden wheel and even a naughty mermaid carved on its prow. But what gave the ship its name – and its beautiful iridescent colour – was the fact that the whole

211

vessel had been carved from a giant conch shell.

Elliot glanced at the wriggling sack on the deck. It looked as though half a dozen baby elephants were wrestling inside.

'Now this here be wind,' said the God of the Sea.

'Thought I smelt something a bit eggy,' grumbled Zeus, wafting his hand in front of his nose.

'That be yer wind,' said Poseidon. 'This be *the* wind. Well, one of them, to be precise. Boreas, the North Wind. He be a right pain in the sailor's poop deck – he can blow ye all over the place. Ye're better off with him in here; he's a stroppy one.'

'It would be more help if you'd just give us our bally Chaos Stones back,' grumbled Zeus.

'They'll be staying with me,' said Poseidon. 'You worry yer beardy brains about finding that there potion.'

Elliot had to agree. The Chaos Stones would have to wait. At least they were safe with Poseidon. All he wanted now was Panacea's potion.

'Where do we go?' he asked Proteus.

'Why not ask your compass?'

'Compass?' said Elliot.

'The one Odysseus gave you,' said Proteus knowingly.

212

'Oh, yeah.' Elliot fumbled for the small silver compass in his pocket, and pulled out Polyphemus's fidget spinner instead. He spun it again. Still cool. He put it back and found the compass.

'I don't know which way we need to go,' he said, opening the lid. 'How will this help?'

'Tell it where you want to go,' said Proteus. 'It will show you the way.'

'Er, the Afterlife. Please?' said Elliot to the compass.

The needle spun until it pointed due west.

'Follow it,' said Proteus. 'You'll end up where you need to go.'

'The Afterlife?' said Elliot.

'Eventually,' smiled Proteus. 'But remember, it's not about the destination: it's about the journey. It's best you don't know more than that, lest you try to change your destiny.'

'Some sat nav you make,' muttered Zeus.

Elliot watched as the Shepherd of the Sea stood on the prow of the ship, ready to dive back into the waves. This was his last chance to ask him. But did he really want to know the answer?

'Proteus!' he called. 'There's something I wanted to—'

'I know,' sighed Proteus.

'Well,' whispered Elliot, steadying his breath.

213

'Do I do it? Do I get Panacea's potion?'

Proteus looked across the boundless sea, before turning his kind gaze back to Elliot.

'One of the worst parts of my "gift" is that, while I will always give the right answers, people don't always ask me the right questions,' he said sadly. 'Yes. Tiresias will give you the potion. That I can see.'

Elliot was confused. This was great news. So why the sad face?

But before he could ask any more questions, the Shepherd of the Sea leapt gracefully from *The Pearl* and vanished beneath the waves.

'Now listen here, sprat,' said Poseidon. 'If ye're heading west, ye need to keep a weather eye on the three terrors of the high seas. Firstly, there's the Sirens. Sure they enchant ye with their song – but, before ye know it, there be a shipwreck. And I'm not just talking about their last album.'

'Highly irrational,' said Virgo. 'No music could possibly have such a potent effect and cause people to lose their minds. Unless it's that curious Gangnam song . . .'

'Ye'll see,' said Poseidon. 'Then, ye'll need to navigate yer way betwixt Scylla and Charybdis. Charybdis be a monstrous whirlpool that sucks ships and all who sail them down to Davy

Jones's Locker.'

'You mean we'd all drown?' gasped Virgo.

'Nay,' said Poseidon. 'Ye'll go down to Davy Jones's Locker. Cheap sportswear store – ye'll end up buying all kinds of flotsam and jetsam ye don't need. Ended up with a trapeze leotard last time I went ...'

'And Scylla?' said Elliot, keen to get the journey underway. 'What's that?'

'She be a fierce one all right,' said Poseidon. 'She have four eyes and six heads, each with three rows of teeth. Then there be the legs ready to snatch ye up and gobble ye down in the dogs' heads around her waist. She be very angry at the world.'

'Because she was treated so unfairly?' asked Virgo. 'Turned into a monster by women jealous of her beauty?'

'Nay,' said Poseidon. 'She says it's a nightmare finding flattering swimwear. Well, it's no use blowing the breeze here, ye need to pull anchor.'

'Farewell, brother,' said Zeus shiftily. 'See you around.'

'Ye too,' said Poseidon absently.

Elliot watched the two brothers try to look as if they didn't care. He exchanged a knowing look with Virgo. Siblings were so stupid.

The rest of the party swapped their farewells. Hypnos hauled up the mighty anchor before flying up to the crow's nest. Zeus took his place at the wheel and *The Pearl* steadily pulled away from the shore and started to bob across the waves.

As Elliot looked out across the ocean, he thought of Josie and how much she would have enjoyed this adventure. They always talked about travelling the world. If only she were here. If only his dad were here. Then they'd all be together. Like a proper family. Like they were supposed to be. If only . . .

'Plop!'

His thoughts were snatched away by Gorgy landing in his lap.

'Ewwwww – get off,' said Elliot, shooing the baby gorgon away. 'Virgo – control your pet.'

'He's not my pet!' Virgo insisted, allowing Gorgy to sit in her lap so she could pet him. 'So . . . I have a question. It's about a friend of mine.'

'I don't believe you,' said Elliot.

'I'm telling you the truth,' said Virgo stiffly. 'It's not *my* question.'

'Not that,' said Elliot. 'I don't believe you have a friend . . .'

'Shut up,' Virgo retorted. 'My friend . . . er, Shirgo . . .'

'Shirgo?' Elliot repeated. 'Seriously?'

'Absolutely,' said Virgo. 'Shirgo is not as experienced as I am in mortal ways and I am seeking some advice on her behalf.'

'Shirgo sounds like an idiot,' said Elliot.

'I – she is not!' Virgo snapped. 'But she is a little concerned that she might have made a slightly . . . sub-optimal decision. This is most out of character, as she is usually correct about everything.'

'I bet she's not,' Elliot muttered.

'I bet she is!' Virgo huffed. 'However, in the unlikely event of her being slightly less correct than usual, she was wondering . . . what should she do? You seem something of an expert on bad decisions. Your hairstyle is a case in point.'

Elliot considered her quandary.

'Can you – your friend – not just go back on the decision?' he said.

'Not without losing something she desperately wants,' whispered Virgo.

'So, she has to choose between what's right and what she wants?'

'Yes!' cried Virgo. 'That is a curiously accurate summary of the situation. So what should she do?'

Elliot looked out over the vast blue ocean, thinking of his mum, the potion and the Chaos Stones.

'You're asking the wrong guy,' he said quietly.

'Siren Rock on the starboard bow!' Hypnos squealed from the crow's nest. Positions everyone!'

'Well, I still don't believe this nonsense about their enchanted song,' said Virgo. 'But I am curious. I am going to lash myself to the mast. I am quite convinced that nothing will happen. But in the unlikely event that I become possessed by their magical music, you are not to release me, no matter how hard I plead. Do you agree?'

'Sure,' said Elliot.

'Even if I beg?'

'You have my word.'

'And here – just to be on the safe side, fill your ears with this.' Virgo handed Elliot some mush from her bag.

'What is it?'

'My in-flight meal from Don'tcAIR. I hoped it would come in handy. Put it in your ears, lest you too are enchanted by the Sirens.'

'Gross.'

Virgo handed him a length of rope. 'Make sure the knots are good and tight,' she said as Elliot tied her and Gorgy to the mast. 'I don't want to escape in the throes of enchantment. And no matter what I say, no matter how fervently I implore, you are not to release me. Do you understand?'

'Trust me,' grinned Elliot. 'This time you've come to the right guy.'

Ahead of them was a series of jagged rocks where the ageing carcasses of wrecked ships told Elliot that this was where the Sirens did their worst. The rocks were a mess – in addition to the shipwrecks, they were covered in broken bottles, discarded takeaway cartons and even a TV set that looked as though it had been tossed into the sea below. Hypnos fluttered over to fetch a single piece of paper stuck to the largest rock, and read it aloud to the group:

'Due to musical differences and several pending murder charges, the Sirens have decided to go their separate ways. They are all working on new solo material and are planning a comeback tour in ten years' time, or whenever they get parole. They'd like to thank all their fans for their support over the years, even if it led directly to their cruel and violent death.'

'You see!' said Virgo triumphantly. 'I knew it was a load of nonsense. Now let me down.'

'Sorry?' shouted Elliot, pointing to his mush-filled ears. 'Can't hear you!'

'Don't be absurd,' said Virgo. 'Untie me at once!'

'No can do,' said Elliot, removing the mush. 'Your orders . . .'

'But I didn't hear anything!' said Virgo.

'How can I believe you?' said Elliot, a wicked gleam in his eyes. 'You'd say anything in the throes of enchantment.'

'But I'm not in the throes of enchantment!' cried an exasperated Virgo.

'Well, you would say that, wouldn't you?' said Elliot, shaking his head.

'Elliot Hooper, let me down from this mast this instant or I'll . . . I'll . . . I'll . . .'

'Wow – they really got to you, didn't they?' sighed Elliot. 'Oh, well, I'm sure it'll wear off in an hour or two. I'll get you down then. Laters.'

'Elliot!' cried Virgo, as Zeus winked at the retreating boy. 'Elliot! ELLIOT!'

'Bad plop man!' growled Gorgy after him.

'Nicely done,' grinned Hypnos, fluttering down to join Elliot at the ship's prow. 'Always good to be the winner.'

'I wouldn't know,' said Elliot.

'But you will,' whispered Hypnos. 'Once you have all the Chaos Stones, no one will be able to come near you. Only you can choose the winners.'

'At the moment I don't have any of them,' said Elliot. 'And I don't care about winning. I just want my mum back.'

'And all power to you,' said Hypnos. 'But you can have both. Remember that.'

An almighty screech shattered the peaceful seascape.

'Troubled waters up ahead!' Zeus bellowed from the wheel. 'Look lively.'

Elliot and Hypnos sprang to their feet. The ship was approaching a narrow channel, with cliffs on both sides. To the right, the sea flowed smoothly past the rocks and back out into open water. But on the left . . .

'I'M TELLING YOU, NO AMOUNT OF INNER BEAUTY IS GOING TO HELP ME WHEN I'M TRYING TO BUY A BIKINI!' screeched the creature. 'SO SHUT YOUR CAKEHOLE!'

Elliot stood rooted to the spot as he took in the sight before him. Perched in a crevice on the cliff-top was a . . . Not for the first time, he didn't know what to call it. The creature had six heads, each with a triple row of teeth, and drooling dog heads around her waist. Twelve clawed feet stuck out from her six legs. Swimwear, Elliot thought, was the least of her problems.

'Scylla,' whispered Hypnos. 'I heard she had a life coach. Looks like it's going well.'

'OK, so, yah – loving your emotion, good to

see you letting all your rage out, yah,' said a bespectacled gnome holding a notebook. 'Have you found your meditation CD helpful?'

'HELPFUL?!' screeched another of Scylla's heads. 'SURE – WHEN I THROW THE USELESS BIT OF RUBBISH AT SOME-ONE'S HEAD.'

And with a scream she hurled the offending CD across the strait, hitting Hypnos square on the head.

'Ow!' he squealed. He caught the CD and looked at the front cover. '*Taming the Beast Within*. There's Thanatos's Christmas present sorted . . .'

'So, the thing is, ya,' the gnome continued, 'if you're going to conquer this anger, you really need to listen to the voice within. Listen. Tell me.'

'YOU REALLY WANNA KNOW?' Scylla screamed.

'Sure. Yah,' said the gnome, stroking his beard. 'What's it saying?'

'LUNCHTIME!' screamed Scylla. She grabbed the gnome with one of her clawed feet and dangled him over one of her mouths, which obligingly opened its gaping jaws.

'So, yah, we talked about this,' said the gnome. 'It's, like, super-important you don't internalize your anger.'

'INTERNALIZE THIS!' Scylla yelled and dropped the gnome whole down one of her throats.

'I'm telling you, yah,' said the gnome from inside her belly. 'You really need to let it all—'

'BUUUUURRRRRPPPP!' Scylla erupted with a satisfied grin. 'You know, he's right. I feel so much better. He's been my best – and tastiest – life coach yet. Whaddya want?!'

'Oh ... don't mind us, just passing through,' said Zeus, steering a course as far away from Scylla's long necks as he could.

'Come closer,' said Scylla, beckoning them with a clawed finger.

'Er, no, thanks,' said Zeus, hastily letting the sail out to speed their journey past the ferocious monster.

'I'm telling you,' cooed Scylla. 'It's for your own good ...'

'Or for your own pudding,' mumbled Zeus. 'Hang on tight everyone, we're nearly—'

The ship came to a shuddering halt.

'What are you doing?' hissed Elliot at Zeus. 'Get us out of here.'

'No can do,' Zeus whispered back. 'We're stuck.'

'HEE HEE HEE!' Scylla cackled. 'Don't say I

didn't warn you . . .'

'What's happening?' Virgo cried. The sea around them parted and turned into a massive pair of jaws.

'Oh, Lordy,' said Zeus as the ship slowly started to turn.

'Charybdis!' said Hypnos, taking flight and grabbing Elliot. 'Come on, you, we're getting out of here.'

Elliot felt the ship tip as the sea around them was sucked into the jaws.

'Help!' cried Virgo, struggling against her bonds at the mast. 'I'm stuck!'

'What about them?' said Elliot, pointing at Zeus and Virgo.

'Winners, remember?' said Hypnos, about to take flight. 'Let's go.'

Elliot hesitated. Hypnos could fly him to safety – if he was sucked down to a watery grave, he couldn't save Mum.

But how could he live with himself if he abandoned his friends?

He wrestled free from Hypnos's grasp and ran to Virgo. His fingers worked at the knots he cursed himself for tying so tightly.

'Elliot – please, hurry!' begged Virgo.

'I . . . can't . . . hold . . . her . . . much . . . longer,' grimaced Zeus, straining at the wheel.

Hypnos flew to help him steady the ship. Water started to slosh over the sides of the galleon, the weight of it pulling the ship further down into the deep.

'Hurry!' cried Virgo amid the lashing waves.

'I'm trying!' Elliot shouted, but the knots were held fast by the wet rope. He looked helplessly at Virgo. She was trapped.

Suddenly, he felt a small slimy hand on his.

'Plop,' said Gorgy softly.

At once, the little snakes around his head began to hiss and wriggle, and the little gorgon stared at the rope, which began to shudder under his gaze. Elliot saw the tight knots begin to melt in front of his eyes.

'It's working!' said Elliot. 'Go on, Gorgy!'

Shaking under the strain, the gorgon kept his eyes fixed on the rope and, with a final grunt, the whole length dissolved. Virgo and Gorgy were free.

'You made sand!' said Virgo, holding her exhausted pet to her. 'Well done, Gorgy!'

'We've got to get out of here!' cried Hypnos. The wall of water was teetering above them, about to come crashing down on them at any moment.

225

'Come on,' shouted Elliot, grabbing Virgo's hand.

'Thank you,' she said quietly. 'For coming back.'

'You're welcome,' said Elliot, looking at the water pouring into the galleon. 'Hypnos – time to go!'

'I can't carry all of you!' shouted the Daemon. 'Elliot – come on!'

Elliot looked frantically around for anything that might help them. How were they all to escape?

'PLLLLOOOOOPPPPPP!' cried Gorgy, bounding across the deck to rescue the writhing sack Poseidon had given them. He grabbed it in his mouth and bounded back, dropping the sack at Elliot's feet like a happy puppy.

'What is it doing?' cried Zeus.

'The North Wind!' Elliot shouted. 'It can blow us free!'

'But Poseidon said—'Virgo cried.

'Who cares what Poseidon said!' yelled Elliot. 'What choice do we have? Brace yourselves . . .'

'Elliot, be careful!' Zeus shouted. 'We have no idea how powerful it—'

But Elliot wasn't listening. With his free hand he pulled at the string holding the sack together. The water crashing around them was determined to wrestle it from his hand, but he was determined too. With an almighty yank, he pulled off the string — and was immediately blasted back across the deck as a vertical tunnel of air roared out of the open sack.

'What was that?' Virgo cried, clinging on to Gorgy.

'I AM BOREAS!' bellowed the North Wind. The air began to take a vaporous, white form — a winged old man with shaggy hair and beard, holding a conch shell. Beneath his billowing cloak were snakes where his feet should have been. 'AND I AM NO MAN'S PRISONER!'

'Got that,' shouted Hypnos, trying to fly away from the North Wind's fury. But it was no use. Sucking in the very air around him, Boreas blew with all his might, inflating the white sails of *The Pearl* so that it began to rise from the whirlpool.

'He's not strong enough!' Virgo shouted. 'Charybdis is pulling us down.'

'NOT STRONG ENOUGH!' screamed Boreas. 'WE'LL SEE WHO'S STRONG ENOUGH!'

With another great gasp, he blew the ship again with all his might.

'It's . . . it's working!' said Elliot. 'Look — the ship's pulling away!'

They looked over the prow of the ship. With the wind's power fuelling the sails, the ship was slowly climbing the wall of water.

'Come on!' Elliot willed the wind. 'Just a little bit . . .'

The ship continued to rise slowly, slowly, slowly . . . until, with an almighty pop, it was free of the whirlpool's grasp.

'Wow – thanks!' said Elliot, as the ship pulled away into clear waters. 'Well, we'll just be on our—'

'YOU DARE TO KEEP ME PRISONER!' shouted the wind. 'YOU DARE TO ENSLAVE THE NORTH WIND! YOU ARE NOTH-ING!'

'I don't have a good feeling about this,' said Virgo, grabbing the mast.

And for once Elliot had to admit she was right. Taking a gigantic breath, the North Wind blew the sails so hard that the ship peeled away from the ocean's surface and took off, up into the bright sky, flying far, far away towards who knew where.

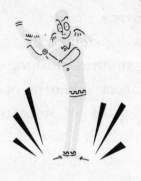

19. Deal with the Devil

Patricia Porshley-Plum could almost taste victory on her lips. One more move and both Home Farm and revenge on the Hooper boy would be hers. At last.

It had been a long and tiring day, but Patricia didn't want to wait. She'd waited quite long enough already. Having come directly from the airport, she approached the infernal fence around Home Farm with caution, but was surprised to find the gate wide open. She couldn't wait to get rid of that fence. Dynamite would do nicely.

She made her way unevenly up the path and knocked on the front door. She drew a steely breath. This was war.

It had been a decade since she'd last seen David Hooper – and good riddance to bad rubbish. But she was taken aback when he opened the door. He'd not changed a jot since the day he was carted off to prison. It was as if he hadn't aged a day in ten years.

'Hello, David,' she said curtly. 'I need to talk to you.'

'Of course,' David smiled back. 'But to whom do I have the pleasure of speaking?'

Patricia was miffed. She also hadn't changed a jot in ten years – if anything, she was younger and thinner than she was last time they'd seen one another. Surely he remembered her?

'You know perfectly well who I am,' she said. 'And I'm here to discuss this house. I want it.'

'Ah – Patricia,' said David with a smile. 'Please come in. I was hoping you might drop by.'

He stood aside to allow her past. Patricia didn't take her eyes off him for a second. What was his agenda?

They walked through to the kitchen.

'Where are all the relatives?' she asked. 'I've got to know them rather well over the past few months.'

'Oh, I sent them out grocery shopping,' said

David. 'You can have too much of a good thing.'

'Indeed,' said Patricia, perturbed by his easy smile as he leant against the door. She looked forward to wiping it from his face.

'Well, now – I'll keep this brief for both our sakes,' she said. 'As you will recall, my late husband took care of all your family's legal affairs. When you were . . . away, Josie approached him and requested a divorce.'

'Oh, dear,' said David, the smile still in place.

'Furthermore,' said Patricia, feeling unusually unsure of herself, 'she requested that in the event of her incapacity, I be named Elliot's legal guardian, a position I now claim.'

'How kind of you,' David twinkled. What was he playing at?

'Now, as you are Wilfred and Audrey's son, the farm legally belongs to you,' said Patricia. 'But I wish to acquire it for my property portfolio. So I was hoping we might come to some kind of arrangement.'

'I see,' said David. If any of this was troubling him, he was doing a good job of hiding it. Under other circumstances, Patricia would have admired his nerve.

'Perhaps I should speak a little more plainly,' she continued. 'I have the son you want. You have the house I want. So either you sell me the house, or I'm taking Elliot.'

'That's quite an arrangement,' grinned David, finally pulling himself away from the doorframe and starting to circle the kitchen.

Patricia frowned. She wasn't used to feeling unsettled.

'Patricia – I'm flattered,' David said eventually. 'All this trouble for me? Faking legal papers? Taking my son? All for this old farmhouse?'

'I always get what I want,' said Patricia. 'And I want this farm.'

'So I understand,' said David.

Why was he so calm?

'So, let me get this straight,' he mused, still circling Patricia. 'You have expertly forged papers claiming that Josie appointed you Elliot's legal guardian?'

'It doesn't matter how I acquired them,' Patricia said calmly. 'They're legally binding.'

'And unless I agree to sell you Home Farm, you're threatening to take custody of my son?'

'Quite. I like to keep things simple. Sell me the farm, or lose your son.'

Dave stood as still as a gravestone. Patricia had to give it to him – he was certainly a worthy adversary. She didn't meet many of those.

Eventually, he walked slowly towards her.

'But you've made a terrible mistake,' he whispered, up close.

Patricia felt a sudden chill run through her. What had she missed?

'You assume,' David continued, 'that I want either.'

Patricia was dumbstruck.

'Come again?' she said.

'I don't want either of them,' repeated Dave. 'The house or the boy. This place is a dump. And I've just got out of prison so why would I want another sentence looking after a kid? You can have both of them. I couldn't care less.'

'I-I'm sorry,' Patricia stammered. 'Are you saying . . . ?'

'I am,' said Dave coldly. 'Make me an offer. Right here, right now. Frankly, you'd be doing me a favour taking both off my hands.'

'If you think this is some kind of joke, I can assure you it isn't funny,' said Patricia.

'I never joke,' Dave glowered. 'So . . .'

Patricia turned her nose up and sniffed in disdain as she looked around the Hooper family home.

'Well, of course I'd have to take into consideration the appalling decor, poor condition, dreadful location . . .'

'I agree,' said Dave, looking around as if he were stuck inside a dustbin.

Patricia pulled a chequebook from her bag and wrote an insultingly low figure in it. She had to start somewhere – he'd be a fool to take anything less than double.

'Now I'm not here to negotiate,' she said, showing him the cheque. 'This is my best and final offer . . .'

'Done,' said Dave, taking the cheque. 'Where do I sign?'

'What about the boy?' said Patricia, handing over a sheaf of papers. 'What am I supposed to do with him?'

'Do what you like,' said Dave, signing the paperwork without a care in the world. 'Put him in a home. Use him as your manservant. Leave him out with the rubbish. I don't care. I'm sure you can have some fun.'

Patricia stepped back to survey this new and improved David Hooper.

'You used to be such an honourable, decent sort,' she said. 'I much prefer you now.'

'Me too,' smiled Dave, handing the paperwork – and with it his family home and his son – over to Patricia Porshley-Plum. 'When do you want us out?'

'Er . . . Th–Thursday?' stammered Patricia.

'Let's say Wednesday,' said Dave. 'No sense in dragging it out. Just do me a favour and clear this lot out. I haven't got time.'

'It's a deal,' said Patricia, straightening her tweed jacket over her perfectly womanly hips. 'I must say, it's been a pleasure doing business with you.'

There was a commotion at the front door as the sisters returned from the shops.

'I'm telling you, it doesn't matter how much low-fat cooking spray you use, you'll still have a bum like a rhino,' the blonde one snapped at her sister. She stopped in her tracks as she spied Patricia.

'What do you want?' she spat, stomping over threateningly. 'Athene . . . !'

'Get out of this house!' shouted the dark-haired sister, storming into the room. 'What is she doing here, Dave?'

'Oh, nothing,' said Dave. 'Just a neighbourly chat. Nothing for you to worry your pretty heads about.'

'I don't trust her,' said Athene, looking squarely at Patricia.

'Oh, she's a wrong'un all right,' smiled Dave.

'But then, so are some of the most interesting people I've known. Excuse me.'

And, with an admiring glance, Patricia watched him walk away without a care in the world.

'What are you up to?' said the blonde sister menacingly.

'You'll find out soon enough,' said Patricia, tucking the paperwork back in her bag before turning on her heel. 'But I hope you didn't buy too many groceries. I do hate to see good food go to waste . . .'

20. Circe Navigating

'Hold tight!' Zeus yelled as Boreas's angry wind finally ran out of puff, several hours after it had blown *The Pearl* from the jaws of Charybdis. The good news was that this meant they were no longer flying wildly through the air. The bad ...

'We're going to crash!' Virgo screamed, clutching her baby gorgon as the ship began to fall through the sky.

'P-p-plop,' trembled Gorgy.

Virgo looked at Elliot clinging to the mast.

'Come over here!' he shouted, watching the ground come up to meet them. 'And brace yourself!'

She ran and linked arms with Elliot around the mast. She scanned the sky above them. Hypnos was nowhere to be seen.

'We're coming in to land!' Zeus yelled from the wheel. 'In three . . . two . . . one . . .'

CRASH!

The Pearl came down to Earth with an ear-splitting crunch, pieces of timber and all its passengers flying everywhere. The mighty mast teetered above their heads. If it fell on them, Virgo thought, it would be highly sub-optimal. And painful. She held her breath as it wobbled from one side to the other, like a tall tree being felled. But after a few anxious moments, the mast came to rest, slightly off-centre, but still upright.

'Is everyone OK?' Zeus groaned, flat on his back.

'Great,' gasped Elliot, winded by the abrupt landing.

'Plop,' squeaked Gorgy softly, emerging from a coil of rope. 'Mama?'

'She's here,' moaned Virgo, pulling pieces of splintered timber from her hair. The baby gorgon bounded towards her and deposited himself in a ball in her lap.

'Mama,' he sighed happily as Virgo gently stroked his back.

'Well, it turns out you aren't such a snotty little runt after all,' said Zeus, coming over to chuck Gorgy under the chin. 'That was some smart thinking there, young gorgon. Thank you.'

'Yeah,' said Elliot, rubbing his head. 'Nice one, Gorgy.'

With a happy grin, the little gorgon leapt from Virgo's lap and bounced over to Elliot. He held his little green hand up proudly for a high-five.

'Thanks, little dude,' said Elliot, returning his high-five with a smile. This made Virgo feel curiously content. Not least because she was clearly correct to have acquired Gorgy as a pet.

'Plop,' said Gorgy happily before returning to Virgo's lap.

'Where are we?' said Elliot, still trying to catch his breath.

Virgo surveyed the horizon. They were in what appeared to be a vast car park – ship park, really. Several roads ran along the perimeter of what was an island, but there was nothing else to see but a complex road system leading to a few twinkling lights in the near distance. The whole place was missing something. Virgo couldn't quite figure out what.

She looked back at what was left of *The Pearl*. They wouldn't be going anywhere in that. By sea or by air.

'Ah – nothing to worry about,' said Zeus. 'Bit of wood glue, a lick of paint, she'll be as good as new.'

The King of the Gods patted the prow.

'Elliot – look out!' Virgo screamed as the mast started to teeter precariously again.

'You what?' said Elliot.

The mast began to fall and Elliot was right in its path. Virgo leapt towards him, yanking him out the way just as the mast came crashing down on the spot where he had been standing.

'Whoa!' said Elliot. The mast splintered around them, destroying itself and what was left of *The Pearl* in the process. 'Er, thanks.'

'You're welcome,' said Virgo. She had been rather brilliant.

'Hmmmm. Might need quite a lot of glue,' muttered Zeus.

'Where are we?' Elliot asked again. 'And where's Hypnos?'

'Here I am!' squealed Hypnos, fluttering down from the sky.

'Where the bally heck did you get to?' grumbled Zeus.

'Listen, boss, some of us don't have your natural sandbags,' said Hypnos. 'That wind blew me miles away. But at least I've done a recce. Welcome to Circe's Island! Home of the greatest witch who ever lived.'

'Witch?' said Virgo. She had researched enough mortal fairy tales to know that things rarely ended well for children when they encountered witches. She would be on her guard against gingerbread houses.

'Oh, top-hole!' said Zeus. 'Circe's a game girl – I'm sure she can help us fix up the ship.'

'Oi – you shouldn't be parked there!' shouted a substantial Nereid, pulling up in a small boat with four miniature sea nymphs in the back. 'That's a parent and child port. Under-thousand-year-olds only!' She rounded on the squabbling sea nymphs. 'Now listen, you lot! If I have to come back there again, so help me, I am going to turn this boat around . . .'

'Parents,' muttered Hypnos. 'Newsflash – no one cares that you had children apart from you . . .'

They walked away from the remains of *The Pearl* and scanned the horizon.

'Which way to Circe, I wonder?' said Zeus.

Elliot pulled out his compass and consulted it.

'Er . . . that way.' He pointed towards a patch of twinkling lights in the distance.

'Come on, then, best foot forward,' said Zeus.

Virgo put Gorgy on her shoulder, but no sooner had they taken a step along the road than a shabby chariot, pulled by a portly centaur, came screeching up alongside them.

'Someone call a blübber?' the centaur asked.

'Er … no, thank you,' said Zeus. 'It's not far. We could all use the leg stretch.'

'C'mon,' said the centaur. 'I'll take you for five obals.'

'No, really – it's fine,' said Zeus. 'We'd like to walk.'

'Three obals!'

'We will walk, thank you,' said Zeus tersely.

'Seven obals!'

'What?' said Virgo. 'That's sub-optimal negotiating.'

'That's what I'll pay you to get in my cab,' said the centaur.

'Oh … very well, then,' grumbled Zeus. 'Come along, kids, hop in.'

The chariot shambled its way along the road, passing the Elementals who lived on the island. Virgo observed that all of them were travelling in some form of vehicle – cars, mopeds, Segways …

'Does no one walk on this island?' Virgo asked the driver.

'Why would you?' said the centaur. 'Circe made travel so cheap, no one needs to walk any more. Ooh – excuse me – bit peckish …'

The chariot drew up alongside a small restaurant with a large golden *C* revolving in the air above it. The centaur heaved his hairy body out of the harness.

'Circe's. Can't get enough of it. Can I get anyone anything?' he asked. 'The Quadruple Bacon Mega-burger makes a great lunchtime snack …'

Virgo felt her stomach starting to rumble. It had been a long time since her last meal.

'Let's get you two some grub,' said Zeus, heading towards the window. 'And see if we can't get some help.'

'Welcome to Circe's – how may I help you today?' droned a voice down the intercom.

'Hello, there!' boomed Zeus amiably. 'We'll take two Mega Mount Olympus Meal Deals, please.'

'Certainly, sir,' intoned the voice. 'Will there be anything else?'

'Yes, actually,' said Zeus. 'We're looking for Circe.'

'Would you like fries with that?'

'No, you misunderstand, my good man,' said Zeus. 'We just want Circe.'

'Do you want that Magnum, Maior or Maximus?'

'No!' shouted Zeus. 'Just Circe. On her own.'

'I see,' said the voice. 'Are you sure you don't want to go Maximus? You'll get a free refillable cup of Oliveade?'

'You're an imbecile!' shouted the King of the Gods.

'Thank you and have a nice day,' said the voice, as two gigantic cardboard Parthenons popped out of the wall.

'Excellent,' said Virgo, grabbing a box. 'I'm starving. Look how much food there is!'

Inside each box were three burgers, two fries, something that once resembled a pie – and a portable electronic device called a 'Lotus'. Virgo had seen how appealing such screens were to mortal children, but never understood the attraction herself. Wasting hours in front of a device seemed absurd. She would look at it later, purely for research purposes.

They boarded the chariot and tucked into their burgers until they reached a high street up ahead.

'That'll be nine obals,' said the centaur, pulling up outside another branch of Circe's and handing over the cash.

'I thought you said seven?' said Elliot.

'I wanted to give you a decent tip,' said the centaur. 'Have a good day.'

Despite polishing off her entire meal, Virgo found herself looking hungrily back at the burger restaurant. She could squeeze one more in, surely? She got out of the chariot and looked up and down the street. Every other shop was either a fast-food restaurant or a games arcade, whirring with brightly lit larger Lotus machines. Virgo watched a tubby merman blasting zombies with one hand while eating fried chicken with the other. On a neighbouring machine, a small zombie was being shouted at by his mother as he drove a pretend sports car while munching on pizza.

'I'm telling you!' the mother zombie screeched. 'If you spend any more time on these silly computer games, you're going to turn into a human . . .'

The roads were full of vehicles and parking spaces, with Elementals using any mode of transport to make even the smallest journey. Virgo watched a chubby fairy waddle out of the fried-chicken shack, get on her unicorn and trot to the doughnut shop next door.

'I CAN'T TALK,' she yelled down her phone.

'I'LL GET SIX POINTS FOR USING MY PHONE ON A UNICORN.'

'Where are the trees?' said Zeus, feeding Gorgy a handful of fries.

'That's it!' said Virgo, finally realizing what was strange about this place. There was no greenery. No grass, no trees, no parks, no fields. It was just a mass of modern buildings, connected by roads, every centimetre of which was designed to feed you, transport you, or encourage you to pump money into computer games. It was artificial, synthetic and soulless.

'This is the most awesome place I've ever seen,' Elliot gasped in wonder.

'This way to Circe,' said Hypnos, consulting Odysseus's compass over Elliot's shoulder. 'Let's head off—'

No sooner had the words left his lips than another chariot sped up to them.

'Someone call a blübber?' said a new centaur.

'Oh, why not,' sighed Zeus.

'Er, before we get on, could I use the loo?' said Virgo, crossing her legs.

'Plop,' said Gorgy, crossing his.

'Sure, toots,' said Hypnos. 'According to the compass, there's a public convenience two minutes walk over—'

'Someone call a blübber?' said a third centaur as another chariot screeched up to the kerb.

Circe's home was a large, modern family house at the top of a concrete hill. The door was opened by a small wooden penate, the knee-high administrative immortals that Elliot recognized from his travels.

'You're in luck,' said the penate. 'Ms Circe works from home on Mondays. I'll let her know you're here.'

'Um ... I'll be with you in a minute,' said Virgo, sitting down in an armchair with the Lotus device she'd not taken her eyes off since getting in the blübber there. At least it was keeping her quiet.

Elliot desperately hoped that this Circe was going to be able to help them get back on their journey. With no ship, no Chaos Stones and no way of reaching the Afterlife, he felt as if Panacea's potion was slipping from his grasp.

The penate whizzed through the hallway to guide them to a bright, large modern kitchen. The first thing that struck Elliot was that everything was sparkling new – the cooker, the fridge, the gadgets all along the side. In fact, all the kitchen equipment looked so new it was almost as if none of it had ever been used.

The second thing that struck him was Circe. Everything that Elliot had read about witches had led him to expect an elderly hag, hunched, cackling over a cauldron, with a wart on the end of her nose and magic spells whizzing around the room.

Yet here was Circe, a dark-haired woman no older than his mum, hunched over a laptop, with her phone clamped to her ear. It wasn't magic whizzing around the room – it was paperwork being darted about by a team of penates. And she wasn't cackling. She was stressed.

'Look, I know!' she cried. She waved to Zeus and gestured that she'd be with him in a minute. 'But what do you want me to do? The Immortal Health Organization can be as concerned as they like about the fat content in my food. But until a bag of organic carrots is cheaper than my Typhon Twizzlers, people will buy my food every time! Deal with it!'

Circe slammed the phone down. Her jet-black hair, cut into a square fringe, framed her pointed face, curling perfectly on top of her shoulders. Her eyes were almost black with make-up and her lips blood-red. A wooden kardia hung around her throat.

'Zeus! Hypnos! Random Child!' she panted in greeting, presenting her cheek for a kiss. 'So great to see you – I'll be with you in just one— What do you want?!'

'Miss Circe – it's *The Sassy Sorceress* – they want you to comment about allegations that your chicken nuggets are seventy per cent centaur meat.'

'That's outrageous!' cried Circe. 'Who blabbed? Tell them I'll call them back. Now, Zeus, forgive me, so good to see you.'

'You too, my dear. Looks like business is booming?'

'Urgh – a little too booming,' Circe sighed, blindly signing a piece of paper waved before her face by a wax penate. 'One minute I'm making burgers to feed my boys and their friends. Next thing I know, there's an insane demand for readily available cheap food with practically no nutritional value. Who knew? And now I've got a business empire on my hands. Anyway – what can I do for you?'

'Well – we're in a bit of a bind,' said Zeus. 'Our ship got a little blown off course and now we're—'

'Miss Circe, Miss Circe!' a silver penate cried from across the kitchen. 'It's your sons' school. Apparently Latinus's lunch box wasn't acceptable.'

'What?' she cried. 'I followed all the rules! No

sugar, no salt, no fat, no sweets, no crisps, no fizzy drinks.'

'Exactly,' said the penate. 'There wasn't anything in it.'

'Oh, I despair!' cried Circe. 'The joys of being a working mother . . . Now, you were saying . . .'

'The thing is—' Zeus began again.

'Miss Circe, Miss Circe,' cried a golden penate, holding another phone. 'It's the school again. Apparently Agrius wasn't dressed in the right costume for his class assembly.'

'Urgh – give it here,' said Circe, snatching the phone to her ear. 'Now listen to me. I am a sorceress so potent I have power over life and death. But let me tell you – no magic IN THE WORLD can conjure up a costume for "Dress Like a Kumquat Day" with less than twelve hours' notice! OK?!'

Elliot's ears rang and his heart thundered. Power over life and death? Forget *The Pearl*. Circe sounded like his ticket to the Afterlife . . .

'Um, Circe—' he began.

'Urgent email from your suppliers, Miss Circe,' the wax penate shouted out. 'They need your order for centaur guts – you're running low on nuggets . . .'

'Drat – that spreadsheet is at the office!' cried Circe. 'I'm trying to work a day a week from home. I find it really helps the work–life balance – massively improves the quality of family time.'

'Circe, I was wondering—' Elliot tried again.

'Miss Circe, it's the school. Again,' called the silver penate.

'WHAT IS IT NOW???!!!' Circe cried, slamming her hands on the table and sending papers flying. 'We made a replica of the Taj Mahal out of recycled toilet rolls, I filled in seventeen forms for them to go on a trip to the park next door, I've baked twelve dozen gluten-, nut- and dairy-free brownies shaped like DNA helices for the PTA, and this school year alone I have sewn name tapes in no fewer than 274 PE socks. What – what could I possibly have forgotten?!'

'To pick up your kids,' said the penate quietly. 'School finished forty-five minutes ago . . .'

'Dammit!' shrieked Circe, reaching for her phone and knocking a cup of takeaway coffee all over her paperwork. 'Noooooooo! It's just all too much . . .'

Elliot looked at the stressed witch. His hand went to his pocket.

'Here,' he said, handing her Polyphemus's fidget spinner. 'I think you need this more than me.'

Circe eyed the small piece of plastic curiously.

'I hardly think this is going to help,' she said,

spinning the outer ring of the spinner. 'I just ... I just get so stressed out.'

She spun the spinner again.

'It's like – between work and the family, I never get time for me any more,' she said, balancing the spinner on her middle finger.

'I really need your help,' said Elliot. 'I need your magic to reach the Afterlife ...'

'Magic?' laughed Circe. 'Magic? I'm a single mother running seven businesses and raising three sons! I DON'T HAVE TIME FOR MAGIC!'

'Look, we've clearly called at a bad time,' said Zeus. 'Perhaps we could help – let us go and get your sons from school. Then maybe we can talk in the morning?'

'Thank you,' sighed Circe, spinning the fidget spinner again and taking a deep breath. 'And please – be my guests here tonight. I have plenty of room. Although I think I promised Teleganus a sleepover with his football team ... And please, order all the takeaway you like. I never get time to cook.'

'I'll steer clear of the chicken nuggets if you don't mind,' said Elliot quietly.

'We'll leave you to it,' said Zeus. 'Good luck.'

'Thanks,' sighed Circe, spinning the fidget spinner before picking up a coffee-soaked sheet of paper. 'I'll be back in the office tomorrow and I'll get back on top of everything.'

'Miss Circe?' said a wax penate, running over with a diary. 'Just to remind you there's no school tomorrow – inset day . . .'

As Elliot closed the door, he heard the sound of a witch's head slamming repeatedly against the kitchen table.

21. Fate Worse Than Death?

He wasn't sure whether it was the decent night's sleep, the fact that he'd eaten two whole pepperoni pizzas for dinner, or the feeling that he was one step closer to finding Panacea's potion, but as Elliot came downstairs on Tuesday morning, there was a very different, more positive vibe around Circe's place.

'Where are all the penates?' he asked Virgo, who was sitting on the sofa chomping on a burger, staring into a portable Lotus device.

'Dunno,' she said, not moving.

'Is Zeus around?'

'Dunno,' came Virgo's reply.

'Circe?'

'Dunno.'

'Thanks. You've been a huge help.'

'Dunno.'

Elliot walked into the kitchen, shaking his head.

When he opened the door, he worried for a moment that he'd wandered into the wrong house. Gone were the teams of penates, the paper-strewn desk, the laptops and the phones.

Instead, there were yoga mats, crystals and incense burners.

'Er . . . morning?' he said into the smoky space.

'Namaste,' came a calm voice.

'Circe?' said Elliot. 'Is that you?'

He waved his hand in front of his face to clear the incense. There, standing on her head in the middle of the room with her feet pressed together, was Circe.

'Um . . . are you OK?' he asked.

Circe came out of her pose and sat cross-legged on the mat.

'I have never been better,' she said, with her eyes closed, putting the palms of her hands together. 'You have shown me the way.'

'I . . . I did?' said Elliot.

'Yes, young mortal,' said Circe, opening her

eyes slowly and revealing what she held in the palm of her hand. 'You have brought me peace.'

'Er, the fidget spinner?' said Elliot, looking at the small disc. He knew they really helped some people to calm down a bit. But this . . .

'Yes, Elliot,' said Circe, stretching her legs out into the splits. 'I have finally found inner peace. I see a whole new path ahead.'

'Right,' puffed Zeus, bundling into the kitchen with three overflowing lunch boxes, a tennis racquet, violin, welly boots and a guinea pig. 'I think I have everything the boys need for the childminder.'

'Forget childminders,' said Circe calmly. 'From now on, I'll be home-schooling the boys. I don't want to miss out on these precious years.'

'But . . . what about your businesses?' said Elliot.

'I'm closing them down,' said Circe. 'The boys and I will run organic smoothie bars at festivals. After I've finished training as a Pilates instructor.'

'Wow,' said Zeus. 'Well . . . delighted to see you so happy.'

'You have given me so much, young Elliot,' said Circe. 'Now what can I do for you?'

'OK,' said Elliot. 'I really need to get to the Afterlife, to save my mum. Can you help me . . . die?'

'You want some of my magic?' said Circe.

'Please,' said Elliot. 'Oh, and I want to live again afterwards. If it's not too much trouble.'

'Of course not,' said Circe rising from the floor. 'I need to rediscover my love of magic. According to *The Seven Secrets of Witches' Wellbeing*, I should take at least twenty minutes of "me" time every day. And sacrifice five kittens every new moon, but I'm not sure how that sits with my newfound veganism. Follow me.'

'Come on, Virgo,' said Elliot.

'Dunno,' said Virgo, rising from the sofa without taking her eyes off the screen.

'I'll just get the boys some breakfast,' said Zeus. 'With you in a jiffy.'

Circe led them downstairs into a cellar filled with magical equipment. Elliot looked around the dark space. Spell books, flasks, herbs and potions filled every corner. Now *this* was a witch's house.

'So,' said Circe, pulling a spell book off the shelves. 'Death is a tricky business. Particularly if you only want to do it part-time. Getting you to the Afterlife won't be easy. Getting you back is even harder.'

'So the Afterlife is another realm?' said Elliot. 'Like Elysium and the Underworld?'

'No,' said Circe, pulping some herbs with a

pestle and mortar.

'Dunno,' said Virgo, not taking her eyes off her Lotus screen and opening another burger carton with her left hand.

'Er – don't you think you've had enough of those?' said Elliot. It took a lot for him to judge – but that was Virgo's third Maximus meal since breakfast. Which had also been a Maximus meal.

'Dunno,' droned Virgo, staring at her screen.

'It's not another realm,' said Circe.

'So . . . where is it?' asked Elliot, all out of ideas.

Circe threw a sparkling powder over her herbs, which immediately burst into green flames.

'It's . . . not another place,' she began. 'It's just . . . a different way of experiencing life.'

'I see,' said Elliot. He didn't really see at all.

'Dunno,' said Virgo.

Elliot looked at Virgo again. Was she . . . putting on weight? Mum always said that a gentleman should never comment on a lady's age or weight. But then, Virgo wasn't really a lady. And he certainly wasn't a gentleman.

'You mortals are so obsessed with your bodies, yet you have no understanding of the soul,' sighed Circe. 'Why do you think that in billions of people, all made up of the same biological components, no two are alike?'

'Because . . . um . . .' Elliot had never really thought about it before.

'Because of the soul,' whispered Circe. 'That unique spark that makes you – you. Bodies age and die. The soul never does. Long after your body is gone, your soul still remains.'

'So where does it go?' Elliot asked.

'Nowhere,' said Circe, pouring her herbs into a small black bag.

'What do you mean, nowhere?' said Elliot. 'You just said it never dies.'

'Correct,' said Circe. 'It just stays here.'

'But . . . what about heaven?' Elliot asked. He wasn't sure how he felt about any one religion yet. But he liked the idea that his nan and grandad were somewhere nice, somewhere there were lots of buttered crumpets, but no draughts.

'Everyone has their own name for it,' said Circe. 'But the principle is the same. Your body goes, your soul stays. Simple.'

'But that would mean that there are souls of the dead floating all around us?' said Elliot, looking around nervously. 'How come we can't see them?'

'Ah!' said Circe, corking a flask and holding it up to the light. 'That's just it! Like I say. You need a different way of experiencing life. That is all death really is.'

She handed Elliot her spell. Elliot looked at the dark herbs rustling in the bag, a single dot of light flickering around within. He accepted it nervously.

'What will this do?' he asked cautiously.

'Oh, not much,' said Circe breezily. 'They're the Herbs of Death. They'll kill you.'

'What!' Elliot spluttered, handing the herbs back. 'No, thanks.'

'Only a bit,' said Circe. 'Just dead enough for you to visit the Afterlife.'

Elliot hesitated. How dead was 'just dead enough'? Could you be 'too dead'?

'Then once you are done, you must take this,' said Circe, handing Elliot a second bag of herbs, this time in a white bag. 'The Herbs of Life will bring you back again.'

'Oh, fine then,' said Elliot stuffing both into his pocket. This was going to be more straightforward than he thought.

'There's just one more thing,' Circe added. Elliot rolled his eyes. There was always just one more thing.

'You must take the herbs no more than twenty minutes apart,' she warned. 'After that, you won't be "just dead enough". You'll be ... "just dead".'

'Great,' said Elliot. That definitely sounded

'too dead'.

'I cannot thank you enough, Elliot,' said Circe, contorting her body into another impossible yoga pose. 'You have brought me back to life.'

'Let's hope your herbs are as bally effective,' said Zeus, walking into the cellar with cereal stuck in his beard. 'Elliot and I are going to need all the luck we can get.'

'No, you're not,' said Circe gravely. 'At least, not both of you. There is only enough for one person. This is powerful magic and it's in short supply. Only one of you can go.'

'Then I must,' said Zeus, gravely. 'It's too risky.'

'It has to be me,' said Elliot quietly.

'No. It doesn't,' said Zeus firmly.

'That's what Proteus saw,' said Elliot. 'He saw me getting the potion, not you. I have to go.'

'He's right,' said Circe solemnly. 'You cannot fight your destiny.'

'But you can kick its butt,' said Elliot, grabbing the herbs. 'Come on, guys. I need to find a good place to die.'

22. Moving On

Josie Hooper had never really cared for objects before. People, time, experiences — they were all that mattered to her. She could hold everything she needed in her mind and the people she loved in her arms. The things she could hold in her hands didn't matter to her at all. It was just stuff.

But now everything had changed. Objects were the vessels that preserved her memories; they held her past when it slipped from her mind. All the things in her home were keeping her memories safe. She needed them now.

She looked at the teapot that her mother-in-law

used to make the tea when she was sad. Josie never knew her own mother, but Audrey Hooper couldn't have loved and cared for her any better. And she always made the best tea.

The coffee table was a wedding present. Josie couldn't remember which of Dave's friends gave it to them – the Hoopers had so many friends – but she remembered the day Elliot drove his toy tank over it.

'Road!' he cried joyfully, looking at the tracks the wheels had scratched into the varnish. And that's what it became – Elly's road. Josie loved that table. It made Elliot happy.

The rug, that lamp, those ornaments – little fragments of Josie's life were stored within each of them. They may have been gathering dust, but whenever she looked at them, the memories they held flooded her grey mind with colour.

Josie looked over at the sisters. She couldn't summon their names, but they were always so kind to her – if not to each other. They were arguing about something – Josie couldn't understand what. Conversations buzzed around her like a broken signal on a television channel. She could only pick up words here and there, and by the time her mind pieced the jigsaw together everyone had moved on to a new puzzle. But the sisters

263

couldn't hide the love between them. Josie could see it glowing around them like candlelight, no matter what their mouths said.

There was a knock at the door. Josie wanted to answer it – but then she remembered she mustn't. Elly had told her that. The sisters stopped their squabbling. Dave appeared like a shadow. Josie wanted to spit at him, but her mouth wouldn't obey her order.

He opened the door. Standing there was Patricia Horse's-Bum. She remembered *that* name.

Josie looked at all the people Patricia had brought with her – men, lots of men with boxes. She didn't understand – who were these people? Why was Dave letting them into their house? She looked at the sisters, but one of them was reading some papers and the other was shouting unmentionable words at Dave and the Horse's-Bum. They looked at each other, they looked at Dave, then they looked at Josie.

Josie didn't like the men touching her things. She didn't want their dirty fingers all over her memories. She wanted the men to leave.

She was holding an ornament in her hands. One of the men tried to take it, but the blonde sister started to scream what she'd do if he laid a finger on her. Josie could sense that he was genuinely scared. And that he was right to be.

Patricia paced over and the shouting started again. Josie hated the shouting, angry words attacked her mind like bullets. She put her hands over her ears to drown out the noise. The blonde sister came over and took Josie in her arms. But Josie pushed her away – she needed to stop these men.

She looked at Dave. Why wasn't he doing something?

The men were putting her things in boxes. Josie wanted to tell them to leave, but it was like she was invisible. No one was listening to her and everyone was shouting. She couldn't bear it – there was so much noise, so much confusion . . .

She screamed.

For a moment, the world stopped. She could feel everyone looking at her, standing in the middle of the kitchen with her hands over her ears, screaming. The sisters had tears in their eyes. Dave had nothing in his. Patricia just smiled.

'Carry on,' she said. And the men went back to packing Josie's things, smothering generations of stories in bubble wrap, so no one could hear them, before stuffing them in boxes.

The men started to take the boxes outside. Josie could feel her memories being plucked out of her house like they had been plucked out of her mind. The boxes were loaded into a van and driven away. She had no idea where they had gone.

Someone had taken her memories away. And she didn't know if she'd ever get them back.

Josie tried to rise to her feet. She had to stop that van. She had to save her memories.

With every atom of her being, Josie found the strength to stand. But then the strangest sensation overtook her. It was as if she were coming away from her own body, almost as though she was flying, leaving behind the body that had shackled her for so long. She felt light, free, almost as if she could float away altogether . . .

'Josie!' the dark-haired sister screamed and ran towards her.

But Josie heard no more. She had already started to fly.

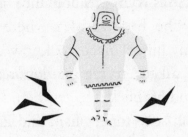

23. After Life

'**W**ell. I guess this is as good a place to die as any,' said Elliot, looking around uncertainly.

Circe had directed them to the only green space on her island – a disused football field that she now planned to use for her first Pilates retreat. Elliot looked around the brown, worn grassy spot. This felt seriously weird. Elliot had often wondered how and when he would die. But he'd never wondered where.

'You're not going to die,' said Zeus, as if reading Elliot's thoughts. 'You're just visiting for a bit. There's nothing to worry about.'

Elliot looked at Zeus's lined face. Who was the King of the Gods trying to convince? Elliot? Or himself?

'Is there anything I need to know about this Tiresias?' he asked, trying to ignore the fear swirling around his chest.

'Don't think so – super chap,' said Zeus. 'Poor soul got stuck in the middle of a ding-dong between Hera and I once.'

'Did you kill him?' asked Elliot.

'Heavens, no!' Zeus laughed. 'But he did end up spending seven years as a woman.'

Elliot paused. He wasn't sure which was worse.

'I'm sure he'll do everything he can to help you,' said Zeus. 'And we'll be waiting here for you. Won't we, Virgo?'

'Dunno,' groaned Virgo as she gnawed on a chicken leg in front of the Lotus. Elliot swore he could see a zit growing on her forehead.

'Don't worry – we'll sort her out,' Zeus whispered, wrestling the Lotus away from Virgo, who made sluggish protests. 'Are you ready for the off?'

Elliot pulled the herbs out of his pocket, the herbs that – however temporarily – would kill him. Could anyone ever be ready for that?

'Yes,' he said weakly.

'Don't worry – dying can't be that bad,' said

Hypnos, stretched out on the patchy grass.

'That's a huge comfort, coming from an immortal who has never had to do it,' snapped Elliot. He sat down on the ground. He figured that if he was coming back to life again, he didn't want to wake up to a broken arm, having fallen down dead on the grass.

'Here,' said Hypnos, handing him a sundial watch from his wrist. 'I've set a timer for fifteen minutes – when it goes off, you only have five minutes to return to your body.'

'Thanks,' said Elliot quietly, strapping the watch to his own wrist.

'I'm not happy about this,' said Zeus. 'Not happy at all.'

'It's the only way,' said Elliot. 'I have to save Mum. And you swore you'd do whatever it took to help me.'

'So let *me* go,' Zeus insisted. 'I've lived umpteen lives – you've barely started yours . . .'

'You heard Proteus. Tiresias is expecting me. It's fate.'

'I don't believe in fate,' said Zeus. 'I believe in choices.'

'Well, this is the only one I have,' said Elliot quietly. 'But if this goes wrong . . .'

'It won't,' Zeus whispered. 'It can't . . .'

269

'But if it does. If I die,' said Elliot, 'promise me
. . . promise me you won't tell Mum.'

'What?' cried Zeus. 'Why would I . . .'

'She's probably already forgotten me,' said
Elliot. 'Don't remind her, just for her to lose me
again. Promise me.'

Zeus let out an exasperated sigh. But slowly, his
head began to nod.

'Right, then,' said Elliot, putting the herbs to
his lips. 'Let's do this.'

'Good luck, Elliot,' said Zeus, taking his position on Elliot's right as Hypnos moved to his left.
'We'll stay here, right by these three trees that
form a triangle, so you can find your way back.
We'll see you soon, old chap.'

Elliot nodded. He brought the enchanted herbs
to his mouth . . .

'Wait!' Virgo suddenly shouted, shattering
the tense moment as she struggled to her feet.
'Elliot . . . ?'

'What?' Elliot cried. It wasn't like he was in a
big hurry to die, but still.

'I just wanted to give you my sincerest wishes
for your safe return,' stammered Virgo. 'And . . .
and . . . and . . . THIS.'

She launched herself at Elliot, in what he eventually realized was a hug.

'Gross,' he murmured and, before he had time to think about the crazy thing he was doing, he swallowed the herbs down whole.

Immediately, he felt as if he were falling. It wasn't an unpleasant sensation – he'd had a similar feeling when he'd challenged his best friend at primary school to a breath-holding competition. The world started to fade out of focus – he could see and hear Zeus and Virgo, but they were growing very faint. He had a sudden urge to stand up, so he clambered to his feet, before looking back at the patch of grass he'd been lying on. There, deathly still, was his body. That was strange. And he really needed a haircut.

He looked around the football pitch – it was precisely the same as before, just with his friends so faint he could hardly see them.

'Tiresias!' he called. 'Tiresias, where are you?'

A low moaning came from the other side of the field. Elliot froze. That didn't sound good. The ground beneath him started to quake rhythmically, as if thousands of feet were hitting the ground at once. He turned away, but the moaning sound began on the other side of the field too. The ground kept rumbling – he was right, he could hear the footsteps now. Something – or someone – was coming for him.

271

Elliot looked around for a place to hide, but the open space offered him nothing. He was a sitting target.

The footsteps sounded closer and across the grass he could see an army of glowing forms coming into focus. Their arms were stretched in front of them like zombies and they continued their low moaning as they advanced. Elliot pulled away towards the other side of the field, but that was soon filled with more moaning figures coming towards him. There was nowhere to run. He looked back at his lifeless body. Should he just take the herbs and come back to life?

No. He only had one chance to save Mum. He wasn't going to chicken out now.

The zombies continued their slow, moaning march. Elliot tried to think about all the zombie movies he'd seen. Was it garlic they were allergic to? Or was that vampires? And there was no garlic. In any case, as the zombies started to crowd around him, there was no time. He closed his eyes and awaited their attack.

'For heaven's sake, will you look at yourselves!' yelled a wonderfully familiar voice. 'Carrying on like a bunch o' bananas. Pack it in!'

Elliot's heart swelled with joy. He'd know that voice anywhere. And if anyone could defeat killer zombies, it was . . .

'Nan!' he cried, and he turned to see the glowing soul of his beloved grandmother.

'My boy!' screamed Audrey Hooper, running to embrace her grandson. 'Wilfred! Wilfred, will you get over here!'

Elliot looked at the zombies, who were standing around laughing and cooing at Elliot and Audrey's reunion.

'Er, who are they?' he began.

'Oh, don't you pay them no mind, they're having you on,' said Nan, shooing them away with a tea towel tucked inside her apron. Elliot smiled – he'd received more than a few swats from that tea towel when he'd tried to steal Nan's baking. 'The old souls do it to all the newcomers, they're as harmless as a newborn runt.'

Elliot looked at the sea of smiling faces waving at him. For dead people they looked kind of . . . happy.

'Now what on Earth are you doing here?' said Nan. 'It's not your time.'

'I know I'm a bit young to die,' said Elliot.

'No, you daft goose,' said Nan, swatting him with the tea towel. 'It's really not your time. Look.'

She pointed up into the sky, where Elliot could see what looked like a massive arrivals board

273

suspended in mid-air – he'd seen one in Waterloo when he and Grandad took their trips to London. The board was filled with lists of names, next to which was a time. Every time a new name appeared on the board, it gave a small ping.

'What does it mean?' said Elliot.

'Just like I said,' said Nan. 'There's no getting around it – when your time's up, it's up. This board just tells us when. Oooh, look – we can be expecting Karen Featherwick from New Orleans any second now ...'

And, with a small jingle, the glowing soul of Ms Featherwick duly came into focus.

'Ooooh,' said Nan, 'it's not going to be a good evening for John Sanderson from Penge . . . But you, my boy – you aren't there. You shouldn't be here. And where is—?'

'Elliot!' puffed a warm voice. 'Come here, you great lug!'

'Grandad!' exclaimed Elliot, hugging his grandfather. He buried himself happily in Wilfred's cardigan, which still smelt of pipe smoke and hay. He felt a toffee being pressed into his hand.

'Wilfred Hooper, I hope you're not giving that boy sweets!' squawked Nan, just like she used to do. '*He's* still got all his teeth!'

'Stop your nagging, girl!' Wilfred winked, waving his walking stick in his wife's direction. 'You've got more chat than a two-headed parrot.'

'It's so . . . it's so good to see you,' said Elliot as he nestled between his beloved grandparents.

'You too, boy,' said Grandad, pinching his nose, just like he used to. 'But you need to listen – you don't have much time.'

'I know – I've got to get back to my body in . . . sixteen minutes,' said Elliot.

'It's not just that,' Grandad began, before receiving a swat from the tea towel.

'Wilfred, I'm telling you – hush!' Nan warned.

'What's going on?' said Elliot.

'Nothing you need worry about,' said Nan firmly, shooting Grandad one of her ferocious 'don't you dare' stares. 'Grandad's just got the wrong end of the stick, that's all.'

'Something's not right,' murmured his grandfather. 'I know it . . .'

'Any road – why are you here?' Nan interrupted. 'This ain't no place for a growing boy.'

'I need to find Tiresias,' said Elliot. 'Where is—'

'Hello, Elliot,' said a voice from behind his grandparents. 'I've been expecting you.'

Elliot didn't know what he'd imagined a prophet to look like. But it wasn't Tiresias's beard

275

trailing on the floor that surprised him. Nor the flowing grey hair. The flowery sundress, however – that was unexpected.

'Dresses are so much more comfortable,' said Tiresias, answering his silent question. 'When you've had the benefit of my experiences and lived as both genders, you learn to adopt the best of both worlds. Overall, despite the lack of pockets and occasional tightness after pasta, they're much better. Although you do need to be careful they don't get caught in your pants. That's embarrassing . . . Welcome.'

'So this is the Afterlife?' said Elliot.

'Not so different, really, is it?' said Tiresias, looking around. 'During life, you see the body more clearly than the soul. Here in the Afterlife, it works the other way around. The soul is clearer than the body. It's simply two sides of the same coin. Like love and hate. Or fear and ignorance. Or heads and tails on a coin.'

That kinda made sense. But Elliot wasn't here for an explanation of the Afterlife.

'I'm here because I need Panacea's potion,' he said, feeling the blood pulsing through his veins. 'Please tell me you have it.'

'Of course,' said Tiresias. 'I've been waiting for you.'

Elliot's heart quickened. He was so, so close.

'OK,' he said, as steadily as he was able. 'Do we need to go to some secret cave or something? Is it guarded by a dragon? Protected by dangerous enchantments? Tell me what I have to do.'

'Oh, it's in the safest place I know,' said Tiresias gravely. 'Somewhere I could be sure no one would find it.'

Tiresias put his hand to his shoulder. Elliot held his breath and watched intently. This was clearly some important prophet . . . ritual . . . thing.

Tiresias produced a clutch purse from under his left armpit.

'Now, I know it's in here somewhere,' said the prophet, pulling tissues, keys and some ancient chewing gum out of his bag. 'I saw it just this morning . . .'

'So, you keep this magical potion, the only known cure for all illness . . . in your handbag?' Elliot said slowly.

'Oh, I keep everything in my handbag!' said Tiresias earnestly. 'Don't understand why more men don't carry one – so useful. Ah – here!'

Elliot looked at the small tube in front of him.

'It says "Cherry Blush",' he said uncertainly.

'Oh, sorry!' said Tiresias. 'Love that lipstick . . . no, this is it!'

277

He produced another tube from his bag. This one was filled with a swirling golden liquid. Elliot's world stood still as he looked upon the answer to his prayers. This was it. This was Panacea's potion. This would give him his mum back.

'Does it . . . does it work?' he asked tentatively.

'It does,' said Tiresias. 'It will cure the afflicted. They will be as new.'

Elliot held back the tears. He had it. He had the cure for Mum. Everything was going to be OK.

But he did have one further burning question.

'Tiresias – can I ask you something?'

'Of course.' Tiresias nodded sagely. 'I am a prophet blessed with eternal knowledge. What do you seek?'

Elliot tried to think of the politest way to ask his question.

'Why are you wearing a girl's dress?'

The prophet paused thoughtfully.

'It's not a girl's. It's mine,' he said.

'Yeah . . . you know what I mean . . .'

'I do not. Where is it written that only certain people can wear certain things?'

'It's not,' said Elliot. 'But c'mon – most men wear trousers.'

'Just because a lot of people do something, that

doesn't make it right,' said Tiresias. 'Look at war. Bigotry. Adult colouring books.'

'Yes, but . . .' Elliot couldn't summon up an argument. Talking to prophets was hard work. Besides, looking at Hypnos's watch, he didn't have time for more chat.

'I have to get back,' he whispered. 'I have to save Mum. I have to save Hermes. I have—'

'No,' said Tiresias, pursing his lips to apply his Cherry Blush.

'No what?' said Elliot, the familiar fist of fear wrapping its fingers around his heart.

'Only one person will be saved by the potion,' Tiresias explained gently. 'It is destined.'

Zeus's words rang in Elliot's mind.

'*I don't believe in destiny. I believe in choices.*'

So, he'd have to choose. Elliot's heart fell. Why was everything an impossible choice? He had to cure his mum, he just had to. But how could he let Hermes die? And how could he tell the Gods?

'I'm sorry,' said Tiresias, putting a gentle hand on his shoulder. 'Nothing is ever simple.'

Hypnos's watch chimed on his wrist, yanking Elliot's thoughts back to the moment.

'I need to go,' he said. 'I need to take the Herbs of Life . . .'

'What did you say?' said a passing soul.

'Nothing – it's just if I don't take the Herbs of Life in the next five minutes, I'll be stuck here . . . er . . . no offence.'

'You've got the Herbs of Life?' said the soul, moving closer. 'Give them.'

He swiped at Elliot's hand.

'Hey!' said Elliot, dodging out of his way. 'They're mine!'

'Did someone say Herbs of Life?' shouted another soul. 'I need to tell my wife where I really hid my life savings – give them here.'

'My brother still owes me a hundred quid!' yelled a third. 'I want the herbs!'

'Is this another game?' laughed Elliot as the souls advanced.

'No, it's not!' cried Tiresias, lashing out with his handbag. 'Elliot, quick – run back to your body!'

As the spirits swarmed towards him, Elliot needed no further instruction. He sprinted across the field and could see his faint body lying on the grass. But the spirits were gaining. And there were loads of them.

'Give them to me – I can solve poverty!'

'I should get them – I can heal the world!'

'I need them most! I never finished that jigsaw!'

The cacophony grew louder as the rabble drew

closer. He was nearly at the spot where he had left his body, but so were the spirits. If he could just reach out . . .

SLAM!

His body hit the grass as a spirit made a dive for his feet and brought him crashing to the ground, sending the Herbs of Life flying across the grass – and a thousand lifeless hands tried to grab them.

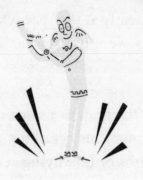

24. Clash of the Titans

'**H**ow long's it been now?' said Zeus for the second time in thirty seconds.

'Relax,' said Hypnos, fluttering overhead. 'He's got loads of time.'

Virgo held her breath as Zeus turned his angry blue eyes on the Daemon. Suddenly she didn't feel like another burger. She handed it to the gorgon on her shoulder.

'Plop,' said Gorgy gratefully.

'Relax?' glowered Zeus. 'The boy is dead! I can't relax!'

'He'll be fine,' said Hypnos. 'Have some faith.'

'I'll give you faith,' muttered Zeus, returning

to Elliot's side. 'It's all right, Elly. We're here. How long?'

'Twelve minutes,' said Virgo, struggling to read her watch due to the curious shaking of her hand. She looked down at Elliot's still, pale body. It made her feel more nauseous than the time Elliot had told her to wash her mouth out and she'd swallowed half a bottle of shampoo.

'Er, chaps,' said Hypnos, looking around the horizon. 'Don't want to be a drama Daemon, but I think we have company . . .'

'Then get rid of them!' said Zeus. 'This is no time for busybodies – we need to keep Elliot safe.'

'Bit of a tall order, chief,' said Hypnos, as a huge shadow started to sprawl across the sunlit field. 'A very, very tall order . . .'

Virgo's heart drummed inside her chest when she saw two enormous figures stomping towards two overweight centaurs, munching burgers on the grass.

'It's true,' whispered Zeus. 'They're . . . they're . . .'

'Titans?!' squealed Hypnos. 'Who let the Titans out?'

'The bally Zodiac Council!' said Zeus. 'I locked them in the deepest pit of Tartarus for good reason – they're monsters.'

They watched as the Titans approached the

centaurs with their giant nets.

'All Elementals are to come with us,' said The Ram. 'By order of the Zodiac Council.'

The centaurs tried to gallop away – but their girth and lack of fitness made it an easy chase for the Titans. They were bundled up in giant nets and the Titans lumbered on.

'I'm guessing they'll be thrilled to see you,' Hypnos said to Zeus. 'We need to get out of here.'

'We can't!' cried Virgo. 'We mustn't move Elliot – he won't be able to find his body again! And he's only got . . . six minutes!'

'Well, what else do you suggest, genius?' said Hypnos. 'It won't be pretty, but *we* can survive a tussle with the Titans. *You* are going to end up in the Afterlife if we're not careful.'

'Zeus?' said Virgo more frantically. 'Zeus?'

'ZEUS!' bellowed The Ram, spying the King of the Gods from across the park. 'Come here and fight! Or are you still a spineless coward?!'

'I'll fight you anytime!' shouted Zeus, withdrawing a thunderbolt. 'And I'll beat you every time! I'll have you back into Tartarus before the sun sets on another day! Take this!'

And with all his strength, Zeus launched the thunderbolt towards the mighty Titan. Virgo watched in horror as the useless weapon simply bounced off. If only he'd had the humility to make friends with his brother, he would have functioning weaponry. But Zeus strode towards the Titans anyway. She looked to Hypnos to take control, but he was clearly going to be as much use as a mortal teenager's deodorant. And Elliot only had two minutes left.

'Um, Zeus,' called Virgo, chasing after him, regretting her fourth Maximus meal. 'Your courage is commendable, but your timing is sub-optimal.'

'I'm no coward!' roared Zeus.

'Your Majesty – please!' Virgo cried, grabbing his arm. 'You are unarmed. And you're my only protection. We – I – need you to stay with me. Please.'

'No!' declared Zeus. 'I will defend you with everything I have. I will keep you—'

'WATCH OUT!' cried Hypnos, snatching Virgo out of the way just as a massive boulder smashed down where she had been standing a split second earlier.

'Whoa – that was close,' said Virgo. 'Gorgy, are you—'

But her little gorgon was clearly not OK at all.

'Plllllopppppp!' growled Gorgy, trembling with rage on Virgo's shoulder. 'Bad plop man!'

'Gorgy – no, don't!' screamed Virgo. But she was too late. Gorgy had already curled into a ball and leapt from her shoulder. He bowled towards the Titans, his snakes hissing angrily around his head.

'Virgo – we need to get you out of here,' said Zeus. 'Come along.'

'No!' shrieked Virgo, as Gorgy threw himself at The Ram.

'BAD PLOP MAN!' Gorgy yelled at the gigantic Titan, focusing his snakes on the Titan's sack.

'Oh, look,' said The Ram, grabbing Gorgy by his hair. 'Takeaway.'

'PLLLLLLOOOOOOPPPPPPP!' squealed Gorgy, his snakes swamped in the Titan's massive hand, robbing him of his powers.

'Gorgy!' Virgo cried, setting off after him.

'He's saving you!' shouted Zeus. 'So let him!'

And before she could protest any further, Zeus bundled Virgo over his shoulder and ran back towards Elliot's body.

'You see!' crowed The Ram triumphantly, stuffing Gorgy into his sack. 'A coward! Well, if you won't come to us . . .'

'Then we'll just leave quietly!' roared The Brain, but a slap from his brother turned him back to face Zeus.

The Ram let out a terrifying howl and the two

286

Titans broke into a run, making the ground shake in their wake.

'We have to get out of here!' exclaimed Hypnos.

'Hypnos – take Elliot and fly him to safety,' said the King of the Gods, scooping Elliot gently into his arms and handing him to the Daemon.

'But how will he find his body again?' said Hypnos.

'We need to make sure he has a body to come back to,' said Zeus. 'And, Virgo?'

'Yes?' said Virgo weakly, thinking of her scared little gorgon all alone in that dark sack.

'RUN!'

25. Time's Up

Before he knew which end was up, Elliot was surrounded by grabbing hands, pulling at his clothing, trying to find the herbs that would restore their lives. Elliot could see the white bag, lying in the grass just out of his reach. But what he couldn't see was his body. There was the triangle of trees . . . Where had he gone?

He knew he didn't have long. He tried to fight the growing panic rising in his throat – he had to get that cure to Mum. He was so, so close . . .

He kicked off the nearest soul clinging to his trouser leg and wrestled his body free of the others. The souls hadn't yet found the bag of herbs concealed in the grass ahead. But it was only a matter of time.

'You get back now!' It was Nan's voice – she was forcing her way through the crowd, hitting the desperate souls with a spatula.

'Ow!' cried one as he received a smack on the back of his knuckles.

'You mind your manners!' snapped Nan.

'Sorry,' mumbled the soul.

'You should all be ashamed of yourselves – scaring a young boy like that with all your carrying on!'

'We thought he had the Herbs of Life,' whined another soul.

'Herbs of Life!' scoffed Nan. 'Honestly! You'd believe anything, you lot. Herbs of Life indeed. I never heard such a load of old—'

'Elliot – over here!' shouted Grandad in the distance. 'I've found your body! Get over here and take the Herbs of Life, sharpish!'

Nan rolled her eyes as the crowd of souls started to mutter angrily.

'Wilfred!' she cried. 'When I get my hands on you, you're a dead man. Again . . . Elliot – run! I love you, my darling . . .'

Elliot didn't need to be told twice. He'd felt that spatula enough times to know when Nan meant business. He dived for the herbs and sprinted across the field, towards the sound of his grandfather's voice.

'Here you go, my boy,' said Grandad, receiving Elliot with a giant hug and pointing towards Elliot's body with his stick. 'Now, listen – I don't have much time. Your Nan doesn't want me to tell you this, but you need to know. Something's not right at Home Farm.'

'Mum?' said Elliot.

'Your dad,' said Grandad sadly. 'There's something . . . wrong. He's not the son I raised.'

'What do you mean?' said Elliot, looking at the approaching spirits. 'I don't understand . . .'

'There's no time,' said Grandad, pulling his beloved grandson to him with a tear in his eye. 'But you look after yourself.'

'I will,' said Elliot, feeling hot tears spill down his cheeks. 'Grandad, I—'

'I know,' said Grandad, as the roar of the souls grew louder. 'We love you too, boy. And we're always with you. Remember that, Elliot. Now go!'

Lying back into his body, Elliot swallowed down the herbs. But as he did so, the arrivals board in the sky above him pinged. A new name, time and location appeared. And this one seared itself into Elliot's heart.

'No – wait!' he said, trying to fight the magic of the herbs. 'I need to—'

BANG!

He spluttered back to life with a gasp and sat bolt upright on the grass, just as Hypnos's watch chimed twenty minutes.

'Thank the Gods, you found us!' said Zeus, rubbing Elliot's back. 'Thought we'd lost you for a moment there, old boy. Thought you'd lost you, come to think of it . . .'

'What's wrong?' said Virgo, seeing the tears streaming down Elliot's face. 'Didn't you get the potion?'

'It's – it's . . .' spluttered Elliot, struggling between the tears and the need to refill his lungs with air.

'Steady there,' said Zeus. 'Take all the time you need. The Titans gave up on us when they caught a group of fairies too busy on Flitter to notice they were being kidnapped.'

'We don't have any time!' said Elliot, scrambling to his feet. 'We have to get home. Now! I saw . . . I saw . . .'

'What?' said Zeus. 'What did you see?'

Elliot took a series of gasping breaths.

'I-I . . . saw her name,' he said shakily. 'In the Afterlife.'

'Wh-what are you—'Virgo stuttered.

'I saw her name on the arrivals board!' Elliot screamed. 'It's Mum. She's going to die at 11.17 tomorrow morning!'

26. True Lies

Thanatos looked on contentedly as the latest batch of terrified captives were shoved through the mighty bronze gates of Tartarus. Their pitiful pleas blended perfectly with the entreaties of the crowds of Elementals already herded into this hellish inferno. There were tearful mermaids, quivering gnomes, cursing centaurs. They were bewildered, scared and angry. Precisely how he needed them to be.

'I CAN'T TALK!' a fairy shouted down her mobile phone as she passed. 'I'M BEING DETAINED AGAINST MY WILL!'

Thanatos watched as the once sparse plains of

Tartarus now swarmed with creatures of all shapes, sizes and sensibilities. Pixies were nearly flattened by giants, unicorns avoided the hungry stares of vampires, werewolves howled at the light cast by glowfairies.

'Will you PLEATH shift your butth!' cried Sisyphus, as a cluster of wood nymphs took refuge on his hill. 'Thith ith a rethricted thpathe!'

'Oi!' shouted Asteria as a group of centaurs drank from her massive urn. 'This isn't the water cooler! Move it!'

'I'm not an all-you-can-eat buffet, you know!' yelled Tantalus at the pixies picking his fruit.

'No – that'th your thon!' quipped Salmoneus, looking anxiously at the gathering of witches stirring their cauldron on his overhanging rock. 'Theriouthly! Have you no thenthe of health and thafety!'

Thanatos smiled at the chaos. It was time.

'Friends!' he called across the scorched plain. 'Lend me your ears!'

A nearby zombie obligingly threw his ears at Thanatos's feet.

'How kind,' said the Daemon, taking a small step away. 'Good citizens of the Earth! I am Thanatos, Daemon of Death!'

A gasp went up from the crowd.

'I thought you were dead,' said a gnome. 'No offence, but whoever's doing your publicity should be shot ...'

'There were times when I wished I were dead,' said Thanatos mournfully. 'Like you, I was falsely imprisoned, shut beneath the Earth for no greater crime than being myself.'

'Uh – thorry, Thanatoth,' groaned Sisyphus, manoeuvring his boulder around a sleeping wizard. 'But in fairneth, you did theriouthly try to theige Zeuth.'

'And now you can see why!' roared Thanatos. 'Even now, he is dizzy with power! The Zodiac Council are mere puppets. Zeus is still in charge. Zeus controls their every move. Zeus put you all here.'

'But what can we do?' sniffed a forlorn pixie. 'We're stuck down here.'

'For now,' said Thanatos. 'But soon, my friends, soon I will have my Chaos Stones and I will free us all from this place. All I ask is that you join me, and you will be FREE!'

A fairy put her hand up.

'Er, is there any kind of membership fee involved?' she asked quietly. 'It's just my local gym made a similar offer and I'm still paying every month ...'

'Oh, don't get me started,' huffed a unicorn. 'I signed up for a free trial of Vetflix – all the best animal dramas on one channel? Tried to take my left hoof when I wanted to unsubscribe . . .'

'I ask for nothing but your loyalty,' Thanatos continued. 'For centuries, Elementals have been treated as second-class citizens. Follow me, and you will be first class!'

'Does that mean we get extra legroom?' asked a giant.

'It means you can have whatever you want!' cried Thanatos. 'For too long, mortals have been allowed to overrun the Earth, pillaging its resources, filling it with toxic gases, polluting its oceans. And how long do they stay here? Mere decades, ruining the planet that we immortals have inhabited for millennia and will inhabit for ever.'

'He's got a point,' muttered a vampire to a group of his friends. 'They're only guests, really. We're the residents.'

'Precisely!' shouted Thanatos. 'And how have they treated our home? Disgustingly. Dryads? Would you destroy acres of trees just to give the mortals a daily newspaper?'

'Noooo!' cried the Dryads, bursting into tears.

'Nereids!' Thanatos called. 'Would you fill the

oceans with waste until marine life is choking on plastic bags?'

'Never!' squealed the Nereids.

'Centaurs!' the Daemon yelled. 'Would you hunt species to the verge of extinction just so a mortal can wear a piece of animal to display their wealth?'

'It's an outrage!' shouted the centaurs, waving their spears.

'Then who do you think should be running the Earth?!' Thanatos roared. 'Mortals, with their wasteful, hateful disregard for our home? Or immortals, who will protect and cherish the place we are bound to for ever?'

'Immortals! Immortals! Immortals!' the Elementals began to chant.

'Then let us take our home back!' Thanatos implored. 'With me as your leader we can—'

'Excuthe me, Thanatoth,' said Sisyphus, leaning on his boulder to hold it in place near the top of the hill. 'Thith ith hardly the motht democratic protheth. It'th all very well you thaying you're the leader, but who thayth we want you?'

'Fair enough,' said Thanatos. 'Then let us put it to a vote. A show of hands will do. All those who wish me to lead them from this hellhole to their rightful place in charge of the Earth?'

A sea of hands shot into the air.

'And all those against?'

'Well, I'm thorry to thay,' said Sisyphus, letting go of his boulder to raise his hand. 'That whiltht I'm sure you have thome of the prerequithite thkillth . . .'

Released from Sisyphus's grasp, the boulder started to roll back down the hill.

'Oh, RATTH!' raged Sisyphus. 'I'll get you for thith!'

But as Sisyphus charged down the hill, chasing his boulder, his cries were drowned out by the mob of angry Elementals, cheering for their new leader.

'Thanatos! Thanatos! Thanatos!' they chanted.

And their new leader accepted their adulation with a gracious nod of his head. Everything was going precisely according to plan.

27. Reunited

'**E**NOUGH IS ENOUGH!'' roared Zeus, slamming his hands down on Poseidon's desk. 'You give us back the Chaos Stones and you get us back to Home Farm. Now!'

Virgo winced at the King of the Gods and the God of the Sea staring each other down. She felt Proteus softly place a blanket around her dripping shoulders. She, Elliot and Hypnos had dived straight into the sea behind a determined Zeus and now they were all in Poseidon's office, having been sucked back down to the Coral Cove. Elliot was standing in a daze as Proteus swathed him in a blanket too. Virgo was going to wrap Gorgy in the blanket with her, but then she remembered – he wasn't there. She brought the blanket to her eyes. Some seawater must have got in . . .

'Now listen here. I got no problem with the little landlubber and I'm sorry for his pains,' said Poseidon. 'I gave you me ship. I gave you me wind. Ye've managed to lose both. Me trident's on the blink. There's nothing else I can do for ye.'

'You can give us the Chaos Stones!' shouted Zeus.

'I told ye, I can't,' said Poseidon. 'That there booty is staying with me. I need to look after me own.'

'You always were a stubborn, ridiculous old trout!' snapped Zeus. 'Don't you realize that Thanatos is coming?'

'Up there on Earth, maybe,' said Poseidon. 'He don't stand a chance down here.'

'You really believe that?' said Zeus. 'You really think that Thanatos will rest before he rules every last immortal, above the sea and below?'

'Zeus is right,' said Hypnos. 'If you think my dearest brother is going to let you carry on your party down here, you're as blind as a pirate with his patch on the wrong eye.'

'Precisely,' said Poseidon. 'Which is why I need those Chaos Stones here with me. Insurance policy.'

'And what's more,' said Zeus, 'the Titans are on the loose.'

'What a load of bum!' scoffed Poseidon.

'You don't believe him?' said Virgo.

'No,' laughed Poseidon. 'I'm just saying he's got a load of—'

'This is no time for your childish jibes!' cried Zeus. 'I saw them with my own eyes – the Titans are free!'

'Don't be so daft,' said Poseidon – a little less certainly, Virgo thought. 'We put the Titans down in the pit of Tartarus ourselves. They're brutes. Beasts. Monsters. Why would anyone be stupid enough to let them out?'

Virgo shifted uncomfortably on her feet. She realized this could be an excellent moment to share what she knew about the Titans in order to give everyone up-to-date information.

'AAAAAAARRRRRRRGGGGGHHHH!' With an almighty roar of frustration, Zeus ripped up the desk and hurled it across the tavern, showering a nearby group of mermaids with splinters.

'I KNOW!' yelled Zeus. 'AND WHEN I GET MY HANDS ON THEM, I'LL GIVE THEM A THUNDERBOLT WHERE THE SUN DOESN'T SHINE!'

Virgo reconsidered. Perhaps now wasn't such a good moment after all.

She looked back at Elliot, standing pale and shaken in the corner. There were other matters that needed addressing.

'Your Majesties,' said Virgo, 'if what Elliot understood in the Afterlife is correct, he needs to return home urgently to administer the potion to Josie-Mum.'

'I wish I could help ye, sprat,' said Poseidon more gently. 'But in truth, there's nothing I can do for ye. I wish ye well.'

'You are an unbelievable, belligerent old piece of . . .'

Zeus ranted at his brother and Elliot shook with rhythmic sobs. Virgo felt the room grow darker, as if it was actually . . .

She looked out of the cave's mouth. There was the giant shadow.

'And that's just for starters – then I'd—'

'Er, Zeus,' she said, tugging at his shirt. 'I think you need to see this.'

'I see it perfectly,' said the King of the Gods. 'My brother is a spineless, useless—'

'Huge butt!' cried Poseidon.

'OH, WILL YOU SHUT UP ABOUT MY BOTTOM?' hollered Zeus.

'No – look out there,' said Poseidon, pointing. 'There's a huge butt!'

All heads turned to the office door, which was filled entirely with a vast Titan backside, muffling the screams of the sea creatures in the tavern.

'What be the meaning of this!' barked Poseidon.

'We saw them on Circe's Island,' said Zeus. 'They're rounding up the Elementals.'

'Well, they ain't rounding up mine!' said Poseidon, reaching under his desk and producing his trident. He held it aloft and slammed it down in the sand. But nothing happened.

'What is the ruddy matter with this?' he said, shaking it.

'I'm telling you,' said Proteus quietly. 'It needs to be reunited with its brother.'

'Or it needs to be reunited with something else,' growled Poseidon. He strode over to the office door and aimed his weapon squarely at the huge buttock in his path.

'Oi, you great whale fart!' he yelled. 'Round up this!'

And, with an almighty thrust, he shoved the prongs of his trident straight into the Titan's bottom.

'YOWWWWEEEEEEOOOOOOUUUU-UWWWWW!' screamed The Brain, leaping in the air, clutching his rear end and clearing the entrance for Poseidon to walk into the main tavern.

'Now this here be my establishment and ye aren't welcome,' said Poseidon. 'So sling yer scurvy hooks!'

'We're following Zodiac Council orders,' said The Ram.

'Pah!' laughed Poseidon. 'Well, I pay about as much attention to them as I do to the hair growing out me ears. Be on yer way.'

'No can do,' said The Ram. 'So what you going to do about it?'

'Don't ye threaten me, ye overgrown whale blubber,' said Poseidon, shaking his trident. 'I've seen off monsters twice the size of you.'

'Have you?' said The Ram. 'Or do you go running like a chicken, just like your brother?'

'How dare you!' roared Zeus, coming to stand beside Poseidon. 'You want a fight? You can bally well have one!'

'Oh, yeah!' said The Ram, dropping his sack to smash one fist into the other. 'So bring it!'

'Suit yourself!' cried Zeus. 'But don't say I didn't warn you! Aaaaaargh!'

The King of the Gods launched himself at The Ram, pounding him with angry fists, landing punch after punch on the Titan's colossal legs.

'And . . . have . . . that . . . and . . . these . . . and . . .' puffed Zeus, starting to tire.

'You done yet?' yawned The Ram.

'Never!' cried Zeus. 'Go on, you great brute – give it your best shot!'

'All right,' said The Ram. 'Now clear off.'

And, placing his giant forefinger behind his massive thumb, he flicked the King of the Gods away like a pesky fly. Zeus sailed across the Coral Cove, slid along the length of the bar and landed smack on the floor at the other end with a barrel of nectar on his head.

'Ye're a useless bag o' britches,' said Poseidon, shaking his head. 'Leave this to the experts. Oi – fish-face! Have some of this!'

The God of the Sea charged at The Brain with his trident. But he was simply picked up by one leg and tossed across the bar to join his brother.

'Ow,' he groaned as he landed on top of Zeus.

'Given up yet?' said The Ram, scooping up a handful of water nymphs and putting them in his sack.

'And this is for Gorgy!' screamed Virgo, running over to The Ram and stamping on his toe.

The Titan stopped and looked down at her.

'Lucky for you you're not on my list,' he said.

'Because someone needs to teach you some manners, missy. Just because you voted for this, it doesn't mean you're above the law.'

'Virgo?' said Zeus incredulously. 'You voted to release the Titans? Why ever would you do such a thing?'

Virgo felt as if she'd just eaten seven Maximus meals. She didn't have an answer for Zeus. She didn't have an answer for herself.

'Not that it's any of my business,' said Proteus, flying in parrot form to where Zeus and Poseidon lay in a crumpled heap on the floor, 'but perhaps your weapons might come in handy?'

Poseidon sighed.

'How about it, brother?' he said, holding out his trident. 'Are ye prepared to reunite?'

'From the bottom of my heart,' said Zeus, unsheathing a thunderbolt.

The two Gods brought their mighty weapons together and shouted at the top of their voices:

'I GIVE YOU MY POWER AND I ACCEPT YOURS. TOGETHER WE'RE STRONGER TO WIN ANY WARS!'

The cave filled with an incandescent golden glow as the two weapons shone with the light of a million stars.

'Uh-oh,' said The Brain, and The Ram dropped

the sack filled with sea creatures.

'Brother!' roared Poseidon. 'I think we be back in business!'

'So let's kick some Titan bottom!' cried Zeus. He unleashed a thunderbolt, sending the Titans flying across the cave and slamming into the bubble wall beyond.

'YE THINK YE CAN COME HERE AND TAKE ME HEARTIES?' yelled Poseidon, raising his trident aloft. 'WELL, YE CAN TAKE THIS!'

And, with an almighty battle cry, he slammed his trident into the ground. At his command, a mighty crack opened up along the seabed, snaking towards the Titans, threatening to tip them into the dark depths below.

'Quick, bruv – run!' said The Ram, pulling The Brain to his feet and bursting through the bubble into the sea beyond. Virgo watched as the Titans swam desperately for the surface.

'Oh, I think ye can go a bit faster than that,' said Poseidon, aiming his trident at the sea. A flash of golden sparks flew from its prongs into the water beyond the bubble, turning into a shiver of sharks that began to nip at the Titans' feet.

'And let that be an end to it!' shouted Zeus at the retreating Titans. 'No buts!'

Poseidon pulled his brother to his feet.

'Ye might not be as quick as ye used to be,' he said, 'but I'm glad ye were here. Brother.'

'Me too. Brother,' said Zeus, and the two Gods embraced one another warmly.

'Proteus!' Poseidon called. 'I need ye to—'

'I know,' said Proteus, transforming back into the Shepherd of the Sea. 'I have it here.'

He produced the watch and walked hesitantly over to where Elliot was huddled in his blanket. Proteus crouched down and placed the watch in Elliot's palm.

'Be very, very careful with these,' he said, his faced lined with worry. 'You can't begin to imagine what they will do in the wrong hands.'

Not till much, much later did Virgo realize what Proteus was truly warning Elliot about. But in that moment, there was only one thing on Elliot's mind.

'I need to get home!' he cried, shaking off the blanket. 'Now.'

'C'mon then, sprat,' shouted Poseidon, striking the floor with his trident. 'What are ye waiting for?'

Immediately, water began to swirl around them, fizzing as if burning pokers had been plunged into it. A head of steam began to form on the surface, at first just a few droplets dancing above the water, but becoming bigger and denser with every drop of vapour until it formed a large cloud. It began to envelop them all, growing and growing until it lifted Elliot, Virgo, Zeus and Hypnos clean off the ground. For a moment everything was lost in a sea of white vapour. But then Virgo felt her whole body rising with the cloud into the air.

'See ye, landlubbers!' cried Poseidon, as the cloud burst through the bubble and up towards the surface. 'Ye know where to find me!'

And with a strong sea breeze, the friends were whisked away by the cloud towards Home Farm, Josie and whatever dangers lay in wait.

28. Daddy's Home

'Come on – we've got to go!' cried Elliot, as the cloud washed up on the banks of the River Avon early Wednesday morning. They'd been travelling all night, but Elliot only had one thing on his mind – getting Panacea's potion to Mum.

'No,' said Virgo firmly. She whistled for Charon. 'You go, I'll catch up with you later. There's something I have to do.'

'Like what?' shouted Elliot. 'We have to get back to Home Farm, to Mum ...'

'I know you do,' said Virgo, as the immortal ferryman burst out of the river before them. 'And

I must do this. I'll find you later. I promise.'

'Mornin' all,' said Charon cheerily. 'Nice to see someone! Business has been deader than a Daemon's doorknob lately. And me bin's not been collected this week. Where to?'

'Elysium please, Charon,' said Virgo. 'As fast as you can.'

'Virgo?' said Zeus.

'I can't explain now,' said Virgo. 'But I need to make the right choice.'

'Then get to it,' said Zeus softly. 'We'll see you later. Charon – lickety-split!'

'Right-o, guv,' said Charon. 'Next stop – Elysium!'

'So . . . see you then,' said Elliot.

'See you,' said Virgo quietly. 'Good luck.'

'You too.'

Elliot felt as if he had more to say. But before he could find the words, the Ship of Death whisked Virgo away down the river.

'Come on!' Elliot shouted again, speeding off towards Home Farm.

'Er – Elliot?' said Zeus, puffing to stay alongside him. 'What's the plan here?'

'I don't care,' said Elliot, quickening his pace. 'We just have to get to Mum and give her the potion before 11.17 this morning.'

'And then what?'

'And then – she and Dad will know what to do,' said Elliot firmly. 'Hurry up!'

Elliot sprinted on across the fields towards Home Farm, leaving Zeus behind. He hadn't mentioned Grandad's warning about Dave to anyone – what was the point? Grandad was mistaken. He had to be.

As he ran over the hill, Elliot saw in the distance a bulldozer knocking down the remains of Hephaestus's fence. Why would his dad do that? But this was no time for questions. His chest was aching from the pace, but he clutched the potion in his pocket. Everything was going to be OK.

He ran down the hill into the final field between him and his beloved home. Ignoring the protests of the builders, he leapt over the remnants of the fence and reached the front door, hammering on it with both fists.

'Dad!' he shouted. 'I'm home! Dad!'

He banged on the door until his fists ached. He didn't care if he had to punch through it. He was going to get to Mum.

'Dad! Please! Open up! Open this—'

The door slowly creaked open, to reveal Dave standing in the hallway.

'Dad!' Elliot panted in relief, throwing himself

across the threshold. 'Where's—'

'Now, now, now, Elliot,' said Dave, holding his son back and pushing him firmly back outside. 'Where are our manners?'

'Wh-what?' said Elliot, pulling the potion from his pocket. 'I've got it, I've got the potion – let's go and give it to Mum. Together . . .'

'I'm afraid that won't be possible,' said Dave slowly. Elliot waited for him to say more. But Dave merely folded his arms.

'I don't understand,' said Elliot, pushing to get past. 'I need to get—'

A firm shove from his father pushed Elliot back on to the path.

'Ow!' he cried, rubbing his chest. 'Dad – what are you doing?'

'I've told you, Elliot, you need to mind your manners,' said Dave coldly. 'You can't just come barging in here without asking.'

'Is this some kind of a joke?' Elliot laughed nervously. 'Because I'll be honest, Dad, it's not very—'

'Can we just stop with the whole "Dad" thing?' sighed Dave. 'We don't really know each other. I think it's best we stay on first-name terms. It's not like we're going to be seeing much of each other anyway . . .'

Elliot didn't understand. What did he mean? Then, for the first time, Elliot noticed his father's bag in the hallway.

'Where are you going?' he asked weakly. 'When will you be back?'

'I won't,' said Dave plainly. 'You see, this whole deal – the family, the farm, the fatherhood – I've come to realize it's just not for me . . .'

'But . . . you . . .' Elliot fought the tears gathering in his eyes.

'No hard feelings, mate,' winked Dave. 'And, like I promised, I've taken care of everything.'

Elliot brushed his tears away.

'Let me in,' he said. 'I need to see my mum.'

'What the bally heck is going on?' panted Zeus, limping up the path behind Elliot. 'Let us in, David, there's a good chap.'

'No can do,' said Dave, picking up his bag and slinging it over his shoulder. 'You see, it's not my house to let you into. But the new owner has very kindly agreed to take you on . . .'

'What?' said Elliot. 'What are you talking about? What new owner? And where's Mum?'

'Oh, dearie me, pickle,' piped a shrill voice behind Dave. 'As your new legal guardian, we're going to have to work on your behaviour.'

The door opened a little further to reveal the

triumphant face of Patricia Porshley-Plum. Elliot felt his fingers wrap around the Chaos Stones in his pocket.

'Legal guardian?' blundered Zeus. 'Don't make me . . .'

The King of the Gods fell silent as Dave Hooper dropped the front door keys into Patricia's grabbing hand and tossed the legal paperwork at Zeus.

'Pleasure doing business with you, Mrs Porshley-Plum,' said Dave, shaking her hand. 'I hope you'll be very happy in your new home. If not with your new son.'

Elliot's stomach filled with burning rage. His dad had betrayed him. His dad had betrayed Mum. And Elliot had stood by and let him.

'You – you – you . . . TRAITOR!' screamed Elliot, launching himself at his father. 'I trusted you! You said you'd take care of everything!'

With a swift lunge, Dave Hooper sent him sprawling on his backside on the path.

'RIGHT, THAT'S IT!' roared Zeus, unsheathing a thunderbolt. 'I'm going to teach you a lesson you'll never forget . . .'

'Uh, uh, uh,' said Dave, waggling a finger in Zeus's face, unmoved by the ferocity of the immortal. 'Sacred Code, remember. You can't hurt

315

me or you'll lose your kardia. I've been paying attention.'

There was a tense moment as Zeus stood poised with his thunderbolt aimed at Dave's heart. Elliot watched the King of the Gods stare murderously at his father.

'I wouldn't waste it on you anyway,' he said finally, slowly sheathing the thunderbolt and helping Elliot up. 'You're evil. No father turns his back on his family. You don't deserve him.'

'No,' said Dave. 'I just don't want him. See ya.'

He barged past Zeus and, without a backwards glance, set off across the fields, taking the last of Elliot's happiness with him.

'Well, now – I knew there was something strange about you,' Patricia said to Zeus. 'Let's see what the authorities make of you and your family of freaks. You'll never be allowed near the boy again . . .'

'Where is she?' Elliot said, as steadily as he was able. Patricia would have to wait. He needed to find his mum.

'Where she should have been months ago,' said Patricia dismissively. 'In the hospital. Best place for her, really. In her . . . condition.'

Elliot's heart froze. The hospital? He had to get to her. Now.

'We have to go,' he cried to Zeus. 'Come on.'

'Oh, no, you can't go!' trilled Patricia. 'We must have some lunch. What are you going to cook for me?'

'Madam – mark my words,' said Zeus, more menacingly than Elliot had ever heard him speak before. 'If it is the very last thing I do, I will see you pay for this. And trust me – I have all the time in the world.'

'Good,' said Patricia. 'You're going to need it. Home Farm is mine. Elliot is mine. And there's nothing anyone can do about it.'

'We have to get to the hospital!' shouted Elliot, starting back up the path.

'You'll keep,' said Zeus, before turning and running after Elliot.

'You can run, my little muffin, but you can't hide,' Patricia called after Elliot. 'You're mine now. And I'm going to make sure you get everything you deserve.'

And with Patricia's triumphant laughter burning his ears, Elliot raced off to save his mum.

317

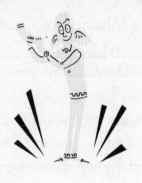

29. Council of War

'**T**his has to stop! NOW!'

Virgo's words echoed around the council chamber like a ricocheting bullet.

'Whatever are you bellyaching about, child?' roared Taurus. 'Is this about the dishwasher-emptying rota again? We've told you before, as the youngest Councillor, it's only right you do it four times more often than your senior colleagues . . .'

'The Titans!' Virgo panted. 'Cole's Law! The detentions! All of it! You have to stop it!'

The Councillors peered intently at Virgo. Excellent. They were taking her concerns seriously.

The chamber filled with peals of laughter. Maybe not.

'Stop it?' said Pisces. 'Why on Elysium would we stop it? Cole's Law couldn't have been more successful! All the dangerous immortals are contained. The threat to our security is all but neutralized. And our opinion ratings have never been higher.'

He threw a graph towards Virgo.

'Zero?' read Virgo.

'I know – marvellous, isn't it!' bleated Aries. 'With all the Elementals in Tartarus, there's no one to participate in the opinion polls. We've never been so popular! And just look at this report in the *Daily Argus*. Sums it all up perfectly, I think.'

Virgo took the paper and read it aloud.

COUNCIL MATTERS
BY PLINY, POLITICAL EDITOR

The new world is safer! A triumph we think
Those rogue Elementals locked up in the clink
Now all decent beings can go through their day
Safe in the knowledge the duds are at bay
All hail the Council! A wonderful measure
Protecting the freedoms we rightfully treasure
We'd happily list how the Council has blessed us
But two great big Titans have come to arrest us . . .

Virgo felt a new sensation bubble up inside her. It was sort of . . . hot – burning hot, even – and it was rapidly spreading from the pit of her stomach, up through her chest and surging into her mouth as if it were volcanic lava.

'NO!' she shouted, throwing the newspaper on the floor and stamping her foot.

The Councillors stopped dead and stared at her in disbelief. No laughing this time. She would remember this tactic for other confrontations. It was clearly very effective.

'Whatever do you mean, "no"?' said Sagittarius. 'No, what?'

'Just no!' said Virgo, stamping her foot again. This really did feel most optimal. 'No to the injustice! No to the imprisonment! No to the . . . just NO!'

'But you voted,' said Aquarius.

'Then I want to unvote!' cried Virgo. 'This isn't right!'

'Don't be absurd,' said Cancer. 'You can't unvote! This is the law!'

'Then the law is STUPID!' yelled Virgo. 'And if you won't change it, I need to find someone who will!'

The Councillors drew breath as one.

'Are you threatening us?' whispered Pisces.

'Not threatening,' said Virgo, searching for the optimal phrasing. 'Just . . . informing you that I will take undesirable actions if you don't do as I ask. I know, for instance, that Zeus is highly displeased . . .'

'What is the meaning of this?' roared Taurus. 'I don't understand!'

'That's just it!' cried Virgo. 'You don't understand! You don't understand anything! You don't understand life on Earth! You live up here on your cloud and you have no idea what it's really like! So life on Earth is bizarre. Some individuals are unkind, others are unhygienic – and, yes, maybe some are dangerous. There are strange habits and customs, many I don't understand. Why must one pledge allegiance to a football team, even when it is sub-optimal? Why are all the worst insults prefaced by "with all due respect"? And what is the point of morris dancing? Mortals disagree about everything – and some disagreements are so bad they hurt each other. But my observations tell me that most individuals on Earth want to be happy. They want other people to be happy. They might not talk to each other on the train, but when something goes wrong they fall over themselves to give money, time, even their own blood, to help. They might never meet their next-door neighbour, but when they hear of strangers in trouble somewhere else in the world, they organize walks, runs or bathe in baked beans to help. There are so many good, kind mortals – far more than bad. They love. They laugh. They like it there. Earth is thoroughly sub-optimal. And yet, the more time I spend there, I have come to believe that it is . . . sort of . . . strangely . . . perfect.'

She took a deep breath. Where had that come from?

The Council was dumbstruck.

'I see,' said Taurus slowly. 'Now I think we all understand.'

Virgo exhaled slowly and silently congratulated herself. Reason would always win the day. She was, after all, entirely right. Again.

'So what do we do?' she said eventually.

'Oh, I think we're all agreed,' said Taurus, looking around at his colleagues for support. They nodded gravely.

'Excellent,' said Virgo. 'I'm ready.'

'Good,' said Taurus, rising slowly to his feet. A huge shadow fell over Virgo. She didn't remember

Taurus being that tall.

'Virgo, Councillor of the Zodiac and former Guardian of the Stationery Cupboard,' he began. 'It is the finding of this Council that you pose a clear and present threat to the security of our world.'

'That's an excellent . . . What?!' Virgo cried. 'I'm sorry, I must have misheard you, I have this beetle in my brain . . .'

'At these times of heightened security, we cannot take any risks with public safety,' Taurus continued.

'Wait – you can't think that I . . . that I would ever . . . You're not seriously suggesting . . .' Virgo floundered as the shadow spread across the chamber.

'Therefore, it is with a heavy heart, that under section 156dolphinThursday7a of Cole's Law, you will be detained in Tartarus until further notice.'

'Don't be ridiculous!' cried Virgo, feeling her eyes starting to sting. 'I am completely—'

A huge net fell over her head.

'What are you . . . ?'

Virgo turned around and found herself staring up at the gigantic forms of the Titans.

'Gotcha,' said The Ram. 'Told you I'd teach you some manners.'

323

'No! Let me out!' Virgo screamed, pulling at the mesh of the net. 'I haven't done anything wrong!'

'Yet,' said Pisces. 'Virgo – this is for your own good. You will be released as soon as the present threat is over. Although who knows when that might be?'

Virgo tugged and tore at the net, but it was no good. She was trapped.

'And I believe that concludes your contract with us,' said Taurus to the Titans. 'As per the terms of our agreement, you may return to Tartarus, where you will be allowed to co-mingle with your fellow prisoners and enjoy greater privileges than in your previous confinement. We thank you for your service and wish you well. Goodbye.'

'Aren't you forgetting something?' said The Ram, pointing to the golden band around his ankle.

'Ah, yes – of course,' said Cancer, jangling a set of keys. 'Stay still.'

She unlocked first The Ram's, then The Brain's golden fetters.

The moment the ankle bands were taken off the Titans, a strange transformation began. Virgo watched in terrified silence – they had been big before, but as soon as they were released they began to grow . . . bigger. The muscles that had bulged from their arms strained and inflated before her eyes. And their eyes . . . their eyes turned a deep shade of blood red.

'Th-th-there you go,' stammered Cancer, cowering in their shadow. 'You are free to leave. Sort of.'

'Mind how you go,' gulped Taurus. He returned to his seat and shuffled his paperwork.

The Titans didn't move.

'Uh . . . as I said, the Council thanks you for your service and wishes you well. You can use the elevator. And kindly take Ms Virgo with you.'

Virgo looked at the Titans. They were still motionless.

'Is there something else?' said Cancer eventually.

'No,' said The Ram.

'Well, then . . . off you go,' said Aries. 'Safe trip.'

Once again, the Titans stayed exactly where they were.

'I'm sorry – have we not made ourselves clear?' said Aquarius. 'What are you waiting for?'

'Further instructions,' said The Ram.

'There are none,' said Pisces. 'Your work here is done. Now please leave.'

'OK, thanks,' said The Brain, but his brother grabbed his arm.

'Sorry, fish-face,' said The Ram. 'We don't answer to you.'

'Oh, yes you do,' snorted Taurus, rising from his seat in a fury. 'We were quite clear – you do this for us and we will downgrade your sentence. If you're not very careful, you will be returned to solitary confinement, where you belong!'

'I don't think so,' said The Ram, flexing his enormous biceps. 'You see – we've had a better offer.'

'A better – what on Earth are you talking about?' roared Taurus. 'You answer to us.'

'Not any more,' said The Ram, as the elevator bell pinged through the chamber. 'We've got a new boss now.'

'A new boss!' Taurus raged. 'Whoever would have the presumption ...'

'Hello, everyone,' drawled a languid voice from the lift. 'Long time.'

Bound by her net, Virgo was unable to see the new arrival. But the voice was painfully familiar.

'Thanatos!' said the Council as one.

The Daemon of Death stalked to the centre of the chamber and bowed slightly.

'Titans – arrest that Daemon immediately!'

Taurus commanded.

The Titans stomped towards Thanatos. But when they reached him, they merely took their places either side of him and crossed their almighty arms.

'Oh, how embarrassing,' chuckled Thanatos. 'Didn't you get the memo? The Titans work for me now.'

'No, they do not!' spluttered Pisces. 'We had a deal!'

'Not really,' said Thanatos. 'You see, I spoke to the Titans too. But my terms were better. You merely offered to upgrade their imprisonment. I offered them their freedom.'

'Er – I think you've rather forgotten something, Thanatos!' said Taurus. 'We're in charge around here! And you're a wanted fugitive!'

'Ah, yes – thank you so much for reminding me!' smiled Thanatos. 'You're quite right, of course. We can't have both of us trying to run the show now, can we?'

'Precisely,' said Taurus. 'Imprisonment is the only option.'

'I couldn't agree more,' said Thanatos. 'Titans?'

'Yes, boss?' said The Ram.

'Seize the Councillors.'

'Our pleasure,' said the Titans together, and

advanced on the Councillors with their nets.

'What is the meaning – what do you think you're doing?' roared Taurus. 'You have no authority here!'

'Oh, I think you'll find I do,' said Thanatos, pulling the Sacred Code from the shelf. 'You wrote the amendment here yourself: *Any immortal posing a threat to security can be detained in Tartarus indefinitely without trial*. It doesn't say by whom ...'

'You can't do this!' said Pisces. 'We've done nothing wrong! We're here to protect the immortal community.'

'Tsk,' whispered Thanatos. 'I've got several thousand Elementals who don't entirely agree. They're rather miffed with you, I'm afraid.'

'You can't put us down there with them!' said Aquarius.

'You're quite right – and I have no intention of doing any such thing,' said Thanatos. 'As tremendous good fortune would have it, now that the Titans have been released, a solitary confinement facility has just become vacant in the deepest depths of Tartarus. I think you'll find it very cosy.'

The Titans caught the Councillors in their nets and dumped them in the lift.

'The Gods won't let this happen,' Virgo said,

struggling in her net. 'We've got three Chaos Stones. They'll come for you.'

'I'm counting on it,' said Thanatos. 'In fact, I anticipate a visit from your friend Elliot any time now. Then I will have everything I need.'

'You'll never take the Chaos Stones from him!' declared Virgo.

'Oh, I won't have to,' said Thanatos, plucking a grape from the table. 'Elliot Hooper is going to hand them to me himself. And then your precious Gods will finally get precisely what they deserve.'

Sweeping the Council's paperwork off the golden table, Thanatos climbed up and stood in the centre.

'Hear me now!' he proclaimed, his voice reverberating around the glass pyramid. 'I, Thanatos, Daemon of Death, King of the Daemons, declare war on the Olympians! I will not cease to fight until their tyranny is overthrown. I, your rightful ruler, take command of the Earth and everyone in it. This is my solemn vow. And I dare anyone to stop me!'

Virgo yelled at him from the elevator: 'They'll stop you! Elliot and the Gods – they will defeat you!'

'I'll enjoy watching them try,' smiled Thanatos. 'Goodbye, young Virgo. I doubt we'll be seeing each other again.'

And with that, the elevator doors slammed shut and Virgo felt herself plummet through the endless darkness to Tartarus.

30. Free at Last

Josie Hooper was ready. For too long she had been trapped within her own body. She needed to be free. And it was nearly time. She could feel it.

But before she could go anywhere, she needed to know that her Elly was safe.

She tried to smile at the sisters. They had refused to leave her, even when the doctors and nurses tried to force them from the bedside.

'If you lay a single finger on me, no medicine in the world will save you!' the blonde one had cried. Josie liked this girl so very much. She reminded her a great deal of herself.

Josie looked around the strange white room again, trying to find something – anything – that she recognized. There was a bed and a bathroom. That was all. It wasn't her home. The only thing that she knew was hers was the patchwork quilt. She remembered stitching it with her mother-in-law when she was getting married.

'This'll keep you safe and warm,' Audrey had said as they sat and sewed for hours. And Audrey was right. Even in this strange place, Josie felt safe and warm beneath it.

The dark-haired sister held her hand and started to sob softly.

'We will take care of him,' she said. 'I swear it. We will be his family.'

Josie could no longer speak, but she hoped that her eyes conveyed her thanks. These were good people. They loved her Elly. He'd be safe with them.

She felt herself start to float away again. No. Josie fought back. She needed to stay. She needed to see her boy. But it was hard, so hard not to go ...

'*Hush, little baby, don't you cry,*' came a voice, pure and clear. It was the blonde sister. '*Mama's gonna sing you a lullaby.*'

Josie didn't know if it reached her lips, but she smiled inside. She loved this song. It always helped her to sleep well.

The dark-haired sister joined in harmony:

'*Hush, little baby, don't say a word.*

Mama's gonna buy you a mockingbird.

And if that mockingbird don't sing,

Mama's gonna buy you a diamond ring.'

The music rang through Josie and her soul joined in. She had to go. It was her time. She began to float, leaving the shackles of her body behind . . .

'Mum!'

The voice hit Josie like a tidal wave. It was him. It was her boy.

'Mum!'

She felt Elliot throw his arms around her. He was safe.

Josie smiled with peaceful relief. Now she could take her leave.

'Mum – you have to . . .'

But Josie had already begun her journey. As she let herself float away, her soul sang out to her beloved little boy:

'*So hush, little baby, don't you cry.*

Daddy still loves you and so do I.'

And with a calm, smiling breath, Josie Hooper was finally free.

31. Broken

Elliot walked numbly out of the hospital, past Hypnos quietly waiting outside. Words and phrases washed around him – 'nothing you could have done', 'incurable', 'only a matter of time'. He didn't know who said them and he didn't care.

Mum was gone.

The only voice he could hear was the one in his one head. That one was loud and clear: '*You failed.*'

'Come on, Elly – let's go,' said Aphrodite, her tear-stained face smiling into his. 'We're going home.'

'Home?' he said in a daze. 'I don't have a home.'

'You have ours,' said Zeus, not taking his eyes from Elliot. 'Mount Olympus. Hephaestus will be waiting for us.'

Elliot knew the Gods were waiting for a response. He had nothing. He couldn't imagine ever feeling anything ever again.

'Let's get you somewhere safe,' said a trembling Athene. 'Something to eat, somewhere to sleep. We'll figure everything out later.'

'She's right,' said Aphrodite, putting her arm around Elliot's shoulders. 'You are exhausted. You must rest.'

'We'll get your house back from that accursed Horse's-Bum if it's the last thing we do,' said Zeus. 'And she'll never get her hands on you. Don't you worry about that.'

'And we'll sort everything out, so you don't have to,' said Athene. 'We'll make all the . . . arrangements – you just focus on you.'

'So let's go, sweetie,' said Aphrodite, pulling his hand. 'Let us take care of you.'

Elliot stayed rooted to the spot, staring blankly into space.

'No,' he said quietly.

'Sorry, old boy?' said Zeus.

'I said – no!' spat Elliot, yanking his hand free

of Aphrodite's.

'Elliot?' said Athene. 'We completely understand how you're feeling . . .'

'You do, do you?' hissed Elliot. 'You – who live
in a family where no one has ever died – you
understand how I'm feeling right now, do you?
DO YOU?'

'Elliot – I'm sorry, that was a stupid thing
to say,' said Athene, trying to take his hand. 'Of
course we don't understand, we just—'

'You just NOTHING!' cried Elliot. 'You did
NOTHING! You swore you'd look after her . . .'

'Elly – we tried, I swear on the Styx, we tried
everything,' pleaded Aphrodite, her eyes filling
with fresh tears.

'Well, you should have tried harder!' shouted
Elliot. 'What use are all your powers, all your
stupid gadgets, all your endless lives, if you couldn't
save my mum when she needed you?!'

'Elliot,' said Zeus. 'There was nothing anyone
could have done. It was her time . . .'

'Time?' said Elliot. 'Her time? No – it was *your*
time that was the problem. We wasted so much
time on stupid Chaos Stones and thunderbolts
and your stupid fight with your stupid brother
that it stole her time! We missed it because of you!
What was the point of this – getting this . . . stupid

potion if we weren't going to get here in time?'

He pulled out the vial containing Panacea's potion and hurled it into a nearby dustbin.

'Elliot,' said Zeus, taking hold of his shoulders. 'There are some things that no magic can change. It isn't fair. It is desperately, cruelly unfair. But it is no one's fault. Especially not yours.'

'Don't pretend you care!' Elliot snarled, wriggling free. 'You never cared about me or my mum! You just cared about your stupid Chaos Stones!'

'Elliot, that simply isn't true,' said Athene, her dark eyes full of tears. 'You're so hurt, please let us help you ...'

There was an eternal pause as Elliot considered his next move.

'OK,' he said at last. 'There is something you can do.'

'Anything,' sobbed Aphrodite, taking his hand.

Elliot stared deep into the eyes of the King of the Gods.

'Give me my mum back,' he said calmly.

The Gods looked helplessly at one another. Zeus sighed from the depths of his soul.

'I would give anything to be able to,' Zeus said softly. 'But you know I can't.'

Elliot nodded.

'Please listen to me, Elliot,' said Zeus. 'Your

mother's destiny was already written, long before we met you. No one could change that.'

'I thought you didn't believe in destiny,' said Elliot darkly. 'You believe in choices. And now, my choice is clear. Hypnos?'

The Daemon nodded his head.

'You want to be on the winning side?'

'Always,' said the Daemon quietly.

'Then take me to Thanatos.'

'Elliot – no!' cried Athene. 'If you go to Thanatos, you'll lose everything. We all will.'

'Tell me,' said Elliot, turning to face them. 'I've lost my home. I've lost my dad. I've lost . . . I've lost my mum. What else have I got to lose?'

He watched the Gods search in vain for an answer.

'Well, then,' he said. He turned his cold eyes to Hypnos. 'You coming?'

The Daemon of Sleep turned towards Zeus and said something to him that Elliot couldn't hear. But it certainly had an effect on the King of the Gods.

'Elliot – please,' cried Zeus, suddenly running over and grabbing hold of him.

'GET AWAY FROM ME!' roared Elliot, yanking the Chaos Stones from his pocket and aiming their mystical beams into the air. At once, the

Earth began to tremble and a cold wind started to blow. A storm cloud thundered above.

The King of the Gods held him for a moment, his eyes boring into Elliot's. Elliot sensed he was trying to speak to him, to enter his thoughts one last time. But Elliot's mind was too full of pain to hear anything Zeus had to say.

After an interminable few moments, Zeus released him, his hands raised in surrender.

'Elliot,' he said calmly. 'If you go to Thanatos, you will be beyond our reach.'

'I know,' Elliot snarled. 'Sounds like the best place to be.'

And with that he allowed the Daemon of Sleep to scoop him up high into the air, far away from the outstretched arms of the Gods.

32. Home Sweet Home

Pegasus landed gently in the centre of the Great Hall.

'Here we are,' said Zeus quietly. 'Home sweet home.'

Pegasus had answered the call of his master's thunderbolt and had brought the Gods back to Mount Olympus, which sat in a realm of its own beyond the clouds.

It had been many centuries since the Gods last spent time on the mythical mountain – and it showed. The vast golden hall that once rang with the feasting of the Olympians now sat quiet and empty, cobwebs drifting in the room that had resounded with music and dancing. Paintings of the Gods' greatest adventures adorned the walls, but they were faded and old. A long, dusty bronze table ran down the centre of the room, lined with fourteen chairs. Those seats had been unoccupied for too long.

'Do you believe it?' Athene asked her father. 'What Hypnos said to you back there?'

'I never believe a word a Daemon says,' growled Zeus. 'But Hypnos promised he'd protect Elliot. What choice do we have?'

'Where's Hephy?' said Aphrodite. 'I want to see Hermes.'

'I'm here,' said a gruff voice behind them. 'And so's he.'

Hephaestus took one look at his immortal friends.

'You look like you've dropped a mina and found an obal,' he said. 'What's going on? Where's the boy?'

Zeus shook his head solemnly. His comrade of many millennia understood perfectly.

'I'm so sorry,' said the God of the Forge quietly. 'I hoped it wouldn't end like this.'

'It hasn't ended yet,' said Zeus. 'Did you find them? All of them?'

'Every last one,' said Hephaestus. 'They're

waiting for your signal.'

Zeus nodded gravely. This was their last hope.

'How is Hermes?' said Athene.

'The same,' said Hephaestus. 'No better. But no worse.'

'Take us to him,' said Zeus.

The immortal blacksmith nodded and limped out of the hall, followed by his friends.

They climbed the mighty spiral staircase which led to the chambers of the Olympians. They approached the door with a tortoiseshell insignia surrounded by wings, and pushed it gently open.

There, in his satin bed, at the centre of a golden chamber decorated with portraits of its occupant, lay Hermes. Athene rushed to his side.

'We're home,' she said softly.

'Hi there, old boy,' said Zeus, holding Hermes's hand. 'How the devil are you?'

Aphrodite held back.

'Aren't you going to come and say hello?' said Zeus.

Aphrodite looked uncharacteristically sheepish.

'If I tell you something, Daddy – you have to promise not to get cross,' she said.

'This is no time for anger,' smiled Zeus. 'What have you done now, my pearl?'

Aphrodite closed her bright blue eyes and

pulled her right hand from behind her back. Between her thumb and forefinger was Panacea's potion.

'Where did you get that?' gasped Athene.

'I went through the bin,' said Aphrodite.

'That was for Josie,' said Zeus quietly.

'I know,' said Aphrodite. 'And we couldn't save her. But we can save Hermy.'

'That wasn't made for Gods,' said Athene. 'It was for mortals.'

'And unless we defeat Thanatos, there won't be any left!'

'That's not the point,' snapped Athene.

'It's entirely the point!' shouted Aphrodite. 'Elliot is taking the Chaos Stones to Thanatos! There will be a war! And in case you haven't noticed, we're not exactly overrun with volunteers here! We need Hermes! The mortals need all of us!'

'We don't even know if it works,' said Athene. 'I, for one, remain entirely sceptical . . .'

'Yer sister's right,' said Hephaestus softly. 'Senseless it going to waste. We're gonna need all hands to the plough.'

'Josie loved Hermy,' said Aphrodite, her eyes filling with tears again. 'If she couldn't have it, she'd want him to have it. He's our best chance of getting Elly back. Josie would understand that.'

Zeus looked at his son lying lifelessly on the bed. This was the only way. He nodded his permission.

Aphrodite walked slowly to Hermes's side. She gave him a soft kiss on his cheek and stroked his head.

'Come back to us, Hermy,' she whispered. 'We need you.'

She pulled the cork out of the phial and held it to her brother's lips. With a deep breath, she poured the golden liquid into his mouth.

No one dared take so much as the faintest breath as they watched Hermes to see what would happen. The seconds piled on top of one another, the tension in the room the only evidence that anyone was there at all.

'I told you so,' said Athene, finally shattering the silence. 'It's a hoax, Panacea's last joke on us all. Why, I bet right now she's in the Isles of the Blessed having a good old chuckle at us for being so—'

'Look!' cried Aphrodite, pointing at Hermes with a shaking hand.

'What?' Athene said.

'Look!' growled Aphrodite. 'There!'

Athene looked from Hermes's face to his chest.

Almost indiscernible to the naked eye was the tiniest golden speck, right above his heart.

'What is it?' whispered Zeus.

'I don't know,' said Athene. 'Maybe it's ...'

'Bbbbbbb ...' Hermes started to mumble.

Aphrodite and Athene grabbed each other in shock.

'H-he's trying to say something,' gasped Aphrodite.

'I know – shhhh!' said Athene, leaning closer. 'It's OK, Hermy, what are you trying to tell us?'

'Bbbbbbbbbbbbb ...' Hermes mumbled again.

'I don't understand,' said Athene, turning to her family. 'Perhaps he's been unconscious too long? Perhaps there's some permanent damage? Perhaps ...'

'What is he saying?' said Zeus, rubbing his tearful eyes.

Hermes's eyes suddenly flew open.

'Perhaps you lot should get a hearing aid. COS I SAID ... BBBBBBBBBOOM!'

And, like a bullet from a gun, Hermes rocketed out of his bed in a shower of golden light. He zoomed around the room like a thunderbolt, whooping with delight as his family cheered.

'MAAAAAAATE!' he cried, as he hovered above their heads, cracking his neck. 'Not being funny . . . BUT THE H-BOMB IS BACK!'

'My boy!' gasped Zeus, tears rolling down his face. 'My brilliant, brilliant boy . . .'

Athene and Aphrodite cried and danced and hugged each other as Hermes whizzed around the room in his feathered slippers. Even Hephaestus, from the corner of the room, allowed himself a small smile.

'BANG, BOOM, BANG AND A DOUBLE PORTION OF BOSH!' yelled Hermes, turning cobwebs into party streamers and dust into confetti.

The Gods celebrated a moment of pure, long-awaited joy as they were reunited with their beloved Hermes. It was good to have a reason to smile again.

After a few more circuits of the room – and more than a few admiring glances at himself – Hermes finally came back to Earth.

'So where's E? Where's J-Hoops?'

His iGod started to ring inside the suitcase that Don'tcAIR had finally returned. 'Actually, not being funny, but where am I?'

'Where's yer trousers?' said Hephaestus in disgust, throwing a pair of jeans at the Messenger God, who was standing there in his pants.

'It's the school,' said Athene, wiping the tears

from her eyes. 'I'd forgotten I redirected the Home Farm number to the iGod. Heaven knows what I'm going to tell them ... Yes ... This is Elliot Hooper's ... aunt. What's that?'

'You'd better sit down, son,' said Zeus. 'We have a lot of catching up to do.'

'Mate?' said Hermes, sitting back down on the bed anxiously. 'Why do I feel like I've just done a high-intensity workout after a night on the vindaloo? This don't end well, does it?'

'But that makes no sense,' said Athene down the phone. 'Are you sure?'

The Gods froze, concerned by the alarm in Athene's voice.

'Of course,' said the Goddess of Wisdom. 'Please let me know anything the second you do.'

'What was that all about?' said Aphrodite. 'You look like you've seen your own reflection.'

'That was Ms Givings, the welfare officer from Brysmore,' said Athene, her hand trembling. 'It's about David Hooper.'

'What about him?' growled Zeus. 'Good-for-nothing wastrel!'

The Goddess of Wisdom looked unusually lost for words.

'He's being released from prison today,' she finally said.

'You're a couple of olives short of a tree,' said Aphrodite. 'He's been with us for weeks.'

'Exactly,' said Athene. 'Ms Givings was waiting for an email from him about his parole officer. When it didn't arrive, she started to do her own checks. She's just discovered that David Hooper is still in prison. She was calling to warn us not to let the man we know anywhere near Elliot.'

'Not being funny, but what are you all on about?' said Hermes. 'Can someone please explain what the bamboozled bosh is going on?'

Zeus, Aphrodite and Athene stared at one another in horror.

'Elliot's father,' said Athene, looking at a shaking Zeus, 'is not who we thought he was.'

'So, wait a second . . . if Dave Hooper has been in prison all this time,' said Aphrodite, 'who's been living with Elliot?'

Athene shook her head slowly.

'More to the point,' said Hermes, shooting up from his bed and grabbing a sword from the wall, 'who the blinking anti-bosh is with Elliot now?'

33. Devil in Disguise

'**W**ell, I'm delighted to have you on the team,' said Thanatos, reclining on his throne of bones in the Underworld.

'I'm not on anyone's team,' said Elliot. 'This is purely business. I don't care what you do with them. I just want her back.'

'Of course,' said Thanatos. 'I am the Daemon of Death. My offer still stands. In fact, I'm now the only person who can give you your mother back. Find me the Fire Stone, hand the others over, and I will return her soul to you. Escort it back to Earth and she's yours, exactly how she was.'

'You swear it on the Styx,' said Elliot.

'I swear it on the Styx,' said Thanatos.

'Because if you are double-crossing me again . . .'

'Why would I do that?' said the Daemon of Death. 'The time for playing games is over. You have what I want most in the world. I have what you want most in the world. It's in our mutual interest to work together.'

Elliot nodded blankly.

'I need somewhere to stay,' he said plainly.

'I have had quarters prepared for you,' smiled Thanatos. 'I had a feeling you might come to me tonight. My associates can show you the way.'

Thanatos clicked his fingers and the Titans came to the door.

'Fine,' said an exhausted Elliot, and stood to follow the Titans.

Thanatos waited for the door to close behind Elliot. Everything was perfect. He turned his gaze to his grinning brother. Hypnos looked insufferably smug.

'So . . . looks like I've managed to do what you and Mumsy couldn't,' he chirped. 'I brought you the boy.'

'The boy brought himself,' Thanatos glowered. 'You did nothing.'

'We still have a deal,' said Hypnos. 'If I kill the child, you can't kill me. As far as I'm concerned, nothing's changed. Once he gets the Fire Stone — assuming that doesn't do the job for me — he's toast. We're allies.'

'Oh, I've had a much better ally than you,' smirked Thanatos. 'In fact, I'm expecting them any second ...'

There was a knock at the chamber door.

'Enter!' Thanatos called.

The door creaked open. His guest walked in with a self-satisfied sneer. Hypnos gasped.

'The boy is here?' said the new arrival.

'He is,' nodded Thanatos.

'What are you ...' Hypnos began, completely at a loss for words.

'You see?' Dave Hooper smiled at Thanatos. 'I told you it would work. Everything has gone like clockwork.'

'Go on, then,' sighed Thanatos. 'Take your moment ...'

'Oh, if you insist,' said Dave, slumping down in a chair. 'Of course some of it was just fun, really — releasing the gorgon and reactivating the magical devices on the day the welfare officers visited was just sport. Especially pushing the mother in that pond ...'

'You're a devil,' chuckled Thanatos. 'You always were.'

351

'Wait,' said Hypnos. 'How do you know him?'

'But selling the house, leaving him with that braying harpy – that was where the real genius of my plan bore fruit,' continued Dave. 'The boy has nothing. He has no one. He's ours.'

'You were right, of course,' conceded the Daemon of Death. 'We're ready. The Elementals are ready to fight. The Titans are free from their bonds. The boy will find the Fire Stone and then ...'

Thanatos allowed his satisfied smirk to say the rest. He turned to Hypnos.

'And so, brother dearest. You need to take the boy to the Fire Stone and make sure he gets it. After that, I want him gone. He dares to think he can barter with me, the King of the Daemons? No one defies me. You'd better remember that too. And you'd better be abundantly clear which side you're on.'

'The winning one,' grinned Hypnos. 'Always.'

'We start tomorrow,' said Dave. 'The Gods are in disarray and the boy is still vulnerable. We need to act fast. We need to—'

'Oh, will you sort yourself out?' snapped Thanatos. 'I can't take you seriously looking like that.'

Hypnos stared into Dave Hooper's dark green

eyes. Thanatos snorted as the realization hit his brother.

'Y-you mean . . . ? the Daemon of Sleep stuttered.

'Oh, all right,' said Dave. 'Although I was getting rather used to it . . .'

He stood up and clicked his fingers. Immediately, his body was enveloped by a thick black plume of smoke, from his feet to his head. Thanatos laughed at his brother's stunned face.

Because when the smoke cleared, Dave Hooper was gone. And, standing in his place, was his true form, stripped of the disguise worn ever since Dave Hooper set foot in Home Farm.

'And that, my boys,' said Nyx, unfurling her long black wings, 'is why you should always listen to your mother.'

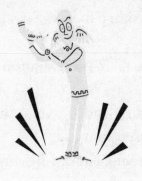

34. Dave Who?

All the worlds were Josie Hooper's to explore now that she was no longer constrained by a single one. There were no more boundaries, no bonds, nothing she couldn't see. Everything was clear to her now. Her soul could fly wherever it wanted. At last, she was truly free.

First she flew down to the Underworld, where she watched her son sob himself into a broken sleep. She wrapped her golden form around him. She knew in time he'd understand that this was the least painful path for them both. But he wasn't going to see that tonight. The way ahead was so complicated, it was no wonder he'd taken a wrong turn. But he'd find his way back, she knew he would.

'I will always be with you, Elliot,' she whispered into his sleeping ear. 'But you are going to need all your strength for the journey ahead. My love will feed your spirit. Sleep well.'

She kissed his sleeping head and floated away, sinking downwards, through the very essence of the Earth until she found Virgo, deep within the darkest confines of Tartarus. Virgo wasn't sleeping. She was looking for the way out. And Josie knew she wouldn't rest until she found it.

'Keep searching, my little star,' she said. 'Josie-Mum is with you and I know you'll find the way. My boy needs you to light his path. Keep fighting, brilliant girl.'

Josie gave her son's friend a golden hug, then floated up, high up through the clouds and beyond the bounds of mortal understanding. She flew to the very peak of Mount Olympus, soaring through the night until she saw them. The Gods were there. They were armed. They were ready for battle. They took five places at a table meant for fourteen. Above them was a giant beacon, to which every head was turned. Zeus looked at his family.

'Ready?' he asked them.

They all nodded their silent assent.

Dressed in the robes of Olympian royalty, Zeus unsheathed a thunderbolt and took aim at the heart of the beacon. With a strong and true arm, he hurled it, exploding the beacon into golden flame. A light burst into the sky, shattering the dark night. A sign, a golden thunderbolt burnished the darkness. It was a signal – a call to arms, a cry for help. But who was it for? Would it be answered? The Gods looked unsure. And Josie couldn't linger to find out.

Because she had to return home. To Earth. To Home Farm. To watch over the one person she knew for certain could save Elliot. The only other person who loved him like she did. The person who was even then wiping away painful, angry tears for them both.

He gathered his breath and knocked at the door.

Josie watched as Patricia Horse's-Bum strolled to the door – the door of Josie's home. It was all so clear now. Patricia's wickedness hung around her like a swarm of flies. What Josie wouldn't have given for one more hour in her body. What she wouldn't have done to that evil old pig-faced hag . . .

Patricia opened the door, a FOR SALE sign in her hand.

'Sorry, we're not interest—' she started, then took in the face before her. 'Oh, it's you again. What do you want?'

Josie watched as Dave Hooper – the true Dave, the husband she'd lost, the love of her life, her Elly's wonderful, loving father – looked this devil in the eye.

'I want to know what you've done with my son,' he said, jamming his foot in the door. 'I want to know what you did to my wife.'

'I . . . I . . . I . . .'

Patricia was lost for words. It was a welcome sight. Dave forced the door open further.

'Listen to me, Patricia Poshley-Plum,' he said, his eyes ablaze with anger. 'I want my son back. I want my home back. I want my life back. And make no mistake, you malevolent witch. I'm not going anywhere until I have them.'

THE END
(*Nearly . . .*)

What's What

ELLIOT HOOPER

Category: Mortal

Realm: Earth

Powers: 1) Current guardian of Earth and Air Stones
2) Hygiene avoidance

This thirteen-year-old mortal male has defied all probability to acquire two CHAOS STONES. The son of David and Josie Hooper, his Wiltshire farm is the present HQ for the Olympians. Scent: worryingly sub-optimal.

VIRGO

Category: Constellation (suspended)/Mortal (temporary?)

Realm: Earth (formerly Elysium)

Powers: 1) Constellation travel (suspended) 2) Stationery supplies

After a failed attempt to regain her kardia, Virgo remains trapped as a mortal. Determined to return to her former position on the Zodiac Council, Virgo is attempting to understand life on EARTH. And her companion, ELLIOT.

ZEUS

Category: Olympian, King of the Gods (retired)

Realm: Earth (wherever licensed for weddings)

Powers: 1) Omnipotent former ruler of creation 2) Wedding planning and cancellation

His Majesty the King of the Gods has been enjoying retirement, and multiple marriages, for over 2,000 years. Previously believed to have vanquished THANATOS, recent information suggests that his pants are, in fact, on fire.

HERMES

Category: Olympian, Messenger God

Realm: Various (excl. Underworld)

Powers: None at present. In coma from poison arrow wound.

One of few working Olympians, Hermes has retained his role delivering information around the immortal community. His responsibilities include communication, transformation and style icon (self-appointed).

ATHENE

Category: Olympian, Goddess of Wisdom

Realm: Earth

Powers: 1) Vast knowledge 2) Transformational powers 3) Handicrafts

Currently working as an esteemed Professor at St Brainiac College, Oxford, Athene has also enjoyed success on several mortal TV quiz shows. Can create any substance from another, but refuses to work with loom bands.

APHRODITE

Category: Olympian, Goddess of Love

Realm: Earth

Powers: 1) Ability to make anyone fall in love 2) She's just lovely . . .

The proprietor of Eros dating agency, Aphrodite exerts a powerful draw over everyone who meets her. This may be due to her immortal powers, or possibly the fact she's a drop-dead gorgeous hottie. I love you, Aphrodite.

HEPHAESTUS

Category: Olympian, God of the Forge

Realm: Earth

Powers: **Invention (esp. swear words)**

The Gods' go-to man for gadgets and gizmos, Hephaestus can fix or build anything. A man of few words, most of them 'Snordlesnot'.

PEGASUS

Category: **Elemental, but considers himself Olympian**

Realm: **Earth (usually above)**

Powers: **1) Flight 2) Crosswords**

The transport of choice for ZEUS, Pegasus is a flying horse with a sky-high opinion of himself.

THANATOS

Category: **Daemon (of Death), King of Daemons**

Realm: **Underworld**

Powers: **1) Strength 2) Touch of death (mortals only)**

Previously believed dead, Thanatos recently escaped from his prison beneath Stonehenge. Determined to regain his CHAOS STONES, Thanatos intends to cull mortalkind with natural disasters, then rule over them. Enjoys golf.

HYPNOS

Category: **Daemon (of Sleep)**

Realm: **Earth**

Powers: **1) Sleep, nightmares, insomnia, sleepwalking (with ivory trumpet) 2) Gambling**

Older twin of THANATOS, Hypnos evaded imprisonment with all other DAEMONS by betraying his brother to ZEUS. Only being who knows location of CHAOS STONES, which he hid at Zeus's behest. Currently under enchantment of his own sleep trumpet.

NYX

Category: Goddess (of the Night); Daemon by marriage and affinity
Realm: Underworld
Powers: 1) Power over the night sky 2) Dissembling 3) Flight

Mother of THANATOS and HYPNOS, Nyx went missing upon the death of her husband Erebus. Believed to have now reunited with her sons, Nyx's precise whereabouts are currently unknown.

CHARON

Category: Neutral, immortal ferryman
Realm: All
Powers: 1) Transport 2) Entrepreneur

The founder of Quick Styx Cabs, Charon can transport immortals to any realm (restrictions allowing) via the Ship of Death on the RIVER STYX. Also available for grocery delivery, courier work and children's parties.

CERBERUS

Category: Elemental
Realm: Underworld
Powers: Security

The three-headed hound of hell is responsible for security in Tartarus. Also, for financing his extensive family.

PATRICIA PORSHLEY-PLUM

Category: Mortal
Realm: Earth (whereabouts unknown)
Powers: 1) Deception 2) Lying 3) Fraud 4) Theft 5) Embezzlement 6) Arson 7) Twinsets

Former neighbour of ELLIOT, Mrs Porshley-Plum is determined to acquire his abode of Home Farm to develop the land for personal profit. Seems untroubled by usual mortal concerns of kindness, generosity and not being a horse's bum.

MR BOIL

Category: **Mortal**

Realm: **Earth**

Powers: 1) **Education (unconfirmed)** 2) **Weapons-grade bodily odour**

History teacher to ELLIOT, Mr Boil's chosen career is sub-optimal due to loathing of mortal children. Exudes a powerful aroma believed to be vegetable-based.

GRAHAM SOPWEED

Category: **Mortal (but you can Call Me Graham)**

Realm: **Earth**

Powers: **Unclear**

The headmaster of Brysmore Grammar School. It has yet to be established what Mr Sopweed's purpose is in mortal life.

———————

Places

ELYSIUM

Heavenly home of Zodiac Council. Not accessible to ELEMENTALS.

EARTH

Mortal realm. Very dirty.

ASPHODEL FIELDS

Formerly destination of aimless souls. Now shopping centre.

UNDERWORLD

DAEMON realm. Also home to Tartarus, eternal prison for the wicked. Not accessible to Gods.

RIVER STYX

Link between realms, accessed via CHARON and the Ship of Death. Also used to swear solemn oaths which, if broken, remove immortality.

Categories

DEITIES

Kardia: Precious metals: Gold (Olympians), Silver (Gods), Bronze (Heroes)
Highest order of immortality including Olympians, Gods and Heroes. Naturally imbued with great powers.

CONSTELLATIONS

Kardia: Crystal
The thirteen members of the Zodiac Council, charged with administering the immortal community.

NEUTRALS

Kardia: Glass
Rare immortals whose special gifts render them immune to other immortals' powers.

DAEMONS

Kardia: Onyx

Immortals with individual responsibility for human experience (e.g. Happiness, Luck, Wealth, Misery etc.). Require instruments to manifest powers. Currently imprisoned in Tartarus, except for THANATOS and HYPNOS.

ELEMENTALS

Kardia: Naturally occurring substances according to class, e.g. stone, wood, rock etc.

Any immortal entity not listed above. May have human, animal or fantastical form. Often used for manual labour.

Artefacts

CHAOS STONES

Four elemental gems with potent powers, given by Chaos to her son Erebus, Daemon of Darkness (former King of Daemons, deceased, father to THANATOS and HYPNOS). Earth Stone (diamond), Air Stone (emerald), Water Stone (ruby) and Fire Stone (sapphire). Current whereabouts of two are unknown – Earth Stone and Air Stone protected by ELLIOT.

KARDIA

Necklace worn by all immortals to denote Category and Class. Materials vary according to above, but all shaped like a heart within a flame.

The Third Thank-yous

I write these thanks at the end of a year that has seen the publication of my first two novels and the completion of my third. It has been a whirl-wind of a voyage and there are so many heroes who have helped me to navigate my authorial Odyssey.

I am indebted to Arts Council England, whose generous support has funded the time not only to write this book, but also to travel to groups who might not otherwise access the arts and work with them and their brilliant imaginations. I am beyond grateful for both opportunities.

I have been overwhelmed by the response to *Who Let the Gods Out?* and *Simply the Quest* and to everyone who has written, tweeted, reviewed and recommended the books; I cannot tell you what each and every one of your messages has meant to me. I must send my huge love to Steph (@eenalol) and Layla (@readable_life) whose rooftop shouting has warmed my heart many times this year. You are Goddesses, both.

The support of the education community for *WLTGO* has been humbling and it's been wonderful to connect with so many of you this year. My huge thanks to Ashley Booth for his early enthusiasm about the book, which I know has encouraged so many other schools to take a look. As someone who sees inside many schools, I am inspired by what you all do, if outraged by what is being done to you. The Author Army has your back – you are all complete heroes.

My wonderful publishers, Chicken House, are always on hand to navigate any stormy waters and I am for ever grateful for your brilliance. Barry, Rachel Hachel, Elinor, Anja (Mutti), Jazz, Laura S, Laura M, Kes, Esther and Sarah – thank you for everything you do for me; I would be a (ship)wreck without you.

I'm still struggling to adequately convey my thanks to my beloved editor, Rachel Leyshon, who I love like the memory of my size-eight figure. I'm conscious I'm running out of attempts, so let's try again: Rachel, you build me up and hold me together until I feel like nothing can get past me.

Leysh: you are my grouting.

My agent, Veronique – I adore you and appreciate every second of time and sanity you've given me this year. I just want to publicly declare that I am TOTALLY over the fact that you turned these books down in 2009. Seriously, I'm completely over it. Really wish you'd stop bringing it up . . .

But, as ever, my heart belongs to my beautiful family, who have kept me afloat during this crazy year. Sharing a home with an author is no pleasure cruise, so thank you for not tossing me overboard when I've been a sea-monster. This tome is dedicated to my daughter Lili, who is one of the kindest, sweetest, most fun people I know. And I get to be your mum. Lucky me.

I will see you all again in 2019, for the final instalment of Elliot and Virgo's adventures. Until then, I wish all my readers plain sailing and exciting adventures – thank you for taking me on this incredible journey.

Love, and other things that don't affect your statutory rights,

Maz
xxx

BEETLE BOY by M. G. LEONARD

Darkus can't believe his eyes when a huge insect drops out of the trouser leg of his horrible new neighbour. It's a giant beetle – and it seems to want to communicate.

But how can a boy be friends with a beetle? And what does a beetle have to do with the disappearance of his dad and the arrival of Lucretia Cutter, with her taste for creepy jewellery?

'A darkly funny Dahl-esque adventure.'
KATHERINE WOODFINE, AUTHOR

'A wonderful book, full to the brim with very cool beetles!'
THE GUARDIAN

Paperback, ISBN 978-1-910002-70-4, £6.99 • ebook, ISBN 978-1-910002-98-8, £6.99

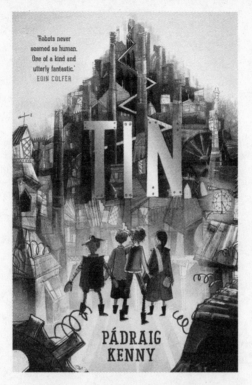

THE SECRET KEEPERS by TRENTON LEE STEWART

A magical watch. A string of secrets. A race against time.
When Reuben discovers an old pocket watch, he soon realizes it has a secret power: fifteen minutes of invisibility. At first he is thrilled with his new treasure, but as one secret leads to another, he finds himself on a dangerous adventure full of curious characters, treacherous traps and breathtaking escapes. Can Reuben outwit the sly villain called The Smoke and his devious defenders the Directions and save his city from a terrible fate?

'There are some genuinely haunting and ingenious moments as the three young heroes combat the villain in his mouldy mansion.'
THE NEW YORK TIMES

'. . . the tension never flags and the hold-your-breath moments come thick and fast.'
CAROUSEL

Paperback, ISBN 978-1-911077-28-2, £6.99 • ebook, ISBN 978-1-911077-29-9, £6.99

MALPAS